Nicholas Mosley

n a t a l i e

Natalia

D1506514

Dalkey Archive Press

First Dalkey Archive Edition, 1996

Originally published by Hodder and Stoughton (London), 1971. © 1971 by
Nicholas Mosley. Revised edition published by Minerva, a division of Reed
Books Ltd (London), 1995. Revised edition © 1995 by Nicholas Mosley.
This Dalkey Archive edition contains additional revisions by the author,
© 1996 by Nicholas Mosley.

Library of Congress Cataloging-in-Publication Data

Mosley, Nicholas, 1923-
    Natalie Natalia : a novel / Nicholas Mosley.
      p.   cm.
    1. Politicians—Great Britain—Fiction.   I. Title.
PR6063.O82N38   1996   823'.914—dc20   96-132
ISBN 1-56478-086-4

                    Dalkey Archive Press
                    Illinois State University
                    Campus Box 4241
                    Normal, IL 61790-4241

*Printed on permanent/durable acid-free paper and bound in the United States of
America.*

By the same author

*Available from Dalkey Archive Press

"He thought that he had discovered in Nature, animate and inanimate, with soul and without soul, something which was only manifested in contradictions, and therefore could not be grasped under one conception, still less under one word. It was not godlike, for it seemed unreasonable; not human, for it had no understanding; not devilish, for it was beneficent; not angelic, for it often showed malicious pleasure. It resembled chance, for it exhibited no consequence; it was like Providence, for it hinted at connection. Everything which limits us seemed by it to be penetrable; it seemed to sport in an arbitrary fashion with the necessary element of our being; it contradicted time and expanded space. Only in the impossible did it seem to find pleasure, and the possible it seemed to thrust from itself with contempt."

"This principle, which seemed to step in between all other principles, to separate them and to unite them, I called the Daemonic."

"Although that Daemonic element can manifest itself in all corporeal and incorporeal things, indeed even in animals expresses itself most remarkably, yet it stands especially in the most wonderful connection with man, and forms a power which, if not opposed to the moral order of the world, yet crosses it, so that one may be regarded as the warp and the other the woof."

GOETHE
Dichtung und Wahrheit

I

Natalie Natalia

1

I N PARLIAMENT SQUARE at night there are the building like a battleship and the Abbey like a toad and the starred sky unseen as if security or long grass were hiding it. I had left the gathering in which I had spent so much of the last few years—Parliament—a turkish bath of society in which discomfort is endured for the sake of satisfaction or the damned —an orgy where lust for power is exorcised discreetly. I had been subject to speeches the contents of which were already known and to which no one listened but which bored holes in the mind through which tolerance and sanity trickled. I was a politician and I was getting out of politics because I was ashamed; but only after knowing the worth of what I had been part of.

There was little traffic in the square at two o'clock in the morning. I was skipping like a child keeping to the lines and squares of the pavement; the skipping was in my mind, the lines and squares in the universe. There was a car parked at the side of the road: I did not think it was waiting for me. I was slightly paranoiac at this time, imagining myself guarded by angels. I had sat up late for several nights and was tired. I did not know whether to pass near to the car or keep away: either course might lead to a loss of magic. I was on my way to a party in Buckingham Gate; the party would go on to three-thirty or four; politicians do not need much sleep, they have bright lights shone on them to encourage them or derange their personalities. Thus they can imagine they are ordering the universe. When I passed by the car it pulled out and followed me. Sometimes our imagination becomes real—in an act of free will or a symbol. We were moving past the squat towers of the Abbey. God might lie in the long grass like a tiger. I thought that if I was attacked I could swing my briefcase: it would be an iron ball and chain with a man on the end; if the iron ball let go, the man would fly out through the universe. The car was in fact following me: up to this time I had thought it was an illusion. Our fantasies are there to feed us as well as give anxiety. The car drew up: the head of a black man looked out. It was a small head, with a green felt hat like an acorn. I felt I should not worry about the smallness of the head since much of the brain is in any case useless. I could explain—I can now bow down and listen to you!

In Parliament we had been debating a crisis in Central Africa. There were always crises in Central Africa, but this time more so than usual. The pacifists were advocating the use of military force and the militarists were pleading for restraint and negotiation. I, as so often, was on the side of neither; imagining the outcome in the hands of angels.

The black man had wide shoulders. He was trying to force them through the front window of the car. This gave an impression of his struggling with a cross.

"Mr. Greville sir!"

"Yes?"

"May I offer transport?"

About Central Africa I thought that some force should perhaps be used but only by those willing to suffer responsibility for it. Debate, however, has to do with the animosities of children.

The black man said "To a destination of your choice, in my capacious limousine!"

I bent down to look in the car. There was another black man driving and a third in the back with an empty seat beside him.

I said "There was an old man of Accra—"

He said "You don't want to ride with me, boss?"

He had a way of talking that seemed to go through me and speak to someone behind my back.

I said "Who went for a ride in a car—"

I walked on. I crossed the space in front of the Abbey. I could have added—When he came back from the ride the old man was inside—. I was approaching the gates of my old public school. I thought—But anxieties are useful, since they expose and prune the personality. I could have kept to the road where there were pedestrians and policemen.

The black man had got out of the car and was following me. He wore a pale brown suit with trousers that ended far above his feet. This was fashionable. His socks appeared luminous. I could not see his face. I wondered if Africans, when they had first seen white men in the tropical sun, had thought they were nothing but shirts and trousers.

He called "A funny man! Good value!"

He held his hands in his pockets so tightly that I thought his buttons might fly off and shoot me.

I had arrived at the gates of my old public school. I stood with my back to them. I remembered a smell of cabbage. I could put my arms up and cry for re-admittance.

He said "Where is this place?"

I said "Where Henry the Eighth was beheaded."

He did a few dance steps. I thought—If his buttons are bullets, I will duck and catch them.

He said "I thought he had syphilis."

I was pleased. Now I need not condescend to him. I could say—But you see, I am on your side about Africa!

I said "What do you want?"

He said "I'm making an enquiry; a personal enquiry—"

He spoke dreamily. Often, at this time, I did not quite hear what people said. They seemed to murmur to someone just behind me.

He said "—about a doggy; a little lost doggy—"

He took a hand out of his pocket. He put it on the gate at my side. He might have done this either in friendliness or to threaten me. I thought—Or both.

He said "—which I thought I might find in this salubrious environment!"

I could see his face more clearly. It was like a nude, face down.

I thought—I should be helping him.

I said "Come on, you can make sense if you like!"

He said "Of course! Pronto!"

He contained enormous silences. In Africa, men sat in the dust waiting for patterns to become apparent there.

He said "About this doggie—"

He put his other hand on the gate. I was now between his two arms which were on the bars behind me. I thought—From a distance we would look like lovers.

I remembered a photograph I had once seen of a baboon being hunted by a leopard. Cornered, the baboon had seemed to float. The leopard had appeared quite idle.

I said "I must go."

I thought—If we were lovers I would perhaps look like the girl.

He was a tall man, rather delicate. His face was sad. He moved a hand and put it on my jacket. His nails were like jewels. I thought—Perhaps his assault is sexual, which is what white women always think.

I tried to remember what to do. We had fought at school. You put your arm round a person's neck and waltzed with them.

The black man did not seem to do anything. He looked at the ground, to his dark past, as if by this he would get power.

I thought—I am like Gordon at Khartoum.

When I did push against him I did this halfheartedly so that he would not know whether or not to resist me. Thus I might get power. He still did not move. I became encouraged. I was not accustomed, after all, to be accosted on the steps of my old public school, with the images of empire behind me. He put both hands on my jacket. He held me tightly. He looked austere in the dark. His head was pushed back and his neck strained like a dancer in a ballet. I thought—They do not have to alter the world; containing this violence within them. I pushed at his hands to get them off. I thought—I have to do this to be of any use. I intended to run a few steps and then look back. I did not think he would turn me to stone. But when I ran I stumbled, and hit my head against a stone. I thought—This is ridiculous. I had been a good runner at school. Now I had just gone a few steps and my legs had given out. The stone was at a corner of the building. I dabbed my head. The blood had not yet come. The pain was like a bell. I was standing on the pavement with one sleeve of my jacket half off. I could say he had assaulted me. I could plant a brick in his pocket; turn him to stone.

"Mr. Greville sir!"

"Yes."

"Can you help me?"

My head was in fact bleeding. I felt relieved. Thus I might be justified. He was standing a few paces from me. He looked somewhat smaller than I remembered. I could say he had been bigger. He held his arms thinly to his sides. There were totems like this, to give the impression of infinity. The car had started up and was coming towards us. The engine roared. I was a man trapped in an alley. The headlights made circles on my eyes. I could run, with my arms like shadows flailing. I was close to Victoria Street where there were pedestrians and a policeman. The car drew up. Its springs sagged. In Africa, women were fat to be attractive.

I said "How can I help you?"

It was as if he were on a soapbox, orating. His hands moved in front of his face like flags. I thought—For him, like kings, the waves will not go back. No sound came from his mouth. The man driving the car had opened the door and was waiting

13

for him to get in. After a time he did so. At the party to which
I was going I could make out I had been blackmailed. I had
been on my way from the House of Commons and a black
man had accosted me. I had run and had hit my head against a
stone. I would have to make sure that my audience knew how
much I supported the Africans. I could explain—But this is the
point!

The car was coming towards me again. I looked for a lamppost to shelter behind. There was a noise like a gunshot as the
car went past. I remained quite steady. I was pleased at this.
Thus you avoided elephants. And empires were lost and won.
I wondered if the driver had done the backfire deliberately.
You pulled the choke out and switched off the ignition. The
car sagged into Victoria Street. My head was still bleeding. I
might in fact have been assaulted. The truth of a happening was
in its consequence. I walked down Victoria Street. I could
have put up a better performance. I was afraid my trousers
might be torn. That they were not gave me confidence. I
could explain—But of course people assault those who support
them! I wondered if the people at the party would know that
"doggy" meant a girl. But I would not mention this. It would
not be to my advantage. I was getting out of politics because I
was ashamed; but I was enough of a politician to know that in
a recognition of one's own advantage lay some sanity and even
a respect for others.

The party to which I was going was given by Sylvia Fisher,
an old friend of mine, the wife of a newspaper millionaire
and the mistress of a socialist ex-Secretary for Housing. Sylvia
lived in a house in Buckingham Gate to which she gave an air
as if Buckingham Palace were her stables. Her parties were
mainly for politicians and intellectuals with a few young potentates from the entertainment world thrown in. The latter
were fashionable; but at Sylvia's parties seemed rather fragile

14

and out of place, as if a sheet had been pulled off them in the dormitory.

I went to Sylvia's parties out of snobbery. I was ashamed of this, but knew it. I thought—One day, I will stop.

There was a Chinese footman at the door dressed like a coolie. He had bare feet. Beyond him guests moved trying to locate centres of attention. They held glasses in their hands like Geiger counters: to indicate importance or to prevent people waylaying them by anything less urgent than a bomb. Some of the young potentates wore their ribbons and beads; they were ponies at society's gymkhana. The older men looked beyond them with the hooded eyes of eagles. The main centre of attention would be Sylvia's small room upstairs, where she would sit on the floor cross-legged and gaze up at the godlike faces round her. They would be the udders of cows, and she a hedgehog. Sylvia was a small masculine-looking woman of fifty whose potency lay in her mixture of childishness and corruption. Her childishness seemed wicked and her corruption genial. This was not a juxtaposition that I liked. There was another conjunction of childishness and corruption which I loved, which was to do with the sweetness and ravenousness of angels.

Sylvia's small room was the inner sanctum of the tribe whose life went on around her. The elders sat on small pink-lined sofas like shells. They were heavy, crumpled-faced men whose power seemed contained not at their centres nor on their surfaces but in between, in the gap between their skin and their clothes. This gave off refulgence like the arse of a baboon.

The socialist ex-Secretary was telling a story. Joe Gregory, Sylvia's brother, waited to take up points with him attentively. The person whom I had come to the party for sat beside him.

Women did not often come to Sylvia's inner sanctum; so this was an honour, or indicated trouble.

Young men hovered round the door not risking going in. When Sylvia blinked the needles of their Geiger counters quivered. I pushed through them murmuring "Gas!" I was pleased at being an initiate.

The ex-Secretary was saying "It's not the principle, it's Eugenie's."

Joe Gregory said "What?"

The ex-Secretary said "What would you do if a black man married your daughter."

Sylvia explained. "Eugenics is his daughter."

When Sylvia laughed she rocked backwards and forwards like a Japanese soldier observing torture.

I sat on a sofa next to the person I had come to the party for. I put my hand on hers. In the room, there was a slight displacement of attention.

Sylvia said in her deep masculine voice "Tell the one about the hand!"

The ex-Secretary said "The hand?"

The elders of the tribe were round their campfire. There was the ex-Secretary, Joe Gregory, the Commonwealth Minister, and the editor of the National Sunday Newspaper. We were in our cave halfway up the mountain. Here the lava would flow to our destruction.

The ex-Secretary said "Oh, if the hand you feed with gets bitten, it doesn't mean it's by a cannibal."

Sylvia rocked backwards and forwards.

Joe Gregory cupped a hand behind his ear. He was in Sylvia's inner sanctum because he was her brother. He worked for the editor of the National Sunday Newspaper. I was fond of Joe Gregory.

I realised it would not be easy for me to tell my story about the black man. I held the hand of the person who sat beside me.

Sylvia said "We kept her for you."

She seemed to be speaking not to me but to someone behind me.

Joe Gregory said "She's yours?"

The Commonwealth Minister was a short man with a long thin face. I had been working for him for some time. He murmured "Who isn't a cannibal?"

Joe Gregory said "I didn't know!"

I thought—We must appear like two children accused of rape.

Joe Gregory said "Old man, you're bleeding!"

"Yes."

"Have you been in a punch-up?"

The person I had come to the party for was called Natalia. Her hand, which had been in mine, withdrew. I thought— Since I have been in trouble, I expected this.

Sylvia said "Oh, what have you been punched up for?"

The ex-Secretary said "In certain states in Africa they've had to invent a rubber mace."

Sylvia rocked backwards and forwards.

I thought—The young men outside this door are like sailors in Antwerp and we are a brothel.

Joe said "What's going on? Have they voted yet?"

I thought—When you go into the holy of holies, you find nothing but a blank room with a blank space.

I said "No. Nothing's happening."

I did not want to look at Natalia. She might be angry that she had had to meet me at this party.

Sylvia said "Do you want some antiphlogiston?"

I said "Is he a Greek?"

She rocked. I thought—And a moment ago, I might never have been asked again to this sort of party.

Natalia would be hating the party, having the sweetness and ravenousness of an angel.

Joe said "I mean, is there going to be a vote?"

I said "Joe, you're not allowed to ask a direct question."

Natalia put a hand up and touched my face. She said "Were you really hurt?"

I shook my head. I thought—I may cry. Her tenderness, in this place, would be a desecration.

Sylvia said "Nanny's watching you."

I thought—We're in Sylvia's nursery; smoking brown-paper cigarettes.

I said "The point is, when it comes to it, will the pacifists fight and the soldiers be conscientious objectors; or will everyone in fact revert to type."

The Commonwealth Minister said "The Marxist Principle."

I said "Yes."

I looked round the room. I was afraid Natalia might take her hand away again. Floodwater seemed halfway up the mountain.

I said "Sylvia, love, we must go."

Natalia jerked as if she had been hit.

Sometimes her jumps, like those within atoms, seemed without reason or location.

Natalia and I were not supposed to know one another in public: we were both married; not to each other.

When I say that I must go I sometimes stay where I am for several minutes. If I stood up I was not sure if Natalia would follow me.

I said "I'm being blackmailed."

Joe said "Are you?"

I said "Perhaps that's the origin of the word, a punch-up with a black man."

Natalia stood. I followed her. I thought—They would not have known how to deal with Natalia; since she has the transforming power of angels.

Sylvia said "Be good, my children."

I thought—In Sylvia's nursery you are prevented from growing up by the harm of brown-paper cigarettes.

As we went down the stairs Natalia and I passed a very pretty girl of seventeen whom I was careful not to notice as if I were looking through her to someone behind.

Natalia was of half-Russian and half-Polish descent. She was also Jewish, which perhaps accounts for her diversity.

Natalia and I sat in a taxi. I pulled her towards me to kiss. She remained rigid and yet limp—a hostile accomplishment.

I could have explained—I've been sitting up late for several nights! I'm tired! But this would have been of no consequence to Natalie.

I sometimes called Natalia Natalie instead of Natalia, when she was the ravenous rather than the angelic angel.

I moved to the far corner of the taxi. With her hand in mine I maintained a bridge by which troops could yet move into hostile territory.

I could ask—What is it?

Natalie's silences, though deathly, could be like a winter in which seeds grew.

I could say—But it doesn't matter that we were seen at that party! Those people would not be interested in anything so straightforward!

The taxi ran through Hyde Park. The night was littered with lights like dead fireflies.

I could say—But I told you those people were horrible!

I wondered whether, if we quarrelled, I could get to bed earlier. But I would not sleep.

I could say—I've been hit on the head by a black man!

But my claim for sympathy was so strong that perhaps justification was unnecessary.

I tried to work this out.

I did not know why Natalie was angry.

I said "Come on! I've been sitting up all night. I'm tired!"

The taxi turned towards Grosvenor Square. I dabbed at my head. The dried blood had crumbled.

I felt myself become angry. I would regret this.

I wondered why women did not give comfort to men when they had been hit on the head by a black man.

But I had not been hit. Perhaps Natalie knew.

In any case, comfort was bad for me.

I was beginning to feel charitable again.

Natalie yelled "Let me out of here!" She heaved at the door of the taxi.

At moments of uncertainty I sometimes pretend to be other people. I became slightly deaf, like Joe Gregory.

"What?"

I held on to her. I had my head down by her waist. She smelled of garlic.

She could never find the handles to the doors of cars.

I thought—Tonight we will make love.

She shouted "Stop!"

The taxi swerved. The driver had such a thick neck he could not get round to see what was happening.

I could explain to him—She is a long way from home; from her natural surroundings!

The taxi came to a halt in Grosvenor Square. Natalie got the door open. She pushed herself out. She wore a very short dress and gold tights with a black bottom. I was pulled closely after her.

I shouted "Oh come back!"

She went off striding round the square like a boxer. I was marooned on the pavement. I had to find ten shillings for the driver. This prevented me from running after her and grabbing her. This was lucky.

It had to stay still. Then everything would come back on the curve of the universe.

I called—"Oh what's the matter?"

Natalie turned and shouted "All right, keep your fucking mistress!"

I could not imagine what she could be meaning. Perhaps the black man had been talking to her.

I should remain calm and dejected.

I could say—But you are my mistress!

She walked on. There was a policeman by the steps of the American Embassy. He was there to prevent demonstrations.

Natalie got as far as the garden in the centre of the square. There she sat on a parapet by a fountain.

She was about sixty yards away. I could wait on the steps of the Embassy, like a protester.

I thought—The policeman is an angel with a flaming sword.

Natalie sat with her head in her hands. Her silences, together with the policeman, gave me space to manoeuvre.

What Natalie said was often a code for what Natalia was meaning.

Anger went on moving while we remained quite still. Then, after a time, it exhausted itself.

The policeman moved. He began walking round the square. I sat on the steps of the Embassy. All round the world there were people sitting on steps of embassies, or on mountains, waiting for annunciation.

It was a cold night. Natalia and I were attached to each other by an umbilical cord; like a fish and an eye that has hooked it.

I thought—We love; try to do what is right: this is impossible. There should be a diagram for this in space as well as in time, where irreconcilables co-exist equally.

The policeman had turned and was coming towards me. I stood and brushed at my trousers. I could explain—I was stealing apples from the Embassy garden.

I walked across the road towards Natalia. The policeman might be a devil instead of an angel. It was a matter of timing.

21

We had only sat for four or five minutes. I could walk past Natalie and wash my face in the fountain. This would be necessary to get the blood off. I had in fact been injured in a struggle with a black man.

I moved at a tangent out of respect to her gravity. If I touched her, there might be an explosion.

Narcissus, looking at his reflection in water, had fallen in and drowned while waiting for his loved one.

I splashed my face.

I was always hurting Natalia.

I touched her shoulder. I thought—I am not condescending.

The heads of small children have not quite closed at the top.

I wrapped my jacket round her to keep her warm.

I said "Let's go home."

I did a few dance steps in the cold.

When Natalie became Natalia again she was like a sea anemone washed by water.

I wanted to call out to someone behind—Don't be too good! There can't be miracles!

She seemed to be crying.

I said "Look!" I licked her tears.

Natalia had a small dark face; clear and gently moulded.

She said "I'm sorry. How can you bear me?"

I tried to lift her with my arms underneath her. We had to lean against the fountain.

"Put me down."

"No."

"Why not?"

"You're too heavy."

The policeman came towards us again. I had one foot on the parapet. I said "Ideally, one should have three legs and several arms."

I pulled at my trousers.

We remained looking at a statue.

When the policeman had gone I said "What was that any-way?"

"What was what?" She put her arms around me.

I thought—So it's not the black man.

I said "My mistress."

She said "Pffft!"

We walked hand in hand past the fountain. I did not know what she meant. I thought—We are in control again; our arms round the universe.

She said "Well, it was something."

"What?"

She said "Well, Sylvia."

She squeezed me.

I said "Sylvia?"

I thought I might shout—Don't you think I could do better than Sylvia?

She said "Oh, I know it's silly!"

I said "But—"

"But you don't know what you called her!"

"What did I call her?"

"Love."

I shouted "But I call everybody love!"

She said "I know!"

We walked into the road.

I thought—I could never, really, be married to Natalia.

I shouted "Do you think, after you, I could lay a toenail on Sylvia?"

She looked pleased.

I thought—This is too easy.

We were waiting for another taxi.

I said "But it's not that. Is it?"

She said "Oh well!"

I wanted to say—I'm so tired, darling; help me.

She said "I didn't want to tell you or it might not come true."

I wondered again when I could get to bed.

She said "Edward's away."

Edward was Natalia's husband.

I could say—I know Edward's away: how else could we have met at Sylvia's party?

She said "So you can come home if you like."

I said "That's wonderful!"

I thought—And that's what it was about?

She said "Oh God, I feel so guilty!" She stood with her fists clenched as if in a gale.

I said "Look! Don't worry! We've got through all this in ten or fifteen minutes! You're brave!"

She put her head on my shoulder.

I thought—In the morning, in my office, I have a lot of work to do.

I said "Look, if we hadn't had a row, you'd have gone on feeling guilty!"

She said "But I am!"

I said "But now it won't make any difference."

She said "That's absolutely true."

A taxi came. We sat in the same corner. We groped beyond each other to some images of ourselves behind us.

She said "Edward's gone to Africa. It's supposed to be secret."

I thought—That might be useful.

Edward was a Member of Parliament.

In Edward and Natalia's house I had an impression of having lived there myself before; perhaps in some previous existence, with the furniture coming awake and pretending not to recognise me.

Natalia went ahead of me up the stairs. She said "Why are you smiling?"

I said "Because I'm so happy."

I thought—There'll be time enough to do everything both now and in the morning.

My office was in Whitehall. Sometimes walking there in the early mornings I did feel happier than I had ever done before in my life; I could fly or breathe under water; by faith, which I could not use, I might move mountains. At other times—or the same—the tension was such that I felt the unaccustomed dimension I was in might break: and I would be hurled, like Icarus, from the furnace.

I thought—To fly too close to the sun is a mark of freedom.

I stopped at an all-night coffee stall. Here were other denizens of the netherworld in which I felt at home: all dazed, through lack of sleep and energy.

My office was in an old block of dark bricks with a cream interior. There were two desks, a hatstand, a filing cabinet, a carpet. Here I could work for an hour or two before anyone else arrived. I would sit in a cell with leaden walls by which impressions from outside were diluted. I could imagine myself ordering the universe.

The files on my desk were to do with Central Africa.

The political situation in Central Africa was not so different from any other: there were certain people who, because it suited them, wished to maintain a status quo: and others who, for the same reason, wanted a revolution.

In either event there would be injustice and cruelty: but each side had to claim that all justice was on its side and all cruelty on the other. I thought—Politicians are machines for justifying self-interest.

This is not a book about politics. A particular set of politics goes out of date like plastic fittings. But there are patterns which recur of a universal predicament.

In Central Africa there was a white minority who suppressed a black majority and explained that this was for the sake of order: a black minority who rebelled and explained that this was for the sake of freedom. In neither event, was there much order or freedom.

I thought—Politicians are components of computers to make the world go round.

In particular, there was an African leader called Ndoula. Ndoula was a pacifist and a Christian, and was held to be a violent agitator. He had recently been locked up, for the sake of peace.

I thought—A computer is a machine whose switches have to be at one position or another.

Ndoula's imprisonment had greatly increased the militancy of his followers. This militancy was welcomed by those who had locked him up, who thus could justify their repression.

I thought—A politician is a right hand who would be dumbfounded at what his left hand is doing.

I sat in my office and outside the traffic swam like muted swans. Without stimulus, I could make up my own solutions.

Ndoula, having been locked up, had become a hero. He thus appeared to be on the side of history.

This, I imagined, might be like the activity of a god.

I had the job, in my office, of writing a report on Ndoula. Freedom-fighters were threatening to attack across the border. Around the world there were calls for military intervention. Ndoula was performing a useful function in being locked up: he was stimulating conscience and activity. However, it was necessary to try to release him.

The Government, for whom I worked, perhaps agreed with this; but could not say so. In order not to come down on one side or the other, they appeared indolent.

I thought—Perhaps a computer works best when it has fused, and people are employed mending it.

In the meantime what was required was a scapegoat. The Government itself was used as a scapegoat, so that people need do nothing about Ndoula. They could say—Why do the Government do nothing? Perhaps the Government needed me as a scapegoat, since I was writing the report about Ndoula.

I thought that by all these means, which were mysterious, there might occur some solution: time being on the side of history.

There was a parallel here with my personal predicament. For instance, I was used as a scapegoat by Natalie. This was part of my paranoia.

On the other hand, in Central Africa, some bloodshed might be necessary.

I tried to imagine Ndoula in his prison camp in the desert. Flies buzzed around him.

I thought—He is someone through whom, like a summer sky, battles are fought: Natalie or Natalia.

I wanted to find some way by which these paradoxes might be held: words being symbols; symbols meaning.

I was imagining all this, and not working, when my secretary came in. She was called Yseult.

She said "Look who's here!"

Yseult was a tall fair-haired girl who did not believe in paradoxes. She thought that young people should go out and die for Ndoula.

I said "I've been up all night!"

She said "I bet!"

Yseult wore a hat like an upturned cup and saucer. She carried a rolled umbrella. I hoped that one day she might throw her hat up in the air and spin it on the point of her umbrella.

She said "I thought you'd been at Mrs. Fisher's party."

I said "What do you know about Mrs. Fisher's party?"

Yseult was a girl who had been brought up with dogs and horses. I thought—To get her boots off, you would have to stand with your back to her and she would put her foot between your legs.

I went back to my report. In the camp in the desert, the prisoners were asking for books and newspapers. They wanted to become like a university.

I thought—Trees grow in a greenhouse; exotic blooms like angels.

Yseult said "What have you done to your head?"

I said "Hit it on a lamppost."

She said "I bet."

"All right. I was in a fight with a black man."

Yseult came and peered at me. There was a faint smell of cooking.

I said "Yseult, you're my only friend!"

She blushed and went away.

I wondered why Yseult was on the side of black men. Perhaps once one had looked over a hedge at her instead of a horse.

I could not get the right style for my report. If I wrote it well enough it would be admired and nothing would be done: if I wrote it badly, the result might be the same.

I said "What about Mrs. Fisher's party?"

"What about what Mrs. Fisher's party?"

"You said it with a note of disapproval."

"Well, there is gossip you know."

Yseult and I sat at an angle to each other at the smaller and the larger desk. Between us was a space like the steering gear of a ship.

I said "What gossip?"

Yseult banged at her typewriter.

I said "About me and Mrs. Fisher?"

She said "About you and Mrs. Jones."

Natalia was called Jones. She was rather ashamed of this.

Yseult's blush deepened. I could say—Grip with your knees, Yseult! Keep your head up!

I put on my calm and dejected face: for protection.

Yseult said "It won't do you any good you know."

I said "Perhaps I don't want it to do me any good."

I wondered if Yseult had lovers. She seemed the wrong component, like a piston.

I said "Perhaps I want it to do me evil, so that out of it a gigantic bloom may grow."

Yseult smiled with half her face. I thought—It is the other half that admires me.

I wanted to say—Yseult! I love you too! Become a cylinder!

I said "I thought your generation was permissive."

She said "I'm not my generation."

I thought—In all women there is something of Natalie: a component like blocked blood.

I said "Anyway, I'll be getting out soon."

"Out of what?"

"Politics."

I hoped she would say—What a pity!

She banged her typewriter so hard I thought it might fire off like a torpedo. She said "Isn't that defeatist?"

I said "Like Parnell. Or Dilke."

She said "Rilke?"

I said "Yes, Rilke."

I thought about this. There were chances ordered by ironic angels.

She said "And what does your wife think?"

"About what?"

Yseult's face had become wooden. I thought—Now she has asked for a fight.

I said "My wife is an admirer of Rilke, who said that in any relationship between a man and a woman the existence of a third person is a necessary illusion. That is, the third person is imagined by the two people so that they can evade the issue on their own. Or perhaps deal with it."

I thought—Rilke didn't say the last bit.

Yseult said "And what does that mean?"

"What it says."

"Perhaps I'm stupid."

Yseult might be on the point of tears. Her skin had gone dark like that of an Eskimo.

I said "Dear Yseult, will you get this typed please?"

I thought—Anything I do may make things worse.

I worked on my report.

Ndoula was in the desert.

There should be some symbol, or style, for liberation.

I said "Look, Yseult, if I didn't risk things, I'd be impossible, wouldn't I?"

I appeared to be waiting for some voice beyond the ceiling.

I said "I'd have money, brains, arrogance, good looks—"

It was difficult to pull this off. I sat with my mouth open.

She said "Good Lord!"

I said "Well then!"

She sucked her finger. She had cut it banging on her typewriter.

I went over to her desk. I laid my papers in front of her. I said "Wait till you see the whites in their eyes Yseult!"

She said "Are you going?"

I said "Yes."

I thought—She may be in love with me.

In the street, I wondered if I could have done any better. I might have let Yseult comfort me, and thus been humiliated.

At ten o'clock in the morning the streets were full. I pushed against people on their way to their offices. I thought—I have not much more to do.

I have a flat in London where I stay during the week and a cottage in the country where I go most weekends. My wife spends most of the time in the country, which helps my impression of schizophrenia.

There is a theory that a schizophrenic is someone who recognises the explosive pressures in the personality that are universal and unavoidable; and thus has fewer illusions than people who are normal.

This week my wife was staying in London; so I was a wolf at the time of the full moon.

Entering my flat I moved into yet another existence: the ruined castle where I hoped to rule in a few hundred years; the broken archways and hidden walls and trapdoor that would bring me back to the future.

There was a body underneath the bedclothes. It might remain there until the prince woke it with a kiss. I said—"Cooee!"

I thought—But nowadays it is not the prince but the beast; whom the princess loves because he lets her lie sleeping.

A hand crawled out from the bedclothes. I sat beside it. I said "Budge over!" The bedroom was a place where I spent much of the time alone. It was now full of my wife's things, which staked out her claims like a prospector.

A dressing case spilled bottles and underclothes and brushes. She kept things she needed on the floor, so that furniture could remain tidy.

I thought—Thus hermits ensure austerity in the desert.

Sometimes when I sat on the edge of my wife's bed she was so slow to move that I sat on her legs; then we would be in dispute like rival prospectors.

She shifted her legs. She said "What time is it?"

I said "Ten o'clock."

The bedclothes were over her face. I could peel them off like a bandage.

Her hand moved towards a bedside table. It hovered over a watch, a handkerchief, a glass of water. I thought—Should one help one's neighbour? She settled on the watch; pulled it under the bedclothes. She jerked up on one elbow. She said "It's ten o'clock!" I said "I told you!"

Her face was a root gathering nourishment.

She said "What have you been doing?" I said "I've been up all night." I thought—Even when it's true, she would not believe me.

I said "And then I went to Sylvia's party."

I had not known whether or not to talk about Sylvia's party. But she might find out I had been there.

She said "And who did you meet?" She blinked. Her face became accustomed to daylight.

I thought—I am tired.

I said "Sylvia's boyfriend." She said "Anyone else?" I said "Joe." She looked away. Her head with its golden hair grew into stems and petals and flowers.

I said "And on the way I was accosted by a black man." I thought—I knew this would be useful. She said "You are lucky!" I put a hand out and stroked her. I said "He was a friend of Marlene's, you remember Marlene?" She said "Of course I do!" I thought—This is not untrue but clever; the truth is in symbols. I said "He seemed to think I'd got her." She said "And had you?" I shouted "Of course not!" I put my head down in the bedclothes. Her smell was warm. She was a mole that had been underground all winter. I said "You don't want to hear about Marlene, do you?" She said "Good God, no!" I said "I'm coming in." She said "How do I trust you?" I pulled down the bedclothes. Her body was like a Titian. I said "The day you trust me—" I looked down. I began to take off my clothes. She said "Yes?" I seemed to be always taking off my clothes. I said "I'm a gangster. Do you know about gangsters?" I turned my back: I thought—I do not want her to see me. I said "They have to be at it every hour of the day and night; they have people lined up for them in the corridors." I got into bed. I said "Like an endless belt." She said "How disgusting." I said "That's why you like me." I pushed at her legs. I thought—Gods used to do this; in the old days, scattering the earth with pollen. She said "You're perky, aren't you!" I said "Fancy noticing!" I thought—If you want seeds to flourish you have to work; then there is the germination all winter. She said "There was no one else at the party?" I shouted "I've told you!" She said "Someone's got into bed the wrong side this morning." I said "That's witty." She held me. I said "I think that's why I like you, because you're witty." She said "Is that all?" She began stretching her legs out. I thought—I am the sun: one day I may burn her. But with my hands I could make her grow. I said "Amongst other things." She said "Tell me a story." I thought—This is a story. I said "About what?" She said "What you like." I thought—People want to be told things. And the more you do it, the more you are able to. I said "Once upon a time there was an enormous black man—"

2

I HAD COME to a time in life when I felt as Dostoievski must have felt just before he had a fit; that the world was so beautiful that my understanding of it could not continue; that it would have to break to make it bearable. Then I could be wheeled out in a bathchair on to a balcony.

There is a subject nowadays which is taboo in the way that sexuality was once taboo; which is to talk about life as if it had any meaning.

Sometimes there was this compulsion in my mind, imagination, skin, as if I contained too many possibilities to be effective. It was this that drove hermits into the desert; Napoleon across Europe with his armies on a tea tray. But if I stayed still, there was the explosion.

I thought—The meaning is in the fit: and therefore hidden.

Before I had met Natalia I had seemed approximately human. I had worked; had worried about responsibility and money. Natalie was a wild man with her hands round my throat in an attic.

I had thought—Perhaps if one got used to fear it would not be so frightening.

At the cottage in the country where I went at weekends I began to build a small courtyard for something to do and for protection. I got a load of bricks and a sack of sand and cement which I carried like a dead antelope. My daughter, aged eight, came to watch me.

She said "What are you doing?"

"Building a castle."

"Why?"

"To keep the dragons out."

The cottage was up a lane from the village. There was a short drive to the back door.

She said "You're barmy!"

"Why?"

"There aren't any dragons!"

"There are in your mind."

The feet of the dead antelope stuck out. I heaved it into the courtyard. I slit its stomach and sand and cement poured out and I put them in a bucket and mixed them. I splashed in water and stirred. The water disappeared in an inland sea. There remained the desert.

I said "Spooks."

She said "Where do spooks come from?"

I said "Stories."

As I stirred the water reappeared mysteriously. There was a migration of matter; a chemical change of birds and animals. I kneaded. My skin scraped off.

She said "Can I do it?"

"It's dangerous."

"Why?"

I showed her my hands.

I said "Each bit is sharp. That's what makes it stick together, and is useful."

She said "Oh please!"

I laid some cement on the row of bricks and put a new brick on top and the cement dribbled down. I wiped its mouth. There were gaps in its teeth. At the far end of the row, the bricks would become neat miraculously.

She said "Just one!"

I said "All right. But I really have to do this myself, you know. It's a sort of magic."

"Oh never mind then!"

"No do. I'd love you to do just one."

I thought—I am mad: my family come to visit me on Sundays.

I gave her the trowel. I thought—It does not matter if the bricks are not neat and beautiful.

She said "That was lovely!"

"Good."

"Thank you. I think I'll go now."

"Don't you want to do any more?"

"No."

"Good-bye then."

"Good-bye."

I went on with my work. The mixing of the cement was tedious. By work that was tedious, at the end of the day was achieved some liberation. Work that was interesting went on and on.

I was an Irish labourer with my shirt off and my trousers falling down. Holding a shovel, I would lean and be whistled at by ladies.

My son came out. He was seventeen. I wondered if my family made arrangements to visit me singly.

He said "That's getting on well!"

I thought—Oedipus should have sent his father to the salt mines.

He said "What is it?"

"A courtyard."

"What will we do in it?"

"Sit."

This was a time when I was not seeing Natalia. I was spending a holiday at the cottage with my family.

He said "I read somewhere of a man who built a lead box, which he sat in and was protected from cosmic rays or something."

I said "And do you know what happened?"

"No."

"There were more rays in him that couldn't get out than outside him that couldn't get in."

He said "Is that true?"

"It might be."

I straightened my back. I was both hoping and dreading that Natalia might get in touch with me. She would sometimes send me telegrams which arrived by an old man on a bicycle.

I thought—Either way I will think she is destroying me.

My son said "Do you think then there are rays and things like that?"

"Oh I don't know."

"But shouldn't one expose oneself?"

I leaned over my bucket. The mixture oozed. I thought— Perhaps God, when creating the world, was being sick into a bucket.

I said "The thing about a protective wall, I think, is to be building and never finishing it."

Natalia would be sitting waiting for the telephone to ring and dreading it.

He said "Didn't Tolstoy build brick walls?"

There was sudden chime of bells from the lane by the back drive. I stayed with my head down. My daughter appeared running round the house as if to a thunderstorm.

An ice cream van would be sitting in the lane like a dragon.

I thought—One day the old man with a telegram will be devoured on his bicycle.

I said "Tolstoy used to have a mistress at the bottom of his drive; when he gave her up, he sent his family crazy."

"Would it have been better if he hadn't?"

"I don't know. Tolstoy believed in God. At various times, he tried to do everything."

My son leaned against my wall. I was afraid he would knock it over.

It was a hot afternoon. Sweat poured off me. There were strands of moss growing already from the bottom row of bricks.

My wife Elizabeth came out of the house. She had been

sunbathing. She was doing up her trousers. She said "Have you seen Sophie?"

Sophie is the name of our daughter.

I said "Yes, she's getting an ice cream."

"Did you tell her she wasn't supposed to?"

I looked at my wall. It would take generations to get it up to the proper level.

Sophie appeared from the lane sucking a cone. Elizabeth watched her.

I thought—My wall is in levels like geology.

My son, who is called Adam, said "Are ice creams bad for you?"

I opened my mouth to say both Yes and No. A fly had time to go in and out of it.

I thought—Like Greeks, we are waiting for a message of disaster: from an old man with wings on a bicycle.

Elizabeth said "Would you like to come for a walk?"

I said "I better get on with my wall."

I thought—The Greeks felt close to the gods because of the low sky and the brightness of the landscape.

I put cement on for another row of bricks. Sweat ran out of my eyes and blinded me.

I thought—For effect, one would have to be both Oedipus and his father.

Adam said "Oh yes, there was a telegram!"

I said "Where?"

"I don't know."

I thought—I will sit on a stone, an old blind man, and wait for someone to comfort me.

Adam said "I think I put it in my pocket."

I said "Do you think you could get it out again?"

Elizabeth went into the house. Sophie followed her.

I thought—When the women have gone you hear the sudden scream behind a portico.

Adam said "Yes here it is!"

I took the telegram. The cement made the paper stick to my fingers.

If I tried to open it I would tear it; if I didn't, it would be the same.

Adam said "I think it was inviting you to the opening of some school or something."

I said "The opening of some school."

"Yes."

I waved the piece of paper. The envelope was like a fungus.

The ice cream van began ringing again.

I said "Abracadabra!"

The paper tore. It extended itself into ladders.

I said "Can you do that?"

He said "What?"

I said "Extend it. Like Jacob's ladders."

In the days when I had first known Natalia and we were innocent—not innocent in that we had not made love because this we usually did—but in that, like Adam and Eve, we had not yet learned how this might be impossible—I used to visit her sometimes at four o'clock in the afternoons, which was a time when both her husband and I were supposed to be running the country and I trusted that at least he was if I were not. I would walk along the alley at the back of her house and there was a door into her garden like the entrance to a fairy tale: I would be imagining myself as Prince Charming, having rubbed my feet in the wings and flexed my muscles; the afternoon beautiful with the sun always shining as it does on great performances or childhood memories; and I would watch for Natalia to appear at her window like a towel or a bright candle, either because she could not wait for me or as a sign to give me warning; for her husband might return unexpectedly from running the country. On the afternoon I am remembering (this story is not chronological; more a demonstration; this afternoon earlier than, though connected with, the days I have been describing) I was walking along the alley at the back of Natalia's house looking at the rooftops for songbirds to lead me to the dragon —Natalie herself the dragon, and, as Natalia, the maiden I might rescue from it—when I saw her beckoning to me fiercely from her doorway. The doorway led into her secret garden. Natalia wore a white dress hanging straight from the shoulders. She was like a child in a thunderstorm. I stopped, with a hand on my heart. I thought—How passionately I am wanted! There is a trick to prolong such a moment; you go up on your toes while the violins play a tremolo. Natalia continued to beckon me: then pointed fearfully to something behind me. I thought the dragon might have got round my back. I began to run. The dragon would be, in this case, Natalia's husband. I thought I should get into the garden quickly. But then Natalia pushed her hands out to stop me. I paused in midair; a technique requiring much discipline. I thought—Perhaps this is how great dancers do it; through some recognition of tension by opposites. Which exists in all art and compulsion. I ran on. Natalia paid me no attention. I went past her into the garden. She remained looking out into the alley. What had happened, I discovered later, was that her husband Edward—I didn't know this at the time—had in fact arrived unexpectedly at the front door of the house just as I was coming up the alley; he had told Natalia he was going to park his car at the back, so she had rushed out into the garden to beckon me or to repulse me—she could not make up her mind. I might turn to face Edward at the entrance to the alley, or Natalia and I might be seen rushing into each other's arms. This seemed a perfect paradigm of love; that Natalia should be both passionately greeting and desperately refusing me; that I should find myself in her secret garden while she was still distraught and looking back. Her white dress, in the small door, made her ghostly. I went up to the house. I had become used to this sort of situation; it seemed that in love people became suspended in midair regularly; like the hanged man, or Saint Theresa. The garden was a small paved courtyard; there were steps up to the house. I climbed them. I found Natalia's husband Edward in the hall. He had his back to me. He was speaking into a telephone. What had happened, I discovered later, was that Edward, having told Natalia he was going to park his car at the back, had changed his mind when he had seen Natalia rushing into the garden and had used the opportunity to telephone privately. I did not know this; it seemed that Natalia must have been beckoning to me in the alley so that I would rush to have this confrontation with Edward. And then she had repented. I stood there quietly. Women sometimes like men to fight duels: this gives them a sense of identity. But their plans go wrong, and men fire into the shrubbery. Edward said into the telephone "Just a moment"; then, with a hand over the receiver, "Will you go away please?" I thought this was extraordinarily polite: if he was talking to me, I could say—Willingly. He had not turned round. What had happened, I realised, was that Edward, hearing my footsteps entering the hall, had thought that I was Natalia: he wanted her to go out again so that he could continue on the telephone. I saw Natalia coming up the steps from the garden behind me. Edward still had his back to us. I gestured to Natalia to keep away. If he heard her come in Edward might think she was me; or at least, that there were two of her. Which there probably were. But this would disturb him. As it disturbed me. Natalia, coming through the door, saw Edward in the hall: she paused in midair like a dancer. I thought—The trick is to believe that it is possible. The door slammed behind her. I thought—Now we are trapped. Edward said "Thank you." He must have thought that Natalia had gone out into the garden again. He continued speaking into the telephone. He was a large roundheaded man with

41

curly hair which came down over the back of his collar. He said "Can I see you this evening?" He spoke huskily. I realised he was making some assignation. I thought it was lucky that Natalia was hearing this: Natalia used to deny Edward's infidelities. She put her head in her hands. He said "Seven o'clock then." I thought—Now I may be able to have dinner with Natalia. But sometimes when Edward was being unfaithful this made Natalia want to be faithful to him: I thought—An event has its own consequences. I realised Edward would soon be putting down the receiver. I could not go back into the garden because he thought that I was there—or rather, that Natalia was. And in this case I was Natalia. But I could not stay in the hall because I was not. I became confused. Natalia was standing beside me. I remembered—Always, when you are in the pit, and in chains, and the dragon is breathing, there is a way out if you jump. There was a door to the basement on my right. I knew about the basement: a lodger lived there who was jealous of Natalia. Sometimes when I visited her he would be standing in his area smoking a pipe; his head and shoulders were like a boiler. I thought I might have time to get to the basement before Edward left the telephone. He was saying "Good-bye!" in his husky voice. It was lucky that lovers took so long to get off the telephone. I opened the door to the basement and stepped down. The door banged behind me. The sound of the door might make Edward think Natalia had come in from the garden; which she had, being in the hall. I tiptoed to the basement. There was a sound of cheering. I thought it might be angels. I could bow and say—Thanks. If I got through to the front area and up the steps it would be as if I had never been there. There would just be trouble, like an allergy, scattered in seeds behind me. The sound of cheering seemed to be coming from television. It was in a room off the basement passage. The door into the room was open. I saw on a television set a football match being played: I recognised it:

it was the final of the World Cup in which England had beaten West Germany. This was a recording. I had wanted to see this since I had missed the match at the time. I had been with Natalia. Natalia did not approve of football; nor television. Now, I might be rewarded. There did not seem to be anyone inside the room. The Germans were just about to take the free-kick that led to their disputed goal. This was the moment I most wanted to see. I noticed the legs of a man up the chimney. It was a large chimney such as Father Christmas might come down. A body seemed to have been pushed up it. Players were lining up to block the way to the goal: they held their hands across their bodies. There was an empty chair in front of the television. I thought I might sit. At least, if the lodger had been murdered, he would not be able to come down. The Germans took their free-kick: the ball slithered across the goal-mouth. I heard a noise of voices upstairs: Edward was shouting "But I asked you to go out!" Natalia shouted "But I did!" Edward shouted "How are you here then?" The English players were scrambling like ninepins: the ball went into the net. It seemed a fair goal. I thought perhaps the lodger might stand with his head up the chimney in order to listen to quarrels between Edward and Natalia. Chimneys were like the horns of gramophones. Natalia shouted "I don't care a bugger!" Edward said "Don't shout at me!" I was sad she used such language with Edward; I thought she only used it with me. The English players were pushing round the referee. The feet of the lodger shuffled in the chimney. I thought—If he suffocates, I may be held to have murdered him. I had seen all I wanted on television. I moved out of the room and down the passage. The way up to the street was clear. I wondered why Natalia pretended not to know about Edward's assignations: perhaps she then found it easier to be guilty with me. And so did not mind Edward. I was walking in the street; it was a bright spring day: I was pleased that I had got so miraculously

out of danger. I thought I might go back to my flat and see the
rest of the football match on television. I realised I was lonely.
I had missed my afternoon with Natalia. My day, and my love,
had become a desert. I was a clown, up to my neck in the sand.
There were lions coming at me; with claws like crabs' pincers.

In a dark wood, at the middle time of life, I went on trying to
explain myself to myself. I might waylay myself like a bandit.

I seemed trying to get rid of some part of myself that was
vital, like a cancer. There was some achievement during the
first half of my life—success, stability, a job, family, money.
This was killing me. Religions understand all this: in prosperity
the heart grows fat: to cut it out, makes the heart stop also.

I thought—But self-abasement too can be a form of spiritual
prosperity.

Sitting at my cottage on a summer evening, lying with
Natalia on a winter afternoon, I thought—There is no need
for self-abasement: if I continue, abasement will come soon
enough from others.

Before I found Natalie I had grown so comfortable that I
had needed something to afflict me. Or I would be a millstone
hung round the world's neck; or the necks of children.

If it was true that salvation came through being strung up,
whatever made this true would provide it.

Or if it did not, I would die comfortable.

When discomfort came, of course, it did not seem what I
had wanted. Natalie, in cutting the cord, had cut my throat. I
saw drain away what life had provided.

I hoped there might be some discipline in anarchy as there
was in restriction. This would be by life rather than death; its
limiting power exhaustion. Discipline by restriction left energy
washed up; thus unused, it rotted.

I thought—Out of a million seeds only one grows to fruition.

Walking through streets at night it was as if I came to a crossroads with a gibbet. From the gibbet was the hanged man. I did not know which road to take because I could take any. This knowledge was a form of choosing. I pilfered the dead man's pockets. I thought—In anarchy, you throw bits of paper into the wind: they become pointers: a key, a coin, a handkerchief.

Sometimes at night the devils came in and I sat up in bed and listened. I wanted to stretch my arms out for satisfaction.

I thought—The sound is Goliath rousing; the only sling is knowledge.

I imagined a mechanism by which satisfaction was only gained by the infliction of another person's pain. There was a balance by which this might be regulated. In tragedy, or farce, there was a gift from the victim to the perpetrator. This gift was potency. But in satisfaction was death. So there was the demand to be a victim.

I thought—Or a cancer might be outside, like the whale that Jonah sat in. Cut it, and you would bob up to the surface like a cork.

Then you would look round for a millstone to land on.

I was involved in some pilgrimage in winter. Because I had no guilt, I was doing penance. I risked wolves and robbers. This was for the sake of people who loved me.

Natalia sometimes joined me in my shelter. There was enough room in so narrow a grave.

Sometimes she sat on a throne and offered me her toe for indulgences. I refused to crawl.

The snow came early one year. We sped down a slope. She ran into a tree and her hair became branches.

I remembered—Suffering is that which gives warning against pain.

Sometimes when I was at the cottage at weekends, I saw myself as gravel being bounced up and down in a sieve. I thought—There must be diamonds; or there would not be so many prospectors.

I tried to explain some of this to Elizabeth. I admitted—Explaining doesn't make it any easier.

We, and other people, were on all fours; some hoped that they were kneeling.

In the night, I sometimes smelled Natalie like the home of a bird a thousand miles away.

There were poles that energy passed between. If the poles fused, or became too far apart, there was apathy. If they were held at the right distance, there was pain.

I could say—This is the spark of being human.

Natalie was a knife sterilised in urine.

Sometimes I longed to be back in the whale's stomach: where I would be white; the acid making us all sinless.

The House of Commons seems to consist mainly of corridors: these are of two kinds, the stone-flagged and vaulted where the public are admitted and which are like a railway station where everyone is on the point of arriving or departing so that any requests made or undertakings given have the air, as if by design, of being untrustworthy and provisional: and the other kind are those in which only the initiates walk in order to fill in time between alighting in one warm room or another; they move to and fro with their hands in their pockets and their thumbs pointing forwards; going about their business, or imagination, of ordering the universe. The doors are guarded by smiling keepers in knee-breeches; the atmosphere is the reverse of that of a madhouse; what is publicly presented is a fantasy, and in private is whatever might be sane.

Politicians are active and predatory people who have little to prey on now except each other. They place themselves in circumstances in which dreams of conquests are still possible: these carpeted and stone-flagged corridors are clearings in the jungle: here the elders gather and rave against their enemies. Their enemies are amongst themselves: but their sanity is still that of hunters. Around them are heroic mosaics of kings and rebels of their past: once there were panoplies to killing; now their descendants have their dreams. In the marble halls where the populace makes demands on them they can still feel martyred: not at the stake, but in listening to triviality when dreams are so grandiose. Politicians are like sleepwalkers: they do not want to wake or the shock might put them to bed. They are large-scale men forced into such proximity that they have no room for expansion: when they put a hand on your shoulder it is as if they are touching wood: you are a platform, or a bead in a rosary. In the central sanctum where on green-leather benches the initiates apparently come to sleep they feel most at home; but they do not sleep, they remember their origins; the whoop and gurgle of hippos, the rustle of leopards in the grass. The gathering of elders has become turned inwards; but it echoes its old sounds to remember its identity. Afterwards, the elders go out to the quiet world and dinner.

My secretary Yseult used to say—If you feel like this, why did you get into it?

I would say—There was not much else.

And besides, there was vanity.

But to get out, I had to achieve some breakdown. The ties of identity were powerful.

People did not seem to notice anything odd in me. They walked past me with their hands in their pockets and their thumbs pointing forwards. The men in knee-breeches smiled. I thought—I may be no odder than anyone.

I would say—Yseult, am I having a nervous breakdown?

She would say—I think you're the only sane person here!

She banged at her typewriter.

In our office papers came in and went out and did not make much difference. They gave employment to messengers who carried them to and fro; to builders, who constructed spaces in which to store them.

People rang, or called, when they did not want to be lonely.

I said "Yseult, do you think this makes any difference?"

"What?"

"Politics."

She said "Without it, wouldn't we all be cavemen?"

I tried to work out what we were doing. If we were a computer, one part would affect all the others. But it would still be affected.

I said "Who does the programming? The bits of paper that are fed into the machine?"

Yseult said "What about free will?"

There was a committee to discuss my report about Ndoula. I moved along corridors with my thumbs pointing forwards. Under my arm was a file of papers which I could set alight and shoot like arrows.

In a small room underground were gathered Clitheroe, Helliman, Peters, and the Minister. Others, who were expected, had not come.

Helliman said "What is it, Ascot or the Derby?"

Clitheroe said "I think Byron's being buried in the Abbey."

We settled round a table. Yseult sat apart, like a hostess at a dance hall.

Peters said "Tony?"

I became a person with mad eyes suspended by my shoulders from a meat-hook. I hunched over the table. I would be transported, bellowing, to where my throat would be cut and I would be at peace: I need not be talking.

Reports had come in that Ndoula and his followers were being victimised in the desert. They were being deprived of visitors and books: they were threatened with solitary confinement.

Freedom fighters were being trained on the border to rescue Ndoula.

We were round a brown polished table on a hot afternoon. We had to stay there for sixty minutes.

"And what does that mean?"

I said "Three boats arrived carrying pig iron."

Air-conditioning hummed. Our voices struggled to get round corners. We dabbled in our papers as if they were entrails.

At the end of the afternoon we would make recommendations which Yseult would bang out on her typewriter. These would be passed back to us for approval; and would be the minutes of the next discussion.

"George?"

"Are we including China?"

"Who sends us this information?"

"Johnson."

"Hasn't he been sent down?"

We tried not to catch each other's eyes. If we did, we might see nothing just behind them.

"I think, Tony, we want more information."

I said "Someone ought to go out there."

I thought—One of us will have to start banging on the table; then we will imagine we are caring about Ndoula.

Clitheroe shouted "All this is balls! Forgive me! There are people dying in Africa!"

Helliman said "I agree."

Peters, the chairman, murmured "Jack?"

Jack was the Minister. He was here as an observer. He had drawn champagne glasses on his blotter. I thought—He is the only one of us who knows what he is doing.

Helliman said "As far as the Chinese go, you could scratch their backs with a walking stick."

Clitheroe said "Are there any operational?"

Yseult made notes on her typewriter.

I said "Nothing else makes sense."

I thought—I will go myself and walk across the desert.

Peters said "You're saying we should do nothing then?"

I wanted the committee to end so that I could go on thinking about Natalia. Perhaps if I thought hard enough, someone might be saved.

The Minister was rounding off his champagne glasses with scrolls and clouds like cherubs.

I thought—He is the dead king halfway up the mountain.

Peters said again "Jack, I'm sorry?"

The Minister pointed to himself: he said "Me?"

He turned to Yseult. He said "Can you read that bit again Miss—"

I said "Yseult."

Yseult blushed. She said "What?"

She read "That someone should go out—"

The Minister began picking up his papers.

Peters said "Did we say that?"

The Minister smiled at him.

I thought—I expected him to smile at me.

Once Natalia and I went away to the country for the weekend: we arrived at a hotel by a river and signed in as couples do for their last day on earth or before the police arrive: we had often talked of going away: she had said—You know what it would mean? I had said—Yes. She had a suitcase as big as a removals van. The hotel was an old boathouse above a lock; the river pushed past with gold scum on black water. I sat on the edge of the bed and watched Natalia unpack. She had shoes and under-clothes wrapped like bacon. I thought—There is nothing to do here but make love: the scum is underneath and you have to dig down to cultivate: there are twenty-four hours a day and we will starve. I could say—Shall we go for a walk? But we had come here to make love. Which was what we wanted. Natalia was wearing one of her short skirts which ended just below her behind. When she bent, there was the stomach of a starving child in India. The river ran to a weir where small boats smashed. Natalie would not like it if I simply made love: she would not like it if I didn't. She moved between her suitcase and the cupboard. I had nothing to do, being happy watching her. I tried to work out when it would be best to make love; this had to be thought of like strawberries. Natalia finished unpacking and sat beside me on the bed. I thought—She is wondering what I will do. I said "Shall we go for a walk?" She looked mournful. I said "Or make love." I thought—It is worse when one has decided. We remained on the bed. I thought—We are in a boat going over the weir. Then—We are going through all this so it will be all right for us. She turned to me. I thought—It is she who has decided then. This was, after all, man's prerogative. Her body, with its slight torso and long legs, was an arena on which several persons might fight: one was part of herself and another that extension of her which she imagined me: I, and part of myself, were also engaged in this battle: two came together on the golden sand, and Natalia and I remained on the sidelines watching. I leaned over her and she held her thumbs against my throat: we moved into dimensions in which only allegories described us. We were toppled off horses and lay in the dust. Banners were flown aloft in triumph. Natalia was a gladiator with soft hair and sweet breath. I offered my life for her.

I said "And I thought we were going to walk by the river!" She pulled hair from her mouth, or sword, laughing.

When we did walk by the river I became dizzy picking flowers. These might make us forget our past lives: they grew below a willow, on a bank between her legs. Where she sat, her body was a formula to deal with the outside universe. A formula was different from a description. The movement of

51

planets, when she walked, was in diagram. Below her waist the slope of a hill ran down. We held hands like tangents. Our muscles were trees which overhung the river. Pollen dropped from her; fed insects.

I said "I didn't think it could be like this."

She said "I didn't think anything could be like this!"

I thought—Words are no use for happiness.

We had dinner on a terrace overlooking the river. From here we might drown. I thought—In happiness there is nothing to do; time stops; the purpose of the world has run down. We would eat each other and grow thin; become snakes in the cores of apples. When she drank, bats tangled in her blood like fireflies. I thought—We are in a place where humans should only dream: in chasms, the roots yawning.

At night she became the sweet child again, innocent and peaceful, whom by the moon I could dismember. Sensations peeled off her like a skin. An entrail slithered. I pulled the cord tight. My head stretched back. She made me groan. I thought—I am on an anthill, tethered; where limbs and castles grow enormous.

The next day we walked as we had done the day before; as we would the day after; we lay on the bed. I thought—This will go on forever. We were by a sea with ruined pillars. Horses stood in the waves. I thought—Heaven on earth is the moment of damnation; the devil waits with his quill and blood of pigs. Beyond us, in a grove of trees, women in black were gathered. They would close our mouths and squeeze our piss out. A god watched. I thought—We will settle by this sea: then one night the crabs will get us.

At our table the second evening—we did not talk much; we had known there was nothing to say—I began to think there was something I might—across the table like an altar—Into thy hands O Lord—that is, I might be ready for this—anything—to give up my life, spirit—though these did not seem quite the words—I might say—Save us—but I was happy enough, now, to choose damnation—but this did not seem quite the word: but I thought I would say something, anyway, whether or not she would follow me—though I did not quite think I was Faust nor she Eurydice—she was an angel, after all, with her gift of all that was desirable—and I was a builder if with one foot in the sand. But an angel is also a death-bringer. I thought we would drink together, from some cup, the water rising past our mouths and eyes and understanding; the candles on the table, which were our wings, burning; so that we would be at peace, like Icarus. I suddenly had a vision of my daughter Sophie riding a white pony by the sea. Natalia put her hand across the table and held me. She gazed at me: she was asking me a question. I thought I knew what she was meaning. And I thought I should say it, because if I did not, I might never have another chance. I had a vision of Assyrians riding across plains. I said "Will you—" She said "What?" I paused. It was, after all, a difficult decision. Natalia had a small straight nose and jet-black hair; her mouth was a bow which the feathers of arrows might brush against. I said "—come away with me." She said "I thought I was away with you." She withdrew her hand. I looked over the terrace to the water. We were sitting out of doors at the end of dinner. We had finished fruit. I thought— If she does this now, I cannot bear it: she will be letting the snake make love to her in front of me. I felt a fury coming up like a limb that has been asleep. I said "You know what I mean." She said "What?" My heart thumped in my coffin. She had said—You know what this will mean? I had said—Yes. The nail went crooked as she smiled. The snake peeped out from between her eyelids. I could shout—But you have be-trayed me! Or—Now we will have to do everything in sweat and crawling on our hands! She pulled at her napkin. She looked at it as if it were a blindfold. I said "Why do you do this?" She said "Do what?" I said "Destroy us." She jumped as if she had been shot. I thought—It is I who have shot her. I held up my hands. I thought—But would it have been different if I had said I would marry her? She said "Can you take me to the station please?" I could say—But we have been happier than we have ever been before in our lives! I watched the river. Bodies, or scum, were on the surface. I thought—I can defeat you. I kicked as if at a stone. Her face was hard as diamonds. I would finish my wine and walk quietly to the bedroom. I said "Did you wait for this?" She said "For what?" I said "Till I said I'd do anything?" She said "Have you said you would do anything?" I thought—We might both be right. I could explain—But I did mean it! Then—But I do not in fact think I should marry her. She finished her drink and walked quietly to the bedroom. She began putting clothes into her case. Here we had been happier than we had ever been before in our lives. When she bent, her body remained hungry as an apple. I thought—And now we have eaten it. I thought I should read a book so I would appear indifferent. She sat in a chair. I thought—Soon she will want me to forgive her. I said "I thought you were going to the station." She said "I am." She picked up a book and began reading. I thought I would go to the bathroom and be sick. There was a sink with white porcelain. I knelt and banged my head against a tile. She said "What a strange noise!" I took her by the throat as if to strangle her. She said "Let go." I said "All right I will." She said "You'll be sorry about this in the morning." I said "I'm sorry now." I put my hand to my head to see if it was bleeding. She said "Have you got any sleeping pills?" I said "How many?" She said "The lot." I said "I'll give you two."

3

SOMETIMES MY WIFE Elizabeth and I meet on neutral ground to go about family business; she does not join me in my business and I do not join her in hers; from our home, all over the world she helps starving children. On neutral ground we both appear in disguise; Elizabeth in a summer frock and stockings, myself in tweeds like a doctor. We were going to see a boarding school to which we might send our daughter Sophie. We did not want to send Sophie to a boarding school, but were going to see one in order to confirm this. I met Elizabeth at the railway station; she travelled like a Victorian with our two children and rugs and a thermos. The children moved up the platform trailing their clothes like hoops.

Adam said "Why are we going to see this school?"

I said "To demonstrate our solidarity against society."

In the car, with my family, I played the role of a Jewish patriarch. Sun blew in our eyes: dust moved across the desert.

Adam said "Do you think one ought to rebel?"

I said "Yes, in order to keep society going."

I thought—I frighten the wolves away with my magician's rod, my bangs and crackers.

Elizabeth frowned. She did not like my paradoxes. She saw them as scarecrows.

Sophie said "At the school, will they have horses?"

Adam said "What's happening about freeing Ndoula?"

With my hands on the steering wheel I guided my family towards the walls of Jericho; which we hoped would fall down, while we shook and peered down our trumpets.

I said "Nothing much."

"Shouldn't we do sanctions?"

"We are."

"Can't you drop paratroops?"

"Would you be a paratroop?"

The school to which we were going was a large country house in a wood. Girls and boys would stand around as if at an Edwardian garden party. At the first call of the trumpet they would have to decide whether or not to volunteer.

Elizabeth said "That's unfair."

"Why?"

Adam said "I wouldn't mind."

I thought—I might be encouraging him, in order to justify my own difficulties.

I said "People get killed."

Elizabeth said "You can't make it a personal thing."

I said "Getting killed is personal."

Sophie said "Adam won't get killed!"

We arrived at the school. Children were bent under the enormous weight of their tennis rackets. They were nuts of which squirrels would have to crack the shells.

Adam said "Perhaps we need a war."

I said "Perhaps we do."

We stood on the drive and were like tradesmen come up from the village. In the distance were the sounds of violins.

I said "School always makes me feel guilty."

Adam shouted "Come out and fight!"

We waited on a parapet. The headmaster would see us in ten minutes. We were travellers in an Arab town, trying to sell our daughter.

I thought—By betrayal we hurt ourselves and perhaps make others human.

We were taken round science rooms and music rooms and libraries. There was a smell of fish. Newts were being dissected in a laboratory.

Adam said "But where are the horses?"

Sophie punched him.

I thought—One day the experiment will blow up; our children will have built a tower too close to heaven.

Boys and girls seemed strung up with hair like Saint Sebastian. Indolently, they pulled out arrows. Their bodies, with pride, deflated.

I said "Can we go now?"

Elizabeth said "We are trying to think of Sophie."

There was a park of oak and elm trees. A family had lived here since the time of Hastings. Indolently, they had pulled out flesh.

Adam said "Could one go out there?"

"Where?"

"To Central Africa."

I thought—Fathers should die as soon as children have reached puberty.

I said "Oh Adam, don't go there!"

Elizabeth said "Why not, if you think society's so rotten?"

I said "I didn't say society's rotten!"

A beautiful boy with auburn hair came out and leaned as if on a spear. He said "The headmaster will see you."

I thought—I will run away and hide in the shrubbery.

The headmaster was a small bright man with gentle eyes. He said "I am one of your admirers!"

I said "Oh are you?"

Adam looked away.

He shook hands with Adam.

Sophie and Elizabeth were whispering in the background.

Elizabeth said "Oh yes! Are there any horses?"

I tried to imagine what Natalia might be thinking. If this story were hers, what might she write of our first meeting—

Darling Anthony, I will be writing this for you: and for you Edward, if only to stop you for a moment haunting me.

I was in an upstairs room talking to a friend. There was this large man like a figure on a ceiling. He came up and asked me to dance. I said—I don't dance. He said—Of course you do!

I went with him to the dance floor. I had not thought he would do this. He lifted me off my feet. I said—Put me down! He said—We're dancing!

I stood with my hands folded. The music had stopped. I looked at the ground. I did not think, if he wanted, I would do anything to stop him.

Edward had been unfaithful to me.

We sat on a wrought-iron bench beneath beech trees. He held me by my side. He was quiet. He rocked backwards and forwards as if in pain.

Darling Anthony, I did not ask you to do this!

I did not know if he wanted me to comfort him: to put his head against my breast.

I used to forget how large he was: he was like the sky, in one corner of the ceiling.

He said—Can I see you?

I thought I could say—Aren't you seeing me?

I had been brought up in a house with the noise of television always going. My mother and father fought in the kitchen. I had waited for someone to come and rescue me, riding across a plain.

After the party I said to Edward—What is his name?

He said—Anthony.

I made an image of it. I find it difficult to use his name.

I am writing this for you; and for you, Edward, if only to stop you for a moment haunting me.

I sat by the telephone.

My ancestors came from a world of wide forests and corn-fields. Men with lances rode across plains.

I thought if I wrote to him he might come. I did not think he would telephone.

Dear Anthony, Will you have lunch with me? I will under-stand if you do not want to.

I thought I would buy some clothes. To make myself pretty. There was a mouth inside me starving.

On the telephone he said—Thank you for your letter! His voice was composed. I wondered if he did this often; in order to be kind.

After lunch we went to a hotel. He was larger than I remembered him. We sat at a bar. He hummed. The air outside him seemed to quiver.

He said—Shall we, then?

I do not know why, Anthony, if it was so difficult for you.

In the room he took me by the shoulders. He said—I must tell you. I could say—I don't want to know. He said—All right then.

It did not seem so different from anything I had expected. He crawled on a rock-face. I groped. He seemed to be reaching for something beyond me.

I said—I've never done this before.

He said—What?

I said—I mean, except with Edward.

We arranged to meet again at the same hotel. I thought I could do this just once more. The ache inside me had become a small soft mouth. Perhaps it is most dangerous, when it does not hurt too much.

Why did you let it, if you knew what would happen?

In the bar again he was attentive and kind. I thought—I may defeat him. I said—Can I have another coffee?

In the room I sat on the bed. He walked up and down. He said—Oh God! He knelt in front of me. He said—Do you know what is happening?

I could not make out whether or not he was suffering.

He was like a vulture chained to a rock.

I thought—He will not defeat me.

I lay on my back with one knee up and my arms above my head.

I had the impression that he was acting. He seemed to be watching himself from somewhere behind his back.

I said—What is it?

He said—I can't tell you!

He did not seem able to do anything.

I felt the ache in my mouth dying, that I had swallowed and had once wanted so much.

That evening I talked with Edward. I said—This comes in a book I've been reading.

Edward said—It isn't anyone?

We arranged to meet once more at the same hotel. I do not know why I did this. I thought—It will be over, and will never happen again.

He seemed in a state of extraordinary excitement.

I said—I've got my period.

He said—Oh that's all right then!

He sat on the bed and hummed.

I said—Don't you want to?

He said—Oh of course!

I lay with one knee raised and my arms above my head.

He was like a corner of the ceiling.

He said—I'll tell you then.

I said—What?

I remembered my mother who was a thin woman with bones like sacking. She said—Give nothing!

He laughed.

I do not know why he did this. The air around him glittered.

He put his hand over my eyes.

My father was a man slamming the door of the kitchen.

He said—It's in the mind: get it out.

He began undressing me.

I tried to think of the holiday I was going on with Edward.

He said—Put your arms round me: hold me.

I said—I can't.

He said—Call me my love.

I said—I can't.

There was the slam of the door: the voices shouting in the kitchen.

He said—I know it's difficult.

It was as if he were peeling me.

He said—Well, you can try!

He was using me as if I were a trophy. I lay in the dust and put a hand up and touched him. I thought I could take it back.

He took hold of my breast between forefinger and thumb; pulled it.

I was hanging at some distance.

I thought—So it is true then!

He put a finger up my behind.

I was underneath him. He was a stone sphinx. Tenderly, birds flew out from him.

There was a time I thought he would never stop.

A bit of rock fell off and lodged in my entrails.

I could shout—Darling!

He laughed and said—There now!

There were knots like ropes: a place where a child's skull had not closed yet.

I said—Why are you laughing?

He said—Because I'm happy!

We were lying on a bed; where he had taken a rib out of me.

I said—What will you do if I fall in love with you?

He said—You mean, you're not in love with me?

He looked amazed.

Darling Anthony, I will be writing this for you; and for you, Edward, if only to stop you for a moment haunting me.

Joe Gregory, Sylvia's brother, came to see me. He said "I've been commissioned to do some articles on Central Africa."

I sat in my office behind my desk. I stretched out my hands.

I thought—I am a drop of oil on the point of touching wood and spreading.

He said "What I want to know particularly is, what arrangements have been made to send in troops."

I said "Joe, you can't know that!"

"Why not?"

"It's the only question of any importance!"

Joe's big black eyebrows went up in arrows. I thought—If he were the devil, he would trip over his tail running across the desert.

I said "Who're you writing for?"

"Ned Symon."

Ned Symon was the editor of the National Sunday Newspaper.

I said "There are always plans to send in troops. There are plans for instance for an amphibious landing in Wales. People are employed to make these plans. They earn their living."

Joe said "Who'd want to land in Wales?"

Joe was a good journalist. He observed events and described his observations.

"Joe, have a drink."

He watched my hands. They did not seem to be shaking.

I said "What else are you working on?"

"Drugs."

"Is that interesting?"

I thought—Like Elizabeth, he would measure interest by catastrophe.

He said "Old man, do you know how many teenage girls have syphilis?"

"No."

His eyelids became concave. I thought—One day, while he watches, I will be taken by Japanese soldiers and beaten on the soles of my feet.

He said "Come along with me old man, and I'll show you

how the other half lives."

I thought—Natalie is another half that lives.

He said "Rather up your street, isn't it?"

I thought—Natalia feels sick when she sees someone eating oranges.

He said "Or do you find it falling off?"

I could say—No, it hasn't fallen off.

I said "Do you?"

"Yes." His eyes went smoky.

Joe's wife, Margaret, was a big fair-haired girl who used to bend over her stove to look into her oven.

He said "It's the old lady."

"She doesn't want it?"

"Yes. She does."

"Oh I see."

I thought—We deserve what we get.

This was one of the afternoons when I was supposed to be running the country. Traffic swam past in the street outside. People came to see me to fill in time between appointments.

Joe said "Do you know what Sylvia makes her boyfriend do?"

"No. What?"

"Eat grass."

"Why?"

"I suppose, over-civilisation."

I wondered how far it would be to run across the desert to rescue Ndoula. I could use Joe's eyebrows as wirecutters.

Joe said "Do you know how much he made out of the budget?"

"Who?"

"Sylvia's boyfriend."

"No."

"Sixty thousand."

I thought—Natalie, Natalia; are you at your back door in your white dress, waiting for a thunderstorm?

He said "Free of tax."

I said "Take me then."

"Where?"

"To this place. Where teenage girls might have syphilis."

His yellow eyes glittered.

I thought—I will do what is proper with publicans and sinners.

He said "I'll introduce you to the pusher."

I said "Yes. Elizabeth will be jealous."

His eyelids came down like a portcullis. He said "How is Elizabeth?"

I thought—Of course, he is very fond of her.

I said "Fine."

"Are you sure?"

I tried to imagine what it was like being Joe. He had flared nostrils. There were dark curves between his nose and his mouth. His face was sad and beautiful. I had once made a pass at his wife Margaret in a taxi.

"Do have a drink, Joe."

He shook his head.

I thought—He might think I'm an alcoholic.

I had once loved Joe.

He said "Old man, you should watch it!"

He might be referring to me, or to Elizabeth, or to what I was thinking about Natalia. I needed more time to try to understand all this; from which such meetings, like my imagination, were diverting me.

Driving down to the country at the weekend I imagined I might say—I had the most extraordinary evening with Joe last night! he took me to a café somewhere in North London—you know—pin-tables like coffins and a coffee- the same as a fruit-machine. Elizabeth would be lying underneath a beech tree: there would be a small pool of sweat upon her throat. I would say—And Joe was asking all his usual stuff, you know; as if he had to go in and out of the room on his hands and knees backwards. Nowadays dope pedlars and addicts are like an aristocracy, you know; because they are victims and can hurt you. Once Elizabeth had liked my stories: we had lain side by side in the long summer grass and I had licked her throat with my tongue. I would say—Anyway, there was a man behind the bar, you know, about six foot four and bulging halfway like a snake with bananas. As if he'd swallowed them, you know. And Joe was asking him questions like when did the next assignment come in; and the man was telling Joe it was held up at the customs. I was on the road driving to the country. I thought—I am making all this up because I have not seen Natalia: without food, the mind goes into fantasies. I could say—Why do you think anyone believes journalists? Is there really a civil war in Africa? Elizabeth sometimes now did not like my stories: she needed seriousness as if it were water in a lifeboat. I would sit in a deck chair above her; would look round at my possessions; my wood and apple trees; my cornfield. I would say—And then the most extraordinary man came in; in a white suit, you know; so tight that he was like toothpaste being squeezed; he was the pusher. I thought this witty. I could explain—I had to see things like this, you see, because Joe was so deferential; he treated the man's white suit like a surplice. So I went over to the jukebox and put on a record. But I was getting tired myself of this sort of story. Someone might come on to the lawn with a telegram. I thought—And Elizabeth will know I am saying this to cover up about Natalia; not only to her, but to myself. I could say—And Joe had to put a hand to his ear. Or I could shout—All right! I know this is awful! it's a story against myself! If I did not love Joe how could I be so awful? Elizabeth and I would sit on the lawn where once we had been so happy; with our woods and cornfields. I would say—Well anyway, there we were, you see, with this black man and Joe doing his salamis—

I mean his salaams—I could not go on. I was driving down to the cottage in the country. It was a journey of about two hours. Elizabeth would be lying on the lawn in a bathing dress. She would have her eyes closed. She drank up the sun like someone in a lifeboat. I could say—And then there came into the room the most marvellous girl, you know; like a champion high-jumper. I wondered why I did this. I could explain—But it keeps my mind off other things. Elizabeth would say—What other things? I had not noticed the road for several minutes. I was driving through beech trees. I wondered what the girls would be like in the café if I ever got there. Elizabeth would say—And did Joe get his story? This time I would make the weekend happy. I would bound across the lawn doing my funny walk like a one-wheel bicycle. Elizabeth would be lying with the pool of sweat at her throat. I would put my head down and drink this. It was easy to make another person happy: you just held them in your arms and called them Darling. I wondered what Natalia would be doing. Elizabeth would say—And who else have you been seeing? I would say—No one. This was true. I had not seen Natalia since we had been by the river. I would sit in a deck chair and stare at the grass. There was a hidden world of tiny trees and enormous insects. I thought—It is impossible to feel what another person is feeling: you climb up a castle wall and the ivy crumbles. I would make Elizabeth a daisy chain. I would fasten this round her throat. I thought—Human beings are made for functions they cannot do: the flowers we give strangle us. I was arriving at the village near our cottage. I thought—Perhaps we are happy only at moments of change; when moving from one transformation to another. In the village there were cigarette advertisements in white enamel. The enamel had holes like those made by bullets. I stepped out by my courtyard. I would not look for a telegram. My last row of bricks was unfinished. I would go and shoot another antelope. I went through the house to the view of cornfields. There were deck chairs. The lawn was empty. The corn was half cut, with a wide path to a wood. There was a combine harvester like a dragon above which the air shook. Beside it stood a boy and a girl. They were holding hands. The girl had dark hair. I thought—Our fantasies feed us. The dragon was wounded. The boy was my son Adam. I did not know the girl. I thought I should go back into the house and look for a telegram. Elizabeth was not on the lawn. There were papers strewn about the sitting room. Adam and the girl seemed happy. I thought—So our life goes on outside us; at the edge of a dark wood.

Natalie said "I'm definitely going to kill myself."

I thought I might say—Do then.

I said "Why?"

There was silence at the end of the telephone.

I was lying on the bed in my flat, where I had returned after a weekend in the country.

I felt as if I had an enormous fish on the end of the line. It was lying at the bottom of the ocean.

I had to stay still, and then I would land it.

I said "You're always saying you're going to kill yourself. You do this in order to get just what you want; which you do, but then you don't want it. If you want to go on wanting what you think you want, you have to try not to get it. Do you see this? Then you get it. Even if it kills you."

I wondered if I might read a newspaper. Natalie's silences often went on for several minutes.

There was a pile of papers at the end of the bed. One of them had an article about Central Africa.

Natalie said "Is that all you can say?"

The article said that everyone had to be absolutely clear in their intentions about Central Africa, or else the situation might result in chaos.

Natalie said "I've been lying here all day in absolute misery—"

I wondered if it might be possible to have dinner with Natalia. I had an appointment at six. It was now five-thirty.

Natalie said "I thought you could help me but you can't. Good-bye."

I was trying to turn over the pages of the newspaper. The receiver of the telephone was under my chin. My arms were stretched as if on a cross.

Natalie said "Are you reading a newspaper?"

"No."

"I thought I heard a rustling."

I thought—I have just got out of a very hot bath. I will catch cold and get pneumonia. I am doing all this for Natalia.

I hoped my silences were not too oppressive.

Natalie said "From the first you've never loved me!"

In another few minutes I would have to get a taxi. I had to get dressed. The timing had to be right, or else I would lose her.

She said "I suppose you do this to all your girlfriends. I hope your new one is nice!"

I said "Oh do stuff it!"

I was trying to reach my trousers. I was hooked like a fish on the end of the telephone.

Natalia said "What are you doing?"

I said "Trying to reach my trousers."

She said "Why haven't you got your trousers?"

I said "Because of my new girlfriend."

I thought I could lay the receiver down quietly while I put on my trousers. I sometimes went too far with Natalia.

I said "Hullo?"

"Yes?"

"Don't you think that's funny?"

"No!" A voice from the tomb.

I wanted to shout—My beloved!

She said "Where are you going then?"

"Out."

"Where?"

"On the tiles."

I expected her to say—Who with? Then I would say—You.

She said "What is on the tiles?"

I laughed. I thought—Perhaps she is like me: she knows all the time we will have dinner.

Or—She does not really care about me!

I had got hold of my shoes. My trousers would not go over them.

She said "So you're not going to see me!"

"I haven't said that."

"You've as good as said it."

I held the receiver between my knees and bowed my head while I put on my trousers. I thought—I am on a tightrope with my arms out.

She said "I just want to see you."

"I want to see you too."

"But you said you didn't."

I almost replaced the receiver. I thought—It is extraordinary how she manages even now to make me angry.

I said "Where shall we have dinner?"

She said "I don't know."

"I don't know either." I felt tired.

I thought—The moment of greatest vulnerability is when the fish is almost landed. You lean too far over into the water.

I said "As a matter of fact, this time when we haven't seen each other has been extraordinarily useful. I've done a lot of work. Seen the family."

She said "Good."

I said "I've been so miserable!"

She said "Oh so have I!"

There was silence again. I thought—God is the fisherman; who provides, or doesn't, dinner.

I yelled "All right come round here then!"

She said "I'm just thinking."

"What?"

Natalia had a long body with a boy's thinness: from the side, amazing projections.

I said "I know what you're thinking."

"What?"

"That you haven't got anything to wear for dinner."

She said "How extraordinary! That's exactly what I was thinking!"

4

OMETIMES AS PART of the job I was still doing—I had
made it clear I was going to give up; had offered as a
reason a lack of enthusiasm as well as health—I went to
that part of the country I was supposed to represent—represent
as a hole might represent a bucket—about twenty miles from
our cottage and along roads where people sat nose to tail on
summer Sundays: and I tried to force myself into some shape
which might not appear ludicrous; a piece of carved wood,
perhaps, like a totem or a judge in a wig; so I would not be out
of place when met by judges themselves or schoolmasters or
policemen; might get through the afternoon even without
wanting to be condemned and tied to a stake. There would be
generals with breasts and behinds like pouter pigeons; a proces-
sion as if at the opening of a Victorian railway station; very
slow, with a man with a red flag in front and someone almost
run over behind; crowds like smoke drifting towards a palace.
I had encouraged the rumour that I was on the bottle; had
thought this would make my way out of public life easier. But
people were tolerant in this envious age, imagining I was worse
off than them. I would arrive at a school hall or municipal
building and would step out on to what would once have been
a carpet—was now more like a bowling alley—a pathway
cleared for a celebrity to roll within—only avoiding, if possible, the gutter. I had accepted that society functioned best if
there were people ready to make sacrifices of their hearts—
these cheerful representatives like totems—but I was supposed
to smile myself at the smell of burning. I would move within
groups with the oiled face of a cricket bat; wished to see myself
disappearing to the boundary. There was not much of a crowd
now: the days had gone when politicians got star billing; now
they were actors mouthing in silent films, of interest only to
specialists. These were the civic dignitaries and party faithfuls

whose function and thus existence depended on a recognition of my own: all still needing to be given proof in photographs. The journalists, like mourners, perhaps turned up out of politeness. We would freeze into drops of water at the moment of splashes; then move on re-formed as a jellyfish. Public life is a business of moving between one centre of attention and another—I had thought this before—it absorbs the energies of people who would otherwise be destructive. Devotion is given to the business of the process going without a hitch; a timetable rigidly to be adhered to. The end product, as often in a modern factory, is waste. We ourselves were probably waste: we moved down lines of people and shook hands as if nuts were being screwed up in us. This was our conveyor belt to the scrap heap. At least, something was happening before death.

The rumour that I was on the bottle or even slightly mad had enabled me to play my role up a little; I would wander off and inspect some stray workmen mending a road; admire flowers growing out of concrete. My fear that my eccentricity might prove acceptable was a dream: a love of oddity was not practical. I created a slight air of boredom round me; men looked at their watches and realised that the conveyor belt was slow; signals were made discreetly for the programme to be speeded. I thought—These are good people who make the world go round; it is my fault if I am dizzy.

—We are so glad—

—My pleasure—

—Found your way—

I hoped to move through these gatherings like salts. But when I smiled, my face had not quite been put together. Cracks showed in the concrete. Flowers might still emerge. The problem was not how to make contact with people but how to avoid it.

—How's the world—

—Not so—

—Treating—

Going in the drill hall, or playground, or club rooms, I thought—It might be easy if we could live with contempt; could thus anaesthetise each other and be safe like beetles in a bottle. I could not have contempt because I was ludicrous. I thought—I have planned this. I moved past tables with raffia and pots of honey; pensioners in bathchairs, boys and girls like formaldehyde. I kept my hands behind my back and bent low out of respect for possible undernourishment. I was a Gulliver on paths of good intentions. I stepped on to a platform draped with flags. The faces seemed familiar. Politicians are photographs touched up to seem the same and stop them shining. A microphone was placed close to my mouth. It hung like an apple. When I bit there was a sound of sucking and gurgling.

—Hear me at the back!—

—Thank you—

—Not my purpose—

Sometimes I could not imagine it was my voice that was speaking. A person inside myself observed myself working. There were knobs and dials and men in white suits facing screens. My teeth flashed like a pin-table. I pulled a lever and no prizes came out.

—Like measles, best to get it over with—

In front of me a youth club, firemen, women's institute, British Legion. They had not wanted to come: might have been affronted if they hadn't. At the end, they wanted to go away and think how pointless it was; having achieved this satisfaction.

—I expect a cup of tea—

—Just one word however—

All that I had to say remained secret. This was not an intention; it was to do with the nature of speaking. There was no structure for words to communicate what I knew. What I did not know, custom made acceptable.

I might say—Keep your wicks trimmed girls: oil your dipsticks.

"There is one thing I have to say about the situation in Central Africa. Many of you may wonder what it has to do with us in this country. Well, often you're right. To protest can be just to protest against the human condition. But there are instances, still, when special responsibilities are forced on us by history."

A voice at the back—"Rubbish!"

I said "The test is not in expediency: you can't count the cost. Also the causes you have to fight for are not the only good ones in the world. But you recognise them by relationship. It is like members of your own family—"

Louder again—"Rubbish!"

I leaned with my fists on the table. I said "Would you explain please?"

He stood up: a small-eyed man with a scrubbed moustache. A lover of his mother and horses.

"I don't see why these people who are no better than ignorant savages—"

"Ah!" A relief in the hall: a wind through baobab trees.

"Should be compared—"

—Bang! An auctioneer's hammer.

The chairman had thick spectacles like targets.

I said "No, let him speak."

I pointed my finger like a prophet.

I thought—We know where we are now.

"Should be expected—"

Another voice—"Sit!"

"I won't! Be treated—"

I clapped my hands. The birds flew up from the forest. Animals paused by the drinking hole.

I said "I don't know about your family!" I smiled.

There was a shout of laughter.

The chairman looked at his watch.

Afterwards, walking past white tables as if they were tapes through a minefield, I thought—This is a safe war; I am in the royal enclosure on D Day; I have made my millions out of hubcaps. Sitting for tea at a flowered table I found the man with the scrubbed moustache there before me. He put down his gloves and his stick.

"You're going to Africa."

"Yes."

"Perhaps you'll tell those buggers—"

A lady with a flowered hat bent over me. In her hands was a fruitcake.

"Your lovely speech!"

"Not at all."

"We do appreciate—"

I thought—She and the scrubbed man should take each other in their arms; like a nurse and a wounded soldier.

"Tell them what they can do with their precious Ndoula."

I said "What are you afraid of?"

"Me?"

"Gentlemen!"

I said "I should be more brave."

After tea, with caraway seeds and ices, the lady with the fruit hat clearing for the scrap heap, I thought—Now I will have to be more brave. We moved on to a playing field where bright boys stood like poppies. They might go out and die there. A goalpost was like a spear stuck in a grave. Our hair blew about in the wind. We held our scalps on. We came to a roadway.

I said "Where's—"

"Who?"

"That scrubbed man."

We were looking for cars in a car park.

"Ah! Perhaps it was unfortunate. He had trouble with his son the other day."

"What?"

"On drugs, you know; and dressed as a woman."

I saw the man walking across a playground. I thought—He has been so often beaten.

I shouted "Oi!"

I wanted to take him to a pub; treat him.

He turned for a moment: his elbows in to his sides like a totem.

I thought—But it would not work: for him, I cannot get beaten.

One of the happiest times Natalia and I ever had was a summer when Edward brought proceedings for divorce: we were summoned by Potterton, my lawyer, and Dangerfield, Natalia's; we had an audience at last to whom we could talk about each other. Potterton was a large man who held his hands on top of his desk like oil; occasionally he spread on to a blotter. Dangerfield, a lady, gave him covering-fire from beneath her pillbox hat. They asked—Has intercourse occurred? I thought—We are like gods being interviewed by the clergy. They asked— How many times? I thought—I would have to have as many fingers on which to count as Vishnu. Potterton made a note. I thought—Our audience at last is moral: as sinners, we will be able to bring light to a suffering world.

Potterton told us we should not see each other in private— in any place, that is, where intercourse might occur. I wanted to ask—Then what is public? It was explained—a restaurant; a bandstand. I wanted to say—You mean, there intercourse might not occur? Dangerfield told Natalia she should remain with Edward: like this, she would not be yielding. Thus we were to fight like children: and love, in persecution, would be kept lively. I thought—Perhaps the point of law and morals is to be a pruning knife to love; which then grows exotic blooms and angels.

In Kensington Gardens we became one of the couples who

lay on the grass; there were toys in the bandstand playing. I thought—Perhaps intercourse, if we had faith, might yet occur. We were the generation of children blessed with nowhere to go. Foxes had holes: I lay my head on Natalia. The sun always shone. Ghosts were around us like detectives. They carried torches, to immortalise us on our pyre.

In the evening Natalia returned to her ogre's castle: I would roam through the streets with my black horse and lonely armour. Or I would rush back through avenues of yew trees; Natalia would float in a white nightdress from her window. I would climb on my toes like ivy. Edward would be downstairs entertaining dwarfs and leopards.

Dangerfield would explain—It is helpful if your husband maltreats you.

I thought—I had not realised that the law might be true.

The summer became luminous in a landscape of blue thunder. Our movements were awestruck like those of innocence. From Kensington Gardens, as refugees, we moved to Hampstead Heath. On the way we sheltered beneath the porticos of the British Museum. There, with the starlings, I wondered if intercourse might occur.

Natalia, when persecuted, became free of guilt; thus tender and almost peaceful. She shone, with her world maltreating her. I thought—Perhaps it is true that sexuality is the forbidden fruit: having given it up, the tree is now back in its compound. I explained—You see, we are innocent! Natalia said—But won't it be bad for us?

There was a man who seemed to follow us in the park. He had a red face and a green felt hat like an acorn. I thought—But his colours are transposed, as in a negative.

Edward had a lawyer called Ell. Ell and Potterton met for lunch at their club. I thought—It is the habits of the old that make possible the happiness of children.

Natalia said—But what do they talk about?

I said—Us; and the formation of new galaxies.

We were once in a public place behind some beech trees. A lady in a flowered hat pointed at us with an umbrella. She said —People at your age should know better! I thought I could say—Are you God, dressed as a clergyman?

Natalia became young dreaming of her ancestors. Uhlans and Cossacks rode across childhood plains. Potterton and Ell discussed the Test Match. Natalia felt for a moment that she would outlive us all: protected by ashes and sackcloth.

She said—Sometimes I feel too many possibilities to continue!

Dangerfield, like the Queen of Sheba, went to see Ell in his Temple. They swept their cloaks round them and sat in the dust. Natalia and I waited in a courtyard. I thought—When the moment comes, we will say nothing.

Men lived and died within their limitations: what became of being immortal?

Dangerfield said—But you can't go on like this!

Potterton said—What's happened in the Test Match?

Once, when parked in my car with Natalia, I put my foot through a window. The glass exploded into millions of small stars. I said to Natalia—I told you!

We had been instructed not to know good and evil: hand in hand we had mocked this by observing the limitation. I thought—Then what would God do? Pain, as a wooden peg, was put between your legs to ease them.

Natalia began to say—But we can't go on like this!

I thought—She is a sculptress: she hacks at me with chisel.

Then—We have always been mythical.

I looked down on the proud earth. This was the summer when people began to worry about Ndoula. I thought—I might go down to the plain as a wanderer with an eye-patch and a spear.

I said to Natalia—Talk to Edward then.

She said—If I do, you know what will happen.

I thought—We are all brothers and sisters: on a mountain pass, at night, my sword will be broken.

I tried to work out what was right. I thought—I know too much, or nothing. The human condition is stretched between two poles. Someone lies on top of you: you are a hammock.

This could not go on: I did not want it to stop. If it stopped, it might be fruitful. I might not see Natalia.

I wondered—Why not admit this?

This was one of the times, I think, when I had faith. I thought—You do what is good; or possibly bad; but trust it. Summer had lasted long; in winter there was ordinariness. I thought—You let life go; it has its rhythms; and thus is controlled by you, because you have let it.

Joe Gregory appeared out of the murk and asked me to go with him to the café in North London. We drove in Joe's small car. The streets were warlike; ruins for children's playgrounds.

Joe said "Old man, you will keep quiet?"

I said "You mean, take my shoes off?"

There was a flyover being built to get the traffic out of London. The traffic stood nose to tail.

Joe said "How's Elizabeth?"

"Very well."

"Doesn't she ever come to London?"

The café was much the same as I had imagined it; a neon-lit room with red-topped tables: a setting for plastic mushrooms and gnomes. There were models of tomatoes containing tomato sauce. A row of pin-tables exhibited women with holes in them.

I thought—People come here to rub off on the dirt.

Joe went to talk to a black man behind the counter. The man was small, in a clown's shirttails. I stood by the pin-tables. Steel balls clanged into women's holes.

Joe said "The bad penny! What have you got for me to-day?"

The small black man wiped his hands on a cloth.

I played a game on a pin-table. You leaned against it and flipped two buttons by your groin. Lights flashed on and off according to chance or tilting the table.

Joe seemed to say "What is it, tea or founder?"

The man said "You want to demander?"

I did not think I would understand much in this place. You sat in a room without stimulus and listened to your ears and heartbeats.

Joe said "I've brought along a friend."

The black man used his cloth to wipe the counter.

I held the table by its hips and tried to steer the balls into holes. The table had its back to me. I thought—Here we are homosexuals.

Joe came over and whispered "I've got to do these articles!"

I said "Sorry Joe, I'll behave."

I went over to the counter. I smiled. I said "Can I have a coffee please?"

The man put his head through a hatch and yelled to the basement.

I thought—I am conducting an enquiry into violence in North London.

Joe said "This is Mr. Greville."

I said "How do you do?" I held out my hand.

The man went on wiping the counter.

I said "Onions, jam, grapefruit."

Joe said "They have quite a clientèle here. They use this as a sort of club. Isn't that right? They don't use the club down the road. It cost a hundred thousand."

The black man said "What did your friend say?"

I said "Pickles, biscuits, tobacco." I thought—We will do a deal behind Joe's back: offer him Bibles and whisky.

We were in the hot dust beneath fruit trees. Guards stood at an entrance to a compound.

Joe said to the black man "I mean, when they come here, do you feel responsible?"

There came into the café two more black men; one old and grey and wearing a purple striped shirt and the other elegant in a pale brown suit with a green felt hat like an acorn. He held his hands in his pockets so tight that I thought his buttons would fly off and shoot me.

He yelled something unintelligible at the counter.

I put my hands over my ears.

Joe whispered "Don't!"

I put my hands up.

Joe said to the man behind the counter "What's that language?"

The man said "English."

When Joe laughed his yellow teeth became like those of a horse in front of sugar. I thought—Joe and I used to laugh like this; years ago, when we loved each other.

I went over to the jukebox. There were labels like those on shrubs. I thought—I was mad to believe that I should come here.

A steel arm came out and wrapped itself round a record.

The elegant man leaned against a pin-table. It lit up as he went in.

I thought—We are like men on an earth waiting to be corrupted.

Joe said "How often does he come here?"

I thought—We are in prison.

Joe said "In our parents' day, everyone talked about sex and money."

The old purple-shirted man had put a hand inside his mouth. He was looking for gold in the desert.

The man with the green felt hat flipped a coin into the air; he smacked his hand where it landed as if it were a mosquito.

The music from the jukebox became part of our brains; an ache inside the tom-tom.

I thought—In an orderly society there is no speech; you twitch to the simpleness of matter.

We were components of a machine: the elegant man was a pillar beside white and gold fir trees; the man behind the counter squatted; the purple-shirted man pirouetted on one leg, a dervish in the desert.

There came into the café a young girl. She wore a suede cap and a leather skirt and dark glasses. As soon as she heard the music she began to dance. She moved her hands in front of her face as if brushing off cobwebs.

Joe was drinking coffee. I was by the jukebox.

The music made such a noise that it pulled your mind like toffee.

The girl lifted her behind into the air like a parasol.

I thought—This is no longer a story I can tell Elizabeth: you only tell about comedy or tragedy.

The girl laid her head against the elegant man's shoulder. Her legs continued pumping.

We were in a café in North London. There was a jukebox playing. Young people, or whatever they were called, came here to pick up drugs.

The girl spread her fingers out and placed one hand above her head and the other at her behind like a peacock.

I thought—Perhaps this is what I require; being so often too conscious.

Joe whispered "I thought you'd like it!"

The music suddenly stopped. We were exposed.

I thought—Where are the photographers?

Joe said to the man behind the bar "Can I ask some questions?"

The girl sat on the elegant man's knee. She drank through a straw from a bottle, like a siren.

I thought—I will pretend to be a rock.

The man behind the counter shouted "Marlene!"

The girl said "Yes?"

Joe said to the girl "Can I ask you some questions?"

I thought—I can go into the street and walk back across the half-built flyover. I have learned this from Natalie.

"Where do you live?"

"Do I live?"

"Yes."

"London."

Joe licked his lips. His tongue was a pencil.

"You often come here?"

"Here?"

"Yes."

"Sometimes."

I remembered—Joe said he has fallen off like a performance.

"What do you do? I mean, what job?"

"Nothing."

"Nothing?"

"No. Should I?"

I pressed the jukebox. A white arm flipped out. The records were black, like a dancer.

Joe said "My friend here's a dancer!"

The girl said "Are you?"

I thought—We are in a world of coloured lights; where tinsel hangs from a Christmas tree.

Sometimes when I was alone at night the devils came in and I sat up in bed as if a bell had been pulled to give me warning.

I felt as if I were breaking some limitations to being human: this was in order to stay human; there was no answer to this; only the ability, or not, to live with it.

Sometimes this seemed a predicament of society; which travelled so quietly to offices in trains, which ran through streets hurling paving stones through windows. It was the quietness that caused the violence; the soft body on the street corner, the crashed car.

Then it did not seem to do with society but with man; who fought his way to the waterhole to stop himself from burning. Again, there seemed nothing to be done. An observer stood with his hair on end like a dog or donkey on a pathway.

There seemed a need to live in perpetual anxiety: thus one was humbled and exposed to experience. Then devils, and angels, came in two by two. You were saved; but the rest of the world perished. Knowledge could not be formulated; only endured.

At night, the body practised death in a rehearsal. Once there had been another body beside me: this the devils could use, to hold us to ransom. Now, alone, the space between the inside and the outside of me became the battleground: and angels watched from the ceiling. They lowered a rope which I could tie round my neck; or toll, if I wanted, like a bell.

Elizabeth had said—But you don't want anyone to help you!

I had said—No: I'm a horse outside Troy.

When Elizabeth had tried to help me I had sat up in bed and tried to prevent the top of my head coming off. I had watched her own face turn to plaster. I had thought—If I go on, the top of her head will come off. Then, inside, I could see the works. One person's suffering was relieved by another's pain. But knowing this, I could not continue. I would lean over a basin as if being sick—as I was to do, later, with Natalie. I could say—Look, you can hold me! But I did not want this to be possible. Which I was to do, later, with Natalia. Perhaps one person's duty was performed by another person's pain. When Elizabeth began to feel the top of her head coming off I would put my arms around her. I would think—For men, it is not difficult. This was a female predicament. She clawed her nails down my face. I thought—I have too much blood. I watched the sap running. I thought—I should carry a small container, to make rubber.

I wondered—Perhaps women, like Venus, have no arms with which to hold you: they are mothers and goddesses, who have tentacles.

Elizabeth said—Have I hurt you?

I said—Yes.

On battlefields, after the battle, no one asks about crimes. Bodies lie in frozen agitation; dead.

In the world of coloured lights I was a stranger. Events happened at random: this made for orderly society. But with nothing different from any other, there was no hope.

Hermits saw devils in the guise of their loved ones. I thought—At least the loved ones, if I see devils, may be left in peace.

Riding through a dark wood in the middle time of life I came upon a provenance of charlatans and witches. Women sat round cauldrons and told men where to go: men, in the steam, rubbed off on trickery. I thought—Success depends on deception: you pick a berry; become a toad; then the foot of the giant misses you. Survival is in appearances being different from what occurs. You bang in knuckledusters; these become the nails of saints.

Sometimes when Elizabeth and I are in the country we are visited by friends, and we climb out of a window and hide in the garden till the raid is over.

I was in my courtyard one Sunday and the cement was going hard in the bottom of my bucket—there is never enough time; you pour in water, stir, and the row of bricks and your life have to be built before energy becomes fossilised—when I heard a car arriving in our back drive and the sound of plaintive, high-pitched voices of friends—they would have to be friends because they were so complaining—and I put the bucket down and hoped that if I lay beneath the level of my wall they might go past like Indians with their jingling beads and red faces. Somewhere in the cottage I had left my shirt and shoes; my bandolier and pistol. I held a trowel like a dagger. From the side of the house was the sound of running footsteps; Elizabeth appeared pulling on her shorts; she had been on the lawn sunbathing. I motioned to her to keep low: we were on all fours in the courtyard. The voices from the car became identifiable as those of Joe and Margaret Gregory; Joe was saying "All right don't!" and Margaret was saying "Why not if I don't want to?" I put an arm round Elizabeth; she tasted of salad dressing. I thought—How hot it is! We lay side by side on the stones. Footsteps came past us towards the cottage. I put a hand up Elizabeth's shorts. As one grows older, one appreciates unusual situations. Joe shouted—"Anybody there?" I thought—Dust will get mixed with the oil and vinegar. Elizabeth made a grab at me and put her knee against my ribs. I rolled with my mouth open. She covered it with her hand. I licked it. Joe said "Their car's here!" I got Elizabeth against the wall and began caressing her. She swatted me. I thought—We are partisans in an occupied hedgerow. Joe's footsteps went back towards his car. I thought it would be a pity after all if we missed Joe and Margaret. It would be a long afternoon. Elizabeth made a noise like a cistern. She was laughing. I crawled out of the courtyard pretending to be a bicycle. Elizabeth followed me and attacked me from behind. I made a noise like a drain. Sometimes when Elizabeth laughs she is like someone having a fit. Joe Gregory said "Hullo there!" I said "Hullo!" When I stood up, I found I had no fly buttons; my trousers were held together by a pin. Joe said to Elizabeth "Hullo darling!" He kissed her cheek. I did not remember his kissing her before. I thought I would go and see Margaret. She was sitting in the front of the car. I was trying to get the pin through my trousers. I drew my stomach in like Mr. Universe. Margaret was behind the windscreen. I said "Hullo love." She did not move. She looked as if she had been crying. The windscreen was dirty. The wipers had made marks on it like a shell. I screamed. Margaret said "What's the matter!" I said "I've got myself with a safety pin!" Joe and Elizabeth came up; Elizabeth was buttoning up her shorts. I thought—They will think we are always doing this. Joe said "She doesn't like my driving." Margaret said "What do you mean I don't like your driving?" Joe said "But you don't, do you?" I had now got the safety pin too high up; it looked as if I had an erection. I said "Don't you?" Margaret suddenly climbed out of the car and walked towards the house. She wore a blue linen skirt with pants underneath in the shape of a V. I thought I should follow her. She stopped by my courtyard. She shouted "Have you got the cigarettes?" Joe shouted "What cigarettes?" She shouted "The cigarettes in the car." Joe was wearing a thick check shirt and black flannel trousers. I said to Margaret "Have you seen my courtyard?" She said "What's it for?" I said "Exercise." Margaret said passionately "You don't need any exercise!" I wondered if I should pull my stomach in again. We could go into the woods. Or upstairs. We went through the house on to the lawn. Here Elizabeth had been lying with the pool of moisture at her throat. There was a beech tree: a sofa hung from a scaffold. We sat. I thought—But it is now that we will have nothing to do all day. Time stretched like the view across the cornfields. The stubble had been burned. The dragon had claimed its victims. Margaret had soft white hairs; a short upper lip. Joe and Elizabeth came on to the lawn behind us.

Margaret said to Joe "Why don't you take any exercise?"

Joe said "I do take exercise."

Margaret said "Why did you say you hadn't got the cigarettes?"

Joe said "I didn't say I hadn't got the cigarettes."

I was looking up at the beech trees. I remembered—Joe has seen Natalia and me at Sylvia's party.

Joe turned to me. He said "Did I?"

I said "What?"

"Have any cigarettes."

I said "No, no, you hadn't got any cigarettes."

Elizabeth lay on her back with her feet towards us so that her thighs were foreshortened. When she was bored, her body became like pincers.

Joe said "That was quite a party!"

I thought—I can pretend he is talking about the girl we met in the café.

He said "Old man, I don't know how you do it!"

I wondered if Elizabeth seemed sleepy on purpose or through exhaustion.

Joe said "Margaret wanted to come to the party but she couldn't."

He waited for someone to ask—Why?

Margaret shouted "I could!"

Joe said "I was just saying—"

Margaret said "Well don't!"

I thought—Perhaps this is so boring, it will save me.

Margaret said "All right do!" She lay back with her legs like pincers.

I looked across the cornfields.

Joe said "I just thought it was interesting."

Elizabeth said "What?"

Joe said "Why weren't you at Sylvia's party?"

At the bottom of the garden I saw my son Adam and the girl with dark hair walking.

Joe said "Your husband didn't stay!"

I thought—Nothing like this can defeat us.

Joe said "You know Edward Jones? Just before the party, he asked Margaret to have tea, in a friend's flat, at four-thirty."

The cornfield was a sea: Adam and the girl were just above the horizon.

Margaret said "Will you shut up!"

I seemed to be watching from a cloud.

I said "And did you?"

Margaret said "What?"

"Have tea!"

"Yes, I did!"

I thought—They are putting on some demonstration for our benefit.

Margaret sat up and spread her legs. Her thighs were white with hair like her short upper lip.

I said "And then what?"

Margaret said "I thought we were going to have tea."

Joe exclaimed "At four-thirty!"

Margaret said "All right I won't tell it!"

Joe said "No, go on."

I thought—We are gods on Mount Olympus.

I said "He pounced on you?"

I thought—It is only polite to ask.

She said nothing.

I thought—Really?

Elizabeth had sat up and was picking at the daisies.

I thought—Is Joe doing this for Elizabeth?

Joe said "What I really minded was that she did have tea, afterwards."

I said "But was this before or after the party?"

Joe said "Before. That was why she couldn't go to the party."

I thought—But Edward wasn't at the party.

Then—Didn't Natalie say he'd gone to Africa?

I looked across the cornfields. Adam and the girl with dark hair were coming towards the garden.

I thought it important to try to work out the timing. I had

been to the café with Joe weeks ago. Then the other day, there had been Sylvia's party.

Elizabeth stood up and went into the house.

The boy and the girl were hand in hand. The sky beyond them was a desert. The cornfields seemed to be flaming.

Joe said "Where's Elizabeth?"

"Gone to make tea."

Joe said "Have you seen that girl again?"

"What girl?"

"That girl in the café."

I did not know what to say to Joe.

I thought I should try to find Elizabeth. I went through the house to the kitchen. She was by the sink, with her back to me. I put my arms around her.

I said "You're the only one I like!"

She said "Good."

I waited for her to turn.

I said "Are they staying?"

She said "I suppose so."

She went on with her work.

I thought—It is about Natalia that I feel anxious.

I said "Who's that girl with Adam?"

"Catherine."

"Catherine who?"

"Joe and Margaret's daughter."

I was still trying to work out the timing. Joe had not seen me between the time when we had gone to the café and when we had met at Sylvia's party. He could not have told Natalia.

I said "They all seem the same to me!"

I thought—Elizabeth knows everything about Natalia.

5

I HAVE A FRIEND called Tom Savile who lives at the top of a long flight of stairs. He is like the Delphic oracle.

When you arrive at the foot of the building Tom leans out of his window and shouts—Ready?—and he throws a pair of keys that you have to run for and catch before they disappear down a gutter.

"Oh it's you!"

"Yes."

"I was expecting someone different."

Tom's flat has Indian hangings and Impressionist prints and picture postcards of Ravenna. Tom is a bachelor. He walks up and down in a long black dressing gown. He is a thin bald man like a monk.

He said "Do you notice anything different?"

"No."

"You're sure?"

"Yes."

"You are impossible!"

Tom and I sometimes adopted slightly homosexual attitudes as if in relief from being heterosexual.

I said "How's Brigitta?"

"Brigitta?"

"I thought it was Brigitta."

Tom and I used to visit each other in order to talk about ourselves. I hoped Tom would talk about himself first; so that when this was over, I could talk about Natalia.

"Not Brigitta: Benedicta!"

"Oh. Benedicta."

Tom lived in an area where foreign girls lodged in attics. Tom waited for them to fall on him like apples.

He said "You're sure you notice nothing different?"

He walked up and down. His skirts swished in the dust. I

thought—He was on his own; having an evening with his loved one.

I said "No."

"I've shaved off my beard!"

I could say—Tom, it's the strength of your face that makes this so unnoticeable.

He went through to the bathroom to make tea.

Tom worked on television. He sat behind a microphone and persuaded goblins and genies to come out.

I thought—The oracle at Delphi was a priestess in a cave.

Tom would be warming the pot, drying it, ladling tea leaves from a fragile wooden box.

I said "Well, Benedicta."

"No, tell me about the Jones woman first."

I thought—Tom and I are inexcusable. Except that oracles have never had any respect for people.

He said "The last I heard, her husband Edward was divorcing her but his lawyer had gone on a kidney machine."

When Tom laughed he sometimes became like Elizabeth; on a rack, being tickled.

He said "Oh dear, oh dear!"

He put his forearms up his sleeves. His face became wise. I thought—Perhaps I am too sad to talk about Natalia.

He said—"She's destroying you. You know this. She's predatory and narcissistic. A woman like that is only conscious of herself; she'd thrive on another person's pain."

I could say—But Tom, yes, I know this.

He said "There's nothing at the centre. She's a vacuum that sucks you in. What you see in her, is what you choose to hurt in yourself."

I could say—But Tom, if this is true, is it what's important?

He said "Now Elizabeth's a decent human being."

I said "Yes."

He said "You won't like my saying this."

People were always telling me—You won't like my saying this.

He poured out tea.

He said "But what do you do about it?"

I said "But Tom, this is the question I'm always asking, what do you do about it?"

He said "I knew you were going to say that!"

I drank my tea. We were underneath the baobab tree. Acolytes stood in the dust. They wore the masks of birds and animals.

He said "But what do you?"

I said "What can she do? Her parents were Jacob and Esau. Her vacuum was at the centre—a dead god. It becomes like a fish—luminous."

He said "I don't know if you take sugar."

I could say—Tom, you know I do!

I said "She was told from the beginning—Get what you can. Put your arms round necks like a millstone."

Tom exclaimed "A bloody great millstone!"

I said "So that's what she does. The first man—" I gesticulated.

Tom shouted "Poor bugger!"

I said "And then me with my lifesaving equipment; a chopper—"

"A what?"

"Chopper. For what can be dragged out of the sea—"

Tom began to roll a small black cigarette. He was telling his beads, or counting gold in a cellar.

I said "Of course she takes it out on me. But if she wasn't a millstone, what's to stop me flying away like a balloon?"

Tom said "But you are a balloon!"

He licked his cigarette. His tongue went in and out like a roulette ball.

I thought—One comes to fortune tellers to confirm that

one's life is not so bad as one had imagined it. Then one goes away refreshed.

He said "Sooner or later you'll have to get back to reality."

I could say—Why?

I said "What should I do?"

"Run."

I could say—Never!

He said "You've told me she wants everything in opposites."

I said "So does everyone."

"That produces chaos."

"No. I think it demonstrates reality."

I thought—One day I will live like a hermit in the desert: then love, like a lion, will ask forgiveness of me.

I drank my tea.

I said "What else have men nowadays got to fight? Except predators and narcissists in their unconscious."

He said "Why are you angry with me?"

I said "I'm not."

I was sitting cross-legged on a bed. I thought—I am a narcissist and a predator in his unconscious.

He said "You're putting yourself outside human experience. The truth is single; not self-contradictory."

I said "I don't believe that."

He said "I know you don't."

It was four o'clock in the afternoon. Soon Tom would be going off to put a programme on the air. He would dream of charlatans and witches.

He said "I may have to turn you out."

I said "Who's coming, Brigitta?"

He shouted "Not Brigitta, Benedicta!"

He went to the window and looked out. I thought—It is I who am the priestess: I am sitting on the bank of a river waiting for Tom to carry me over.

He said "The trouble with you is, you don't recognise good and evil."

I thought—There are sounds of children in the street crying.

I said "Shall I go?"

He said "Not for a minute. This one really is something!"

He turned from the window. He rolled his eyes.

He said "A figure like an amphora!"

I thought—Then I will be oil; or a Roman soldier.

He said "And from a nice family too!"

The doorbell rang. Tom turned back to the window.

He said "Now don't try any funny stuff!"

I put my hand on my heart.

Tom shouted out of the window "Oi! The gutter!"

I ran my fingers through my hair.

The front door banged. Footsteps came up the stairs. Tom tightened the cord of his dressing gown. A girl's voice groaned. Tom went on to the landing.

The voice called out "Oh aren't you gorgeous!"

I thought—But this should not have happened so quickly!

She came in wearing her small suede cap and leather skirt. I could say—But you're not Benedicta!

Tom said "May I introduce Madeleine."

I thought—But you're called Marlene!

I said "But you're not Benedicta!"

Tom said "I never said this was Benedicta!"

I thought—It is too unlikely. There should be contradictions between good and evil.

Tom said "Do you two know each other?"

I was asked to do some articles on Central Africa by Ned Symon, the editor of the National Sunday Newspaper. He said "You're the one person who can do it!"

I said "I thought you'd asked Joe Gregory."

He flashed his eyes at me. He was a large man behind his desk with his palms spread out like oil.

I thought—One day someone will put a match to him.

I said "I'm supposed to be having a nervous breakdown."

His shoulders moved up and down as if he were using a loofah. I thought—He should get other people to scratch his back.

I said "How much?"

"Seven fifty."

"How many?"

"Three."

I thought—He might increase it.

He said "You are going there?" He walked up and down. The carpet muffled and protected him.

I said "What could I say? Ndoula's locked up. This is a great injustice, but is useful. He should be freed; but then there would be violence. This also could be useful. Can I say this in an article?"

He said "What about guerillas?"

I said "The unemployed are being trained. It's like the dole, on the border. Everyone's happy so long as they never leave camp. But they may have to, because that's what they're trained for. Then the camps and their homes will be bombed. And what will they come back to?"

He smiled. "And the Chinese?"

I said "The Chinese have sent armoured cars. These are labelled pig iron. They break down, and are sold to the Arabs as pig iron."

He said "I'm just thinking aloud. Don't pay any attention."

I said "Would you print this?"

He said "You write; we print."

He spread himself again behind his desk. He brought out bottles and glasses. I thought—He must have heard I'm on the bottle.

"How do you like it?"

"A little."

He said "I've always thought the pretensions of history non-sense."

I thought—Did I say that?

I said "People don't make decisions: decisions occur from the style in which they let things happen."

He said "Who're you going with?"

"Jack."

"Will he be good?"

"Very."

He handed me a glass. I thought—He's probably asked me here for something quite different.

I said "What should be sent out there is a dummy: to be carried by soldiers in kilts like a bagpipe."

He laughed.

I thought—This sort of thing is expected of me.

I said "The people who went out to Central Africa were NCOs. They hadn't been to public schools, so weren't used to being buggered."

He said "Good!"

I said "Marx was right. The lower classes are useless as colonialists."

He said "Did Marx say that?"

I swirled the liquid in my glass. I turned to the door behind me suddenly.

I said "I'm being followed."

He said "Who by?"

"A man in a green felt hat."

His shoulders shook up and down. I thought—I've been too long in the bath with him.

He said "I hear you're getting divorced."

I said "I'm not. Who told you?"

His small eyes glittered.

I said "If you knew a load of dirt about me, would you print it?"

"It depends."

"What on?"

He said "When are you going to Africa?"

I said "I'll write your story. But it will be about what life is, instead of what it's supposed to be. From the inside, which is imaginary; and the outside, which is the same; and how they're joined together, which is different."

He went on smiling.

He said "I'm sure anything you wrote would be enormously stimulating."

I thought—He may even believe that.

Natalia said "I'm definitely coming to live with you."

I said "That's marvellous!"

I looked round the flat. I thought—I will be leaving Troy for the last time, with my ancestors on my shoulders.

I said "When?"

She said "Now."

I said "Right!"

I put down the telephone.

I got the flat ready. I cleared some drawers and hid the few relics of Elizabeth's.

I sat on a chair.

I thought—All this will have to be gone through in time: what I do now will affect the future no more nor less than anything else would.

I noticed I had holes in my socks. Armies were entering Troy. Around us was the burning city.

When Natalia arrived she had her suitcase like a removals van. I carried it upstairs on my shoulders.

I said "What's happened?"

"Edward's being reasonable."

"What about?"

"The divorce."

"How?"

"He says I can divorce him."

I sat on the edge of the bed. I put my arm round her. I thought—At these moments it is important to be comforting. Outside in the streets the crowds were running.

I thought—This is the end of our beautiful summer.

I said "I've cleared out the drawers and cleaned the kitchen."

She said "I could have done that!"

I said "No I'll do it."

I thought—We will cling to each other now because we can do anything.

Natalia unpacked. She hung out washing. I thought—She will put a line out and I will come through the trees on a motorbike and decapitate myself.

She said "Look! I've bought you some socks."

I said "That's just what I wanted!"

I was determined to make a success of this. I thought—It will not be for want of trying.

We should dress up and go out. Run through the streets like playing children.

I thought—It is now Thursday. Elizabeth will be in the country till Tuesday.

I said "I'll cook you dinner!"

She said "No I'll do dinner."

I looked at my new socks. They were black and gold. We would spend the evening as a normal married couple. This was what we wanted. I thought—Like Joe and Margaret Gregory.

Natalia worked in the kitchen. I watched her through a half-open door. Steam rose as if from a cauldron.

I thought—In the streets are the screams of fires and children.

I laid the table. I became a monk with my hands in my sleeves moving between refectory and the kitchen. My skirts swished in the dust.

We set up an altar and sat on either side of candles. We were representatives of a memory in an upstairs room. One day, the streets would fall in on us.

I thought—Or we could stay here all our lives, if we were dying.

She said "I'm afraid the meat is overdone."

I said "I think it's perfect."

We listened to music on the gramophone. We sat with our heads propped against each other's shoulders. Beyond, in the streets, the noise of crowds retreated. I thought—When it is dark, perhaps I can climb down and go for a short walk in the garden.

She said "Bach has such austerity and yet passion, don't you think? as if he did not have to ask any questions."

I said "Yet he lived an absolutely humdrum life, as a courtier with his family."

There was something I did not understand about all this. We seemed part of a larger mechanism which went on behind our backs, with the sound of pickaxes clinking.

She said "What are you thinking?"

I could say—Of you, and the formation of new galaxies.

On the bed there were her breasts and small waist like a rosary. The sea formed millions of delicate shells and then crushed them into beaches. I sat beside her like a Buddha. I wanted her to place wreaths against me. I thought—I will become starved; my ribs like Jacob's ladder.

I had got used in the evenings to going for walks and thinking about Natalia.

I thought—My life is a rainbow between one chasm and another. If it were a bridge, I could balance there.

I heard rain falling.

I said "Thank God you're here."

She said "Thank God I'm here."

She was an idol looking out across the ocean. I was an old man walking across a desert with his child. When I arrived at the place of sacrifice, there was a thicket. I thought—What does that prove? That God has potency?

I thought—If I raised my knife, there might be no one to stop me.

On her back, she looked up from between my legs as if I were a sphinx and she were a desert.

I thought—To love Natalie, and Natalia, one would have to be omnipotent.

Her hands, in the cold behind me, flew like bats. I became the stake in the heart of a witch.

I thought—At midnight wolves become human.

I lay in bed and thought of the world outside. I should be out fighting dragons.

I could hear the men with pickaxes through the walls. They were coming closer: rescuers or destroyers.

They would take us by the feet and drag us. The crowds would cheer. We would be grateful for the air: a glimpse of sky from the tumbril.

She was quiet as Cleopatra holding the snake, her lover.

She said "Is the window open?"

"I think so."

We lay a long time. I thought—There must have been a moment like this when love, who could not sleep, came down for a cup of tea. If he had not, he would have had no love for what he had created.

We were in an old mine shaft. Our rescuers had long since dug their way through and gone.

In the early hours we became cold. Our bodies were images formed from wax.

I knew she was lying awake beside me. I thought again—

There is something quite different going on. The graven image, which had formed, was deserted.

She said "Are you awake?"

"Yes."

"What are you going to do?"

"Nothing."

I thought—Perhaps we cannot bear to be used for such grand purposes.

She sat up in bed and held her head in her hands.

I thought—Perhaps, like me, her head is so full of birth pangs that the top is coming off.

I said "What's the matter?"

She suddenly jumped out of bed and began dressing.

I thought—She is thinking of her children; her children's children.

Then—This is what I try to think of; and find so hard.

She said "You don't really want me."

I said "That's a lie."

I watched her dress. She put on armour.

I thought—Now she will be able to go out and fight dragons.

I sat up in bed.

In the streets there would be boys and girls running. I could put an arm out and pull another one in through a doorway.

She said "Good-bye."

I said "Good-bye then."

I thought—All this has happened, as I knew, without my knowing it.

I shouted "And this time don't come back!"

She said "Oh God I hate you!"

I said "I hate you too!"

I was walking through the park during my lunch-hour break one day and was watching the pelicans with their necks like racing motorists when a man came up to me from behind and gripped me by the elbow and said "Got you!" He was a tall man with a bright pink face and a brown hat with a curly brim. He seemed familiar. I could not make out if he was an old friend or a member of the Secret Service or a private detective put on to me by Natalia's husband. I thought—Or by Natalie! But this I could not hope for.

He said "Guilty conscience!"

I said "Yes."

We walked side by side. I was beginning to find it difficult to place people, because people in this sort of context had stopped seeming to have much significance.

He said "Long tide no sea. How's Elizabeth?"

As an old friend, he might be someone who had admired Elizabeth in our youth. There had been a time when Elizabeth and I were like polar bears; our friends gazed at us across chasms.

He was still gripping me. He had a large chin and protruding eyes. I thought—Perhaps he is drowning.

He said "Do you know who I am?"

"No. Are you a member of the Secret Service?"

He pulled up sharply. He seemed astonished. He said "What a terrible thing to say!"

This was about the time when it was known I was implicated with Ndoula.

I thought—But if he were in the Secret Service, or if he wasn't, he would still act the same: in this area there are layers of complexity like onions.

We walked on.

I said "Or a private detective."

He reeled again. It was a windy day. I thought—Perhaps like the rest of us, he's just unbalanced. Hair escaped from his hat like steam.

He said "Look! What is this?"

I said "I mean, I know a lot of people who have taken jobs in the Secret Service. Or as private detectives. They are sometimes very old friends. It's to do with a search for identity: or money."

He said "You do lay it on don't you!"

He was carrying an umbrella. He whacked the ground with it. I thought—It won't obey his commandments.

He said "Just because I asked you—How's Elizabeth?"

"Very well thank you."

"Are you sure?"

People were always asking me—Are you sure?

We walked on. The wind made tears in our eyes. I wondered—He is down on his luck; a bookie; an army officer.

He said "I heard you were splitting up."

"No."

"I'm glad."

In days when Elizabeth and I had had admirers they had often thrown bread to us which had fallen out of reach in the chasm.

He said "Why did you ask was I in the Secret Service?"

"A joke."

"You're going out to Africa?"

"Yes."

I thought—He does look like a private detective.

He said "I mean, what about Ndoula?"

He stood to attention again. I thought—In the wind, he might hear the National Anthem.

"What about him?"

"Shouldn't one do something? What?"

I could say—Would you run across a desert?

He sat on his umbrella. I thought—It might run through him, or close up like a telescope.

He said "You know Ned Symon?"

"Yes."

"Will you see him?"

"I have."

He said "Good. Good." He frowned.

We moved on. There were always people waylaying me like this. They were the sounds of pickaxes clinking.

I said "Do you think there might be something in a conspiracy theory of history? Certain people work for powers and principalities and whatnot; but the point is they don't know each other or even what they themselves are doing; they're like people picking up clues of paper in a park."

He stopped again. He said "Look, why are you saying this?"

I thought—It might even be true.

He said "Can't we just walk?"

"Yes."

He said "You will do something then?"

He suddenly pointed his umbrella at a taxi. He was a red-faced man with blue eyes. The taxi stopped.

I thought—We have no technique for describing this.

When he had gone, I continued with my walk. These were incidents in my journey from one form of consciousness to another. A jellyfish crawled up a tree and became an ape. An ape made wings. I thought—People are not characters, but indications about aim. Faces popped up like targets on a shooting range. If I did not fire, they smiled and nodded and disappeared. I had an ache, or an emptiness, at my heart. I thought I should run through streets and listen for the cries of children. I thought—What I do not want to be is a jellyfish stuck in branches.

Or—But I know where I may find Madeleine, or Marlene—

And—My flat is empty.

"I thought you were the intellectual type."

"I am."

"You looked so mild. Studious."

"Who was that man in the café? Your boyfriend?"

"Which?"

"You don't have two!"

"No, he's with my sister."

"Do you have a sister? Impossible!"

"Thank you kind sir, she said, dropping him a curtsey."

"Come on then, let's get it over with."

"You know, I do like being with you."

"I like being with you."

"I'm not like all the others then?"

"Which?"

"They're so boring!"

"They only want one thing you know!"

"They do!"

"How terrible! What is your sister?"

"An actress. She is, really."

"And you? A little modelling."

"Oh aren't you informed."

"Act something."

"Will you pass me the cucumber sandwiches Gwendoline."

"Cicely."

"Oh, aren't you gorgeous!"

"Rhubarb."

"What's the name of your girlfriend?"

"What girlfriend?"

"Spooks."

"Why do you call her spooks?"

"Well she is, isn't she? Very dark. Silent."

"Who told you?"

"Oh have I hurt you! Diddums!"

"Tom?"

"Ladies and gentlemen, will the member in the brown suit stand up again please."

"Is that what your boyfriend does?"

"What boyfriend?"

"The one in the brown suit."

"Ha ha. I told you. That was my sister."

"Was it Tom?"

"Yes. Which one do you like?"

"The one in the middle."

"You're so witty. Honestly."

"What does Tom do?"

"I haven't been with Tom."

"Did you catch the last bus home then?"

"What does that mean? Sometimes I don't understand what you mean."

"That's because I'm so mild and intellectual."

"Come on then."

"All right."

"Why did you ask me out? To make spooks jealous?"

"Yes. Shut up about spooks."

"But you've got a wife."

"Yes."

"And children?"

"Yes."

"All right! I'll be silent. Dark! Boring!"

"Because you're good for me. Corrupt me."

"Oh! I know I'm stupid!"

"Use me. Cast me aside like an old glove."

"James! my little ones are starving!"

"Ow. That tickles."

"How old's your wife?"

"Sixteen."

"Is she really?"

"No."

"Honestly, I never thought you were going to."

"What?"

"Would you—er—like to—er—come back—er—I think I should warn—ow!"

"I didn't!"

"There there!"

"It was you who asked me!"

"Oh yes it was, actually."

" 'Don't worry—I'm a modern girl—I've got my—' "

"Do you think that's awful?"

"No."

"Most men are so boring."

"Carrying it round in your handbag."

"Would you like it if I didn't?"

"No."

"Mister, I'm an orphan!"

"Where do you come from?"

"A cowshed."

"Come down from Liverpool on a lorry."

"Do you mind!"

"To the lonely castle."

"Where there was no help within five miles. Jasper!"

"Yes? Fuck! I've broken a tooth!"

"Do you say fuck with spooks?"

"Sometimes."

"Do you say fuck with your wife? Ow, we're touchy, aren't we!"

"You're made of blubber."

"Please, can I use the basin?"

"Yes. It'll give me pleasure."

"This is what my boyfriend liked. He was an agoraphilic."

"A what?"

"Open spaces. Trains. Oh now I've upset you!"

"I've told you, you're good for me."

"Why?"

"To exorcise me."

"One two three. One two three. This is for the stomach."

"You're like an advertisement for safety belts."

"That's the end! Never, never, will I darken your doorstep!"

"I'm so sorry! So terribly sorry!"

"You do like me?"

"Yes. Have you really got a sister?"

"No."

"And is he your boyfriend?"

"Which?"

"The one in the brown suit."

"I've told you."

"And what did Tom say?"

"What about?"

"Me."

"That you were rich and arrogant."

"What else?"

"Ah, you like that, don't you!"

"Is he?"

"Yes, actually."

"What?"

"My boyfriend. The one in the brown suit. Why aren't I like spooks?"

"You're just not."

"What is she like then?"

"Dark. Silent."

One day there came into my office a priest, a man with a black cloak and a long straight nose like a broomstick. He came to talk about Central Africa. Priests were always talking about Central Africa; it was one of the few places left where they felt they still had some function, being both primitive and deathly.

He said "Very good of you!"

"Not at all."

He sat down. His skirts swished in the dust.

I had an ambivalent attitude towards priests; I thought they had some vital function, but this was perhaps to get themselves martyred quickly.

He said "You know Bill Harris?"

"No."

"You don't?"

"Never heard of him."

I had never seen a priest laugh so much. He became possessed, like Elizabeth or Tom Savile.

"What a relief!"

"Who is he?"

"He said he knew you. He was at school."

"You were at school?"

I simulated amazement. I slid down slightly behind my desk; spread my hands out like oil.

He had small bright eyes. I thought—Fire is underneath his black cloak; which he carries for the purposes of magic.

He said "You're going out to Africa?"

"Yes."

"You'll see Ndoula?"

I thought—Everyone wants to see me now I am seeing Ndoula.

His shoulders hunched. He became a vulture. He gazed at a tangent. I thought—Perhaps he has learned this from Natalie.

He said "Could you do something?"

"What?"

He moved his lips.

He said "Give him a message."

I could say—Are you mad? In my position?

He seemed to be having some struggle inside his chest. He twitched his eyebrows and pushed his mouth out.

I thought—The fire inside him is a child.

I said "Do you believe in a just war?"

"Under what circumstances?"

"Any."

"I think I do."

I thought—If he wants to get help to Ndoula, shouldn't he be questioning me rather than the person inside him?

I said "If, in Central Africa, an African came to you and asked for asylum—he'd been blowing up a bridge or something—people had been killed—would you, or wouldn't you, protect him?"

"Probably."

"Depending on what?"

"Conscience."

"And how would you inform your conscience?"

I had at last succeeded in catching his attention. He looked up for a moment from inside his cloak.

He said "By a consideration of the social and historical situation."

I said "I don't think that's any good."

I had expected him to say—By prayer.

I walked up and down behind my desk. I thought—What if the African asked for dynamite?

He said "Why, what is any good?"

"A certain instinct."

I thought—The people who keep on turning up in my life seem to be asking for asylum.

I said "Do you know Ndoula?"

"Yes."

"What's he like?"

"A very good man."

"Perhaps he's better locked up."

"Why?"

"He can be a martyr."

He said "But one can't choose to be a martyr."

"But he doesn't."

"No. Perhaps we choose him."

I thought—This is the first serious conversation I have had for weeks.

I said "Can you choose to betray things?"

"What sort of things?"

"What if the African asked you for dynamite?"

When he looked at me directly, I felt as if he were wounded and lying on a battlefield.

I sat behind my desk. I said "Do you come from Africa?"

"Yes."

"What do you do there?"

"Run a school."

"Things have to get worse."

"Probably."

"But you have to make them better."

"Yes."

He chewed his lip.

He said "I know it makes nonsense."

I thought—When he blushes, he is like someone in love.

I said "What message do you want me to give Ndoula?"

I thought—Perhaps I should pick him up and bandage him.

He looked at the ground.

I walked up and down behind my desk.

I said "I suppose one can betray things that are not historically proper."

He said "That are not right."

I thought—I must have sounded cynical.

I said "Why is it that everything of importance has to be said in the form of a parable?"

He said "To give the other person choice."

I said "Yes. We do have choice." I sat down behind my desk. I said "What do you want me to tell Ndoula?"

He said "Just that we've been trying to get books and papers through to him, and they've been stopped."

I said "Books and papers."

"And we'll try again at the very end of the first week in December."

"I see."

I could not think what else to say. I thought—Our air is running out. Or—So I might be part of rescuing Ndoula?

He had closed his eyes as if exhausted.

I said "You know, soon, I'm getting out of politics."

I thought—He is one person who won't say—What a pity!

He said "What a pity."

I wondered—Is he praying?

I said "Did you really come to see me because of someone at school called Harris?"

"And other things."

"What?"

"We do have a mutual friend."

He had opened his eyes. He seemed again unaccountably embarrassed.

I said "You might as well ask me if I play cricket!"

"But you do!"

I wondered—Why do I not ask him who is our mutual friend?

I said "If odd people keep on popping up in your life, do you think they are emanations?"

He said "Things are betrayed anyway."

I said "What?" Then—"Are you going back to Africa?"

His eyes seemed full of tears.

"Probably."

"Perhaps I'll see you there."

"I hope so."

"I've got one or two things I'd like to talk to you about."

He said "Very good."

I said "I mean, things like if God loves a sinner then you've got to be like God not to sin."

He said "Yes, I see that."

6

NATALIA WOULD BE MOVING through streets with her long hair flying; her breasts and hips a sea-spray. She would come to the small door of Sylvia's house; have to bend to get in. Her bright eyes would be carried like coals in a censer.

"Am I late?"

"How lovely!"

"I've had such trouble!"

This was what I imagined. I didn't stop imagining about Natalie.

Edward Jones would be standing with his hands on the back of Sylvia's chair. Natalia would put down her shopping basket to kiss him. With a taper, she would light up his red skull.

"What have you got?"

"I'm so stupid!"

"Natalia, you know you do everything perfectly!"

From her basket she would take out materials, toys and trinkets; a few old lamps and snakes.

"Will they do?"

"Natalie, what big eyes you've got!"

There would be other men in the room watching her. She would wear a white net dress with a see-through bottom. The men would carry magnifying glasses in their hands. Fish swam inside her.

"Natalia, what are you doing now?"

"Oh, everything!"

"Where did you get that dress? to put your shopping in?"

Once I had met Natalia in this room. She had been talking to a friend. I had said—Will you dance? she had said—I don't dance. She had immediately become compliant.

—Natalia, will you lie on your back please; raise one leg.

I could say—Darling, I hope you are sometimes suffering.

In Sylvia's drawing room there were soft pink sofas like shells. Sylvia was a judge in a pageboy wig. She would lead Natalie along to a bedroom. Someone would ask—Whatever happened to poor old John the Baptist?

—That was a long time ago: and besides, he betrayed me.

Natalia and Edward would sit with their children round a tea table. Two by two, they formed a mandala. When they ate, they were framed by gilt on their chairs like honey. Natalia leaned forwards, upsetting a breast.

"Mummy, look what you've done!"

"It was you who did it!"

Like a pelican she would clasp her children to her breast. Blood ran down on to the table.

I said to myself—Of course, I would dream of her as prostitute or mother.

"Mummy—"

"Yes?"

"You won't leave us, will you?"

Once, in fact, I thought I saw the four of them. They were in a car. There was a uniformed chauffeur in front. Natalia and Edward were on small centre seats facing back. Their two children were on the back seat facing forwards. I did not know why they were in this peculiar arrangement. They were like royalty—or people escorted by police. I thought—A mandala is true in the mind: in reality, it is moving.

Sometimes when Elizabeth came to London she used to stand in the doorway of my flat and sniff; strange smells and objects seemed to emanate that I thought I had eradicated and tidied.

I tried to make jokes; the hanged man with his sausages.

"What is it this time?"

"You tell me!"

"The woman downstairs! She sprays her tobacco plant!"

Elizabeth sat on the sofa with her feet curled up. In London she had nothing to do. Her distaste created a vacuum which spirits rushed in to fill.

I said "The bedroom's clean."

"Good."

"The bath powdered."

I put my hands in my hair. I was in a tree, caught out riding. I thought—She wants to be rid of me.

I said "What do you think I get up to?"

"I'd rather not think."

"I sit here watching telly—"

I could make anything a fantasy. What did I want?

Elizabeth went to the bedroom and opened a drawer. There was a piece of tissue with lipstick on it. Elizabeth left the drawer open and sat on the bed.

I gazed at the tissue. I thought—My unconscious must have left it there.

I said "A wicked magician!"

I wanted to say—All right then stop me! Fight me!

I said "It's an old one of yours!"

I wondered if it was Natalie's or Madeleine's.

I was confused at so many possibilities. I thought—Innocence is just a lack of knowledge; not necessarily of good and evil.

I sat on the bed with my back to Elizabeth. I felt the top of my head coming off.

Because I had done Elizabeth an injury I wanted her to comfort me.

I said "I'm ill. I've got to see someone."

I had begun to see life as this spiral on which you climbed. The steps were the ability to hurt and be hurt by other people.

She said "Yes why don't you see someone?"

Elizabeth had come to London to go to one of Sylvia's parties. I had said—But you don't go to Sylvia's parties!

I had not known whether or not Natalia would be there.

I said "I have such thoughts: like devils!"

I wanted her to say—I'm so sorry. Then take my head upon her lap. Then I could stop worrying about her.

I thought—But I want her to come to Sylvia's party if Natalie is there.

I might go and walk in the streets. I had one or two appointments before evening. If I quarrelled with Elizabeth now, I might have time to do my work and to be free to see what happened later.

I thought—So I do not want Elizabeth to be too sorry for me!

I said "I'm appalled by evil: I mean, my own. I see everything as fantasy and duplicity. One tells no truth, knowing it can be the opposite: makes nothing better, because worse can be useful. The more one knows, the more contempt there is. Of course, I don't think like this always."

When I talk like this Elizabeth's face becomes old as if she has travelled too far in space too quickly.

I said "Which is why I'm getting out. Going away. Where I can think. I know this is ridiculous!"

I thought—Asking for pity is no good: you see the arteries hardening.

Then—But I'm too hard on myself. This is genuine!

I said "Do say something!"

"You're always thinking of yourself."

I shouted "I've said it's ridiculous!"

Holding my head, and with great effort, I thought I might do something that was not to do with myself. Logically, this was impossible.

She said "This is a sort of smokescreen."

"A smokescreen for what?"

"What?"

"A smokescreen conceals something. What does it conceal?"

I thought—This is despicable.

I felt better.

She said "How do I know what it conceals?"

I walked up and down. By my appearing normal, I thought the top of her head might come off.

She said "I find a piece of tissue with lipstick on it—"

She began to screw her face up. A hand clutched at her windpipe.

I thought—I am a devil.

I said "I'm sorry! Sorry!"

If she was hurt too much, I might not get away before evening.

I said "Why don't you stay with me in London then?"

She said "Because you don't want me to!"

"But I do!"

I thought—What we both want is to be able to say that the other person doesn't want us.

But it was true both she and I wanted her to stay in the country.

I said "There's been no one here except Tom's ridiculous girlfriend."

"What girlfriend?"

"Marlene. You know. I met her in a pub. She wanted to talk about Tom."

The pain in my head was getting less. I thought—She will believe me because she wants to; and it's almost the truth anyway.

I said "You don't want to hear about her do you?"

Elizabeth said "Good God no!"

She went back to the dressing table and began brushing her hair.

I thought—We know each other so well; what she wants is simply for me to have courage.

I said "That's the horror!"

"What?"

"No one can help."

I had a vision of Elizabeth's strong back: she was striding through a battlefield: the hem of her skirt swung above the wounded.

I picked the piece of tissue paper from the dressing table and dropped it in the wastepaper basket. I thought—It was Natalia's.

I said "Never mind. I'll be going out to Africa."

She said "I don't want you to."

I said "I may be there some time."

"Why?"

I said "I think, to be any good, one has to squat in a desert."

I noticed her handbag on the floor. In it there was a long letter in her handwriting.

She was making up her face in front of the mirror.

I said "Are you coming to the party?"

"Yes."

"I have one or two things to do first. Do you mind?"

I could not read the letter in her handbag. I wondered if it was to Joe Gregory.

I said "I do admire you."

She said "Good. What's happening about all that?"

"All what?"

"Africa."

I thought—What I admire, and what will save us in the end, but not yet, is that we both want, and want the other to want, everything: and will fight for it.

Madeleine, or Marlene, was a girl who lived in a building in Soho where you went up a stone staircase black with damp and on every landing there was a lavatory with flowered wallpaper peeling. Madeleine stood at the top of the stairs: she wore a pale suede skirt. I thought—You could write your name on her behind on it.

She said "So you found this salubrious establishment."

I said "Oh yes, like a pigeon."

There were two rooms; the outer one a kitchen.

I said "Is this where your clients wait?"

She shouted "Look—!"

I said "I'm only joking!"

Marlene was material for a pinup. Pouting, she could be hung on a soldier's wall. She stood with one knee bent and her foot turned out. I thought—There is some image of this in the mind: the shape of a mandala, or testicles.

She said "Why are you so horrid!"

"I'm nervous!"

"You don't really think I'm a tart?"

"No. I like imagining it."

There were wicker chairs and a bed. I could say—Look, we'll sit and talk about our families.

"I'm afraid I can't offer you a drink."

"I've brought some whisky!"

We sat opposite each other and drank. I thought—When you are in trouble you double up on it, like a mad and bankrupt gambler.

I said "How's the job?"

"I've left."

"What are you doing then?"

"You needn't be nice!"

She lit a cigarette; avoided the smoke like cannonballs.

I thought—This may at last be something not to do with myself: my bread will be returned after many days.

She said "Have you been seeing spooks?"

"No."

"That's why you're seeing me then!"

Her feet were up on the wicker chair so that her ankles were pressed against her groin. Bits of straw appeared between them.

"Have you been seeing Tom?"

"No."

"Why does he call you Madeleine?"

"I am called Madeleine!"

My whisky seemed to be going down the wrong way. It made a cushion of air which kept me floating.

I thought—When she pouts, it is to make her face more comfortable like a cushion.

She said "Why don't you like me?"

"I do."

"Look, will you take me out tonight? I'll pay for it."

I gazed into my glass. There were bubbles rising. I was a few inches above the ground, having been raised and made holy.

I said "Madeleine, no one has ever said that to me before!"

"But will you?"

"I don't think I can."

Once Marlene and I had gone dancing. There had been a cellar like the inside of a drum. Fuses had gone off like Roman candles. Bones had beaten our ears. There had been red-plush tables like a coffin.

She said "Are you going out to Africa?"

"Yes."

"To see Ndoula?"

"How did you know that?"

When we had been dancing there had been a black man who held up his wrists as if they were broken. He had come and spoken to Marlene. His socks and fingernails were luminous. Marlene had crouched and gritted her teeth.

She said "I do have some influential friends, you know."

"Who?"

She picked at the pieces of wicker between her legs. I thought—Coloured lights are what babies grope for just after they have been born.

She said "A priest as a matter of fact."

"What?"

"Told me you were going to Africa."

I said "Father Whatnot?"

I was amazed.

I said "The man who came to see me at my office?"

I tried to concentrate on this. The whisky was becoming transformed into coloured lights. He had said—We do have a mutual friend, you know. I thought—Of course, I am on the bottle: this is the illusion that the world has meaning.

I could say—Are you a member of the Secret Service?

She said "I'm not a complete nonentity, you know!"

I said "No, you're an angel!"

She came and stood close to me. I put my hand up her skirt.

I said "How do you know that priest?"

"Why shouldn't I?"

Her body seemed halfway to the ceiling.

I said "What else do you do? Knit?"

I thought—It is the oddity that gives meaning.

I was in a small room in Soho. It contained wicker furniture and a bed. Marlene was a roundfaced girl with a body like balloons.

I said "What have you put in this drink?"

She sat on my lap. She said "It's your whisky!"

I tried to work out what was, or was not, fantasy. Father Whatnot had been to see me in my office. I had gone out with Marlene once or twice after I had met her with Tom. I had first seen her with Joe Gregory. She had been once or twice to my flat. I did not know about Father Whatnot.

Marlene said "Try this!"

Her cigarette was sweet. I supposed it was marijuana.

She said "You're tired."

She put her mouth down full of smoke.

I said "I keep on telling you." I breathed some smoke in.

"Why don't you see this doctor then."

"Which doctor?"

"This doctor I keep on telling you about."

I said "Whichdoctor Witchdoctor." I thought this funny. I began to laugh.

I could not think how I had got so drunk on so little whisky.

I said "I must go now."

"You won't have dinner?"

"I'm so sorry, I've got to see some Africans."

"Who are you having dinner with? Spooks?"

"I've told you—"

"I'm not stopping you!"

Madeleine was a huntress walking in a forest. She wore a white smock just to the top of her thighs. A dog jumped up and got its teeth in her.

I said "Madeleine, thank you!"

"For what?"

"For being so kind."

"Are you having dinner with your wife then?"

I knelt by the bed and put my head down on her knees. I thought—I will be boring.

Then—We live like lilies.

I said "What does your doctor do; give one pills?"

She said "Are you all right?"

I said "I need a lavatory."

"It's outside."

"Look! A Christmas tree!"

From my mouth there were extraordinary strands like tinsel. At the top, I could pin an angel.

I began to watch my feet from my head floating above them. They moved out on to the landing. Gusts of wind took them. I trailed a cable which might catch against wires. Madeleine was left above me. I was surprised how well I floated.

Madeleine shouted "Be careful!"

I shouted "We've got wings!"

I thought that if I tripped over too many wires at once, I might light up like an aurora borealis.

Edward Jones was a large roundfaced man with fair curly hair that came down over his collar. He wore pale grey suits on which drops of oil might spread. He was an upper-class Englishman with invulnerability sprayed on to him by not having lost a battle on home ground since Hastings.

Edward was one of a delegation that came to see me about Ndoula. I sat in my office while they established themselves like ambulance men. They deposited coats and briefcases. They were the silver of the earth; sixpences in the Christmas pudding.

Edward said "We just want to put the other point of view."

I said "Everyone knows the other point of view."

He had a soft voice to show his gentleness.

I had the impression we were talking about Natalia. We faced each other across my desk. I did not know how matters stood between Edward and Natalie. She had sometimes said he was cruel, but this was to make me kind: sometimes that he was kind, but this was to be cruel.

He said "The point for law and order. I think a government is meant to govern, and the best people to do this are experts on the spot. This is not a popular theory."

I sometimes had sympathy with Edward. We waxed hot or cold according to what wind Natalie blew us. I could say—She is your, and my, lifeblood; should we expect her to have only one breast?

I said "I agree; but the best people to know about opposition are also experts on the spot."

He smiled. "I take your point."

I could say—We are stuck in some infinite regression.

When Natalia is with you she wants to be with me; when with me, you. There is no place, except on a tightrope, where there is room for all.

I said "Then what do you want me to do?"

"Leave them alone."

"We can't."

"Why not?"

"Because your lot of experts have got the other lot of buggers locked up."

Edward always asked for a decision. He would say—I must have her wholly or give her up! But people had to be cared for, and to grow.

He said "But what's that got to do with us?"

"We're responsible."

"Why?"

"We just are."

Once he must have worshipped Natalia. She had seen him as a god. Then, when they became human, there was too much to do.

He said "Charity begins at home."

I said "That's not in the Bible."

"Ah! Who is my neighbour then?"

There had been times when I had wanted to ring up Edward. He and I could have met for a drink in a pub. In no-man's-land, on Christmas Eve, we would have made a nonsense of those generals—Natalie and Natalia.

He said "The Church! I sometimes think those priests are at the back of it. There are some, certainly, who are the dupes of the communists."

I said "You don't believe that."

I thought—Natalia's being Jewish may make us cling to her: She sits with her young and like a pelican tears her breast.

He said "All we're asking is, you don't get carried away by the current idea that revolution is praiseworthy just because it's revolution."

"What do you suggest then?"

"Accept the status quo."

"We can't."

"Why not?"

"It won't work."

One day, in a restaurant, I had seen Edward with his mistress. I had not told Natalia because it would not have done me any good. Edward had not told her he had seen me because it would not have done him any good. I thought—There is an economy.

He said "Otherwise there'll be bloodshed."

I said "There's bloodshed anyway."

He said "But justice isn't the prerogative of the weak and unsuccessful."

I said "They usually win."

He stared at me.

I thought—Perhaps he is imagining me, as I imagine him, with Natalia.

He put his hands on his knees, ready to go.

I thought—I should be a person in a courtyard by a court-house; having come down from an upstairs room.

I said "Surely things are not so much in our control."

He said "Thank you for seeing us."

I thought—It is because there are two of us that Natalie, or Natalia, can double up like the mad bankrupt gambler; so that her bread may return after many days.

A delegation of Africans came to see me. I said "I'm sorry, I've been very busy."

I sat behind my desk. I tidied papers. I thought—At least, I look exhausted.

The Africans sat in a row. They were large men with their hands on their knees. I thought—The three wise virgins.

They said "We just want to put the opposite point of view."

I thought—I am Jonah; they will not know it is the acid of the fish's stomach has burned me white.

They said "The point for law and justice. A government governs, surely, for the benefit of all the people."

I said "In theory."

"Not in practice?"

They had tired eyes. I wondered if any of them knew Madeleine. Her boyfriend wore pale brown trousers.

They said "All that we ask is that responsibility—"

"—Yes—"

"—Troops—"

"—Yes—"

I walked up and down. I wanted to say—Do you wish to stay as children?

But then, they might take over the kingdom of heaven.

I said "Don't you have to fight? On your own? If not, you'll be fighting soon enough among yourselves."

They watched with their yellow eyes. The gods had fallen down and were making love in front of the children.

I said "For your own identity."

They said "We just advocate a return to the constitution."

I did not know if they believed this. One of them, at the end of the row, was a small quiet man with eyes like an Assyrian.

I thought—God must have felt like this when searching the sea for Jonah.

I said "Some peaceable change is possible but not here; you're stuck in some blockage of history."

I thought—I have this new theory of biological evolution.

They said "We ask you to place the strongest possible pressure—"

"—of course—"

"We understand Mr. Edward Jones—"

"—that doesn't matter."

127

I could explain—I'm friendly with his wife.

I thought the best I might do when I got out to Africa was to get drunk and behave like a clown, for a diversion.

I said "Do you know Father Whatnot?"

"Who?"

"A priest. A long nose. He runs some school out there."

They shook their heads.

I thought—They are wondering why they trust me. I'm so unpredictable.

My new theory of evolution was, that once you thought you understood something your counter was removed from the game. Then, you found yourself back in the garden.

The small quiet man said "You'll be seeing Mr. Ndoula?"

"Probably."

"Yes." They waited.

I said "But I may not be going."

Their anxiety seemed genuine.

I explained "I've been slightly ill."

I thought—They're thinking of their children.

I wanted to say—Look, Europeans have fought each other almost into the grave!

I said "Africans may manage it. You may just sit and things will fall into your lap."

I was behind my desk. My hands were spread out like oil.

I said "History is on your side."

The small quiet man said "When has history ever been on the side of people who sit?"

I shrugged. I said "It goes where it wants anyway." I lifted my hands and looked at the palms. I added "Of course, every-one has to do what he can."

I had the impression, which I had had several times before, that such incidents as these were mysteriously being performed for my benefit. I was in a curtained box; a mad king; while elsewhere enormous events occurred as part of an unknown strategy.

The small quiet man said "But you will be going?"

"Yes."

I thought—At the edge of a wood, on a dark night, I, and he being black, would still recognise each other.

In Parliament Square at night there are the building like a battleship and the Abbey like a toad and the starred sky unseen as if security or long grass were hiding it.

I was going to a party at Sylvia Fisher's; the party would go on till three-thirty or four; I had been sitting up late for several nights and was tired. The party would be mainly for politicians and intellectuals, with a few younger potentates from the television world thrown it.

There was the Chinese footman at the door. I pushed past him murmuring "We've only got four minutes!" Inside were the guests holding their glasses like Geiger counters. I found Sylvia upstairs in her inner sanctum, sitting cross-legged on the floor.

She said "I hear you're working for the Russians."

I said "On whose side?"

I kissed Sylvia on the cheek. Her skin was like a Ping-Pong bat.

I thought—Her shadow will be discovered in this position in a thousand years.

I looked past her down the stairs. People's heads were moving like particles of molecules.

I said "Anyone seen my wife?"

Sylvia said "Which one?"

It was as if a scientific experiment were being attempted in which a mass of people were put together and then bombarded with perception. This either did, or did not, create new patterns.

I saw my old friend Tom Savile on the stairs. He was behind a television camera or a gun. I thought—He is halfway up the stairs of the Tuileries.

I said "Tom, what are you doing?"

"I've a bone to pick with you!"

He was dressed in a smart blue suit; a diagram of a technician with two legs and two arms.

I thought I could say—Tom, I was just dusting her and she came to pieces in my hand!

There were arc lights in the corners of the ceiling; and behind them, possibly, angels.

I said "Does Sylvia know she's being televised?"

Tom said "You're drunk!"

Television rays were going through us all the time. People did not notice these. Perhaps soon, we would not notice the cameras and technicians.

Tom shouted "A few inches to your right please!"

There was a sketch for television going on beneath some potted palm trees. The Prime Minister was being pushed towards the leader of an African delegation. The Prime Minister was in a dinner jacket. The African wore flowers. They were acting—The Proposal: or—What Shall We Tell the Children?

Tom shouted "Can we have that again please!"

I wondered whether, if I moved through the crowd, it would form up again when I had passed; or whether I would create a vacuum in which I would be shot in the back.

Tom said "Why haven't you been to see me?"

I found myself in the line of fire between the Prime Minister and the machine gun. I ducked. There had been a number of assassinations recently.

Tom said "Why are you drunk?"

I thought—The experiment is to discover the mechanisms of the brain. But the instruments are constructed by these mechanisms, so the operation is impossible.

Then—So what you are bombarded with is coconuts.

I saw Elizabeth on the lawn. She was talking to Ned Symon,

the editor of the National Sunday Newspaper.

I walked through the early morning dew. I thought—The world has been made a corpse and swells to our destruction.

I said "I'm off the day after tomorrow!"

Elizabeth said "Oh you're here!"

Ned Symon said "I've just been asking her if she's going with you."

I looked up to the window where I had once sat with Natalia: where we might be sitting: where I had imagined her. It was an empty room, where I had been with Sylvia.

I thought—We are parts of a limb struggling across a desert.

I said "Don't you think it's an apotheosis, that Sylvia should be re-enacting the storming of the Tuileries while politicians do it as a sketch for television?"

A man with a pink face bumped into me. I said "Don't I know you?"

"Of course you do!"

"What are you doing now?"

"Look, what is this?"

They were putting makeup on to the Prime Minister. If they entirely covered him, he would die.

I thought—The man might be his bodyguard; or an old friend of Elizabeth's.

I said "Don't you think there's some worldwide conspiracy? To place two mirrors opposite each other, so that a beam of light is thrown to and fro, forever."

He said "You will remember?"

Joe Gregory was standing by the leader of the African delegation. He had a notebook open as if it were a hungry mouth.

I said "Yseult, Yseult, will you go to Africa with me?"

A strange woman answered "No!"

I said to Ned Symon, "In Africa there are monkeys who, to defend themselves, shit on people's heads."

Ned Symon said "You do that."

It was very hot. Lights for television poured down. We were out in the garden under plain trees.

Elizabeth was wearing a black net dress. She fluttered her fan above the necks of gladiators.

A black man had come up and was talking to me. I said "How do you do."

"Very well thank you."

"It's very hot."

"Yes. Would you care for a drink?"

"That's very kind of you."

Elizabeth said "Who is that man?"

I said "I think, a waiter."

I went back up the stairs towards Sylvia's inner sanctum. Here Natalia and I might have sat: here we might still be sitting.

I found no one there except a small grey man with whiskers.

He said "Hullo."

"Hullo."

"Are you looking for someone?"

"Yes."

"Who?"

"A doctor."

"I am a doctor."

"Ah!" I sat down. I said "Then perhaps you can help me."

I thought—I should explain that I have come here quite by chance. No one has sent me, except my wife and one or two girlfriends.

I said "I think I'm suffering from paranoiac delusions."

He was unscrewing a fountain pen. The inside came out like a bladder.

He said "What are your paranoiac delusions?"

I said "I see life as if it had some meaning. And I imagine I have some slight control."

He said "And you want me to stop you?"

I said "No."

He wore a pink silk shirt with glimpses through to his grey stomach.

I thought—Rub it, and a lamp might come out.

I said "But is there such a thing as a pill which would make me humdrum?"

He sighed. I thought—Or he might move one hand in a straight line above his head while the other went round and round on his stomach.

He said "Have you got a headache?"

"No."

"You touched your face."

On this sofa Natalia had sat. This had been at a previous party.

I said "What we want is a new mythology."

"Such as?"

"Of time, spatially. So that we can move backwards and forwards with control."

He said "I only bought this pen two weeks ago."

I thought—His technique is never to be caught in the same place at once: thus he creates mystery.

Ink suddenly spilled out over his shirt.

He said "How's Madeleine?"

I sat like a Roman emperor.

I said "All right thank you."

He said "She tells me you only like destructive women." His face lit up with gentle radiance.

I thought—I might not have heard correctly.

I looked out through a window. There were couples at random on the lawn.

I said "Are you really a doctor?"

He pulled an inhaler out of his pocket and pushed it up to his nose. He banged the side of his head like a mouth organ.

I had the impression of screens having been placed around

me. These were to filter sensations coming in.

He said "And what happens in your new mythology?

I said "Oh, well, we see everything in stories. These are constructions of our minds."

"Right."

"But what are the patterns of construction? What we want is a myth about myths."

Looking out of the window, I saw Natalia with Edward on the lawn.

The doctor said "Would you like some of this?"

"What is it?"

He held out his inhaler.

I said "No."

Edward had had an arm round Natalia's throat.

I thought—I must get a long way from here.

The doctor put a hand to his face. He said "Excuse me, one of my patients committed suicide this morning."

I said "What was wrong?"

There would be the detention camp in the desert. It was a formation of wooden buildings surrounded by wire.

The doctor said "When you've written your myth, will you send it to me?"

"Yes."

He put his inhaler away.

I thought—A diagram, to work, would not be a story but a formula.

I walked down the stairs. I thought—I am a spiral, like everyone, walking up and down; or parallel, one inside the other.

At the bottom of the stairs I met my son Adam. We stood at the edge of the garden. I was glad to see him. I said "Adam, what on earth are you doing here?"

"Oh hullo!"

"Hullo!"

"What is going on?"

"A party."

"But I mean what's that television?"

I said "I suppose, for some reason, someone's televising Sylvia's party."

Adam and I were in some straight line within which time did not flow up and down; but like a tree.

I said "But how did you get here?"

"Catherine asked me."

"Who's Catherine? Oh yes! Joe and Margaret's daughter."

I thought—How extraordinary he should be here!

A girl with dark hair stood on the edge of a flower-bed. I thought—Natalia and I are close, without touching.

I said "I've been talking to a doctor. He takes a sort of inhaler, to make himself better."

"And does he?"

"I don't think so."

Jack, the Minister, came up. He put his hand on my shoulder. He said "All set for safari?"

I said "Yes. This is my son."

Adam said "How do you do."

"How do you do there! Are you looking after your father?"

We were standing on the edge of the lawn; clouds were beneath us.

Adam said "I don't know."

The Minister said "Do. He's an important man."

Natalia was standing at some distance to me talking to Edward. Elizabeth had her back to me talking to Joe Gregory. I was side by side with Adam, facing the Minister, an old man like an apple.

I thought—Perhaps I am having one of those hallucinations, or revelations, that are not worked out until you have lived with them in the morning:

—I will construct my myth about how our minds make myths: about how we are, or are not, trapped in them.

II

Natalie

7

ROWING INTO THE harbour from the sea the water was dark and clear and scum floated on it like flesh on a cold cauldron. The oars stirred the water into whirlpools that followed the blades and beneath them the seaweed on stones moved sluggishly. The quay was a low stone wall with iron rings. Crouched, I had to prevent the boat running into it and breaking. With my arms I supported the universe. The scum was scattered beneath me like lights from a stained-glass window. I stood on her shoulders; seaweed moved like hair in the wind.

I tied the boat with rope to an iron ring. The ring was rusted, and I pushed the rope between it and the stone. The end of the rope was frayed spraying outwards like a fountain. I remembered a lawn with marble statues. When I stood up the boat rocked. I could see above the quayside to a row of white-washed houses. Beyond them were dark hills. The boat moved up and down and the houses moved up and down in front of the hills. My fingers hurt where I had pushed them against the stone.

I walked up a cobbled street past the whitewashed houses. The sky was dark. The houses appeared luminous as if lit from behind. Through an open window I saw a group of men round a bed. They wore white cloaks. They bent over a figure who was giving birth to a child. They had the masks of birds and animals. I was walking up the street away from the harbour. I had been rowing all night and was tired. I had come from a place I could hardly remember. There had been a city with tall towers and masts of ships. I had crept, keeping to the shadows. I became aware of someone walking parallel to me against the line of whitewashed houses. When the figure was upright its speed was equal to mine but when it moved away or towards me its speed was infinite. Sometimes it rushed flat on the ground as if it were hiding. I came to the end of the row of houses where the lights ceased: it would not be able to follow me. The lights were street lamps so that it went swinging round like a scythe. I stood between two lamps and it pointed in two directions at once. One was to where I was going, and the other could become this by manipulation. I held my arms out to keep my balance. The wind blew the smells of the sea up from the harbour. Standing on shoulders, her hair had spread out like the wind.

The path led up a valley. Beside me was a stream which ran back to the sea. This was a thread I could return by. The shadows had left me and were rushing round behind hills. If they moved fast enough they might be there before me. I was on my own with the impression of myself walking. There were men inside me in white coats facing dials. Men had been grouped round a bed attending to the birth of a child. They sat facing screens that looked out over a landscape. When my foot hit a stone there were mechanisms to balance me. A pipe ran back to the sea. I was walking up a valley with dark hills on either side. At the end was a cottage with a lighted window. The shadows which had followed me were out of sight behind hills. After a hard day's work, you return up the valley to your home.

I reached the cottage and looked through the lighted window. She was sitting in front of the fire alone. Above the fire was a cauldron. The cauldron was hung from an iron ring. She stirred the cauldron, and the blades of the oars made whirlpools. The seaweed, like her hair, moved sluggishly after it. I had to get into the cottage without being seen. If I was seen, she would turn and face me and disappear. I put my fingers against a window which was like a grating. My fingers would grow tendrils: there would be flowers through the stone. I was inside the room with my back against the wall. I had leaned against the wall and it had moved. The room had not changed.

There were oak tables and oak benches; the fireplace with seats on either side. Ash fell on the carpet. It made a noise of heat going down. Here we had sat all summer. I had gone each day to the harbour to get food. Blades had cut into the water. In the chair, my arms and legs were at right angles forming squares. The squares were unfinished between my knees and hands and between where I was sitting and the ground. She sat opposite me, alone. There was an iron bar between us. From this was hung a cauldron. The cauldron was held by an iron ring in the stone. If I moved towards her she had to move towards me; if I moved away, she moved away on the other side of the fire. I had to move without being seen. There were mechanisms for doing this in the body and brain. She sat beyond the cauldron, facing me. Here we had sat all summer. I had gone each day to the harbour to get food. She had stirred the cauldron the blade had gone into the water. I remembered a cell in which I had spent all winter alone. If I moved away from her, she moved away from me and I fell back on the other side of the fire. If I moved towards her she moved towards me and we became pressed against each other like stone. I wanted her to remain seated so I could move towards her and put my head in her lap. When I tried to do this she moved towards me and her face became terrified. She could lean over me and put her head against my back. Staying where I was, my arms and legs were in squares: there were gaps between them and between where I was seated and the ground. Her eyes were watching me, so that there were reflections of myself watching her. There was an iron bar between us in the stone. She was asking me something that I did not understand. When she smiled a gap appeared inside her; men rushed up and down on ladders facing dials. Here we had sat all summer. I had gone down each day to the harbour to get food. By signalling behind my back, I could summon the people who had come up from the valley. When I had left the harbour they had run round

141

behind hills. They could hold me, while I crawled towards her. Then she could stay still. There are mechanisms for doing this in the body and brain. She put a hand behind her against the wall. I had climbed out on to the quayside. A hand would come through the wall and hold her. Tendrils had grown through a window. Then she could crawl towards me without being seen. Without turning, I could hear the people beyond the walls. They had come up from the valley. They were breathing and stamping in the snow. Here we had been all summer. Every time I moved she had to move away or to-wards me: her knees became pressed against mine like stone. Or when she fell away, there was no one to hold us. She had sat stirring the cauldron. The people who had been with us had disappeared behind hills. I had looked through a lighted window. There had been men round a body giving birth to a child. A hand came through the wall and held her. Her wrist was fastened to an iron ring in the stone. With her face to the wall she could not see me. Standing on my shoulders, she had looked out over the harbour. The people who had left us had moved behind hills. I could hear them outside the cottage: they were in the snow. By stretching my fingers I could move through the walls and beckon them. Then they could hold me, so I could crawl towards her past the fire. I could put my head in her lap. There were mechanisms for doing this in the body and brain. She was watching me from the other side of the fire. We had been like this all summer. I remembered a cell which I had sat in, alone. There was a town with tall towers and masts of ships. Men in white coats had climbed ladders: they faced switches and dials. A stream ran back to the sea. Every time I moved she fell back on the other side of the fire. Or our fists became pressed against each other like stone. Outside, we could hear the men stamping and breathing. They wore the masks of birds and animals. Their hands came through the walls and held me. She had beckoned to them with her fingers. I had been trying to reach them through the walls. I was outside in the group stamping in the snow. She had looked beyond me to where they might come in. There were mechanisms for doing this. If I put my head on her lap, she would lean over so that I carried her; if I moved away, we would escape on the other side of the fire. We had been here all summer. When they held me, I could crawl towards her and put my head in her lap. Arms came through the stone and held her. Putting my hands out, I felt the hands through the walls. Like this, we moved across a landscape. We were hand in hand through the snow. Behind us, I could see where we had sat in our chairs. We had been there all summer. Men wore the masks of birds and animals. One, with the beak of a bird, had put his head down against her throat. Blood ran on to the snow. We were walking hand in hand across a landscape. People had come through the walls and held us. We were outside, stamping in the snow. I had crawled forwards and put my head in her lap. She had moved towards me and stayed still. There were mechanisms for doing this in the body and brain. One, with the beak of a bird, had put his head against her. Blood had dripped on to the snow. She had joined me. We were walking across a flat landscape. Looking back, we could see where we had sat. There were men with white masks grouped round a bed. They were demonstrating the use of another person's pain. We were going on a journey across a level plain with snow. Our footsteps made no sound. All around us was light; there were no shadows. We were moving on a line, seeming to get no closer nor further away. The plain was empty. When we stamped, the ground sounded hollow. Beneath it I remembered gardens where men and women had lain on grass. There was a pink light on the horizon; if we turned to one side or the other, the sky became split. We moved in a straight line so that it remained still. The line on which we were walking was drawn on a map. The line went from the cottage to a walled city:

another line went from the city to the harbour by the sea. From this, the path led up to the cottage in the valley. These three lines formed a triangle, which was supported on a wire. We were walking across a landscape covered with snow. The landscape moved. At the three corners of the triangle were the cottage, the walled city, and the harbour by the sea. These were illustrated by drawings. The cottage was a small thatched house with smoke coming out of the chimney; the walled town had a moat and battlements and towers; the harbour reflected an iron ring in the stone. Beneath the water, her hair had been like seaweed. On the path between the harbour and the cottage I had been alone; the shadows had left me and had rushed behind hills. There had been the impression of myself walking. Men in white coats had sat on ladders facing dials. On the line across the plain we walked together. There were no shadows because the light was all around. The shadows had rushed ahead of us. We did not appear to be moving towards or away. We had the impression of our bodies working. Hands were touching the faces of switches and dials. If we stamped, the earth could be sent spinning. We were walking across a landscape covered with snow. Our feet made a booming. We were moving towards a walled city, where the sky was pink. Here the men with masks of birds and animals would be waiting; they would have gone behind hills. They would watch for a hand to come through the walls and beckon them. Fingers would grow like tendrils through the stone. We had joined the group outside the walled city. Their leader was the man with a beak who had put his head down to embrace her. When he saw us, he put a hand to his mouth and blew. The town was surrounded by a high stone wall with a tower. The battlements were like fingers rising out of the plain. There was a moat with a drawbridge. High up in the tower was a window. Here you had been imprisoned all winter, alone. You would lean out of the window and give a signal like tendrils. Then we would break in. We stood around, stamping and blowing in the snow. In the moat, scum floated on the water. There was iron in the stone. Your hair, beneath the water, had spread out like seaweed. You had gone ahead of us into the tower. We were outside in the cold. I was one of the men with masks of birds and animals. We had gone behind hills to get there before you. We were waiting for your signal from the tower. You would wear a white nightdress: carry a candle like a dove. The candle was beneath your breast and would burn you. The blood dripped down against the snow. I had rowed into the harbour from the sea; the oars had made whirlpools. A light appeared in the window: your breast, above the candle, burned. We wrapped our cloaks round us: ran with our shoulders against the drawbridge. Hands came through the door and held us; they were tendrils through the stone. You watched from an upstairs window. We were in the hallway of the castle. You stood with the candle and one hand against your breast. The candle burned: it made blood against the snow. The man with the beak of a bird put his head down to embrace you: with one arm round his neck, you were a tunnel through which he could breathe. On the stairs were figures in suits of armour. Firelight flickered. You were laid on a table with one leg raised. The man with the mask of a bird rummaged inside you. He was looking in you like a suitcase. I had been in the cell all winter alone. Turning you on your front, you had been split up the back by an axe. Men in white coats stood around you. They had instruments in their hands with which to handle coals. They flipped them over. You had your face to the wall and were fastened to iron rings. The man with the beak of a bird tore the lining. Hands had come through the wall and held me. Your arms were round the neck of the man with the mask like a swan. He reached to the entrails and the liver. Men leaned over tables and shovelled coal. Their pink cheeks glowed. You stood with a hand at your breast and the candle burning you. On the stairs were men in armour; their swords flickered. With your back towards them, they heated irons in the coal. They lifted your leg up and put it on the table. Moving with my hands behind me, I felt an iron ring in the stone. If I pulled, there would be a tunnel: I could put an iron bar across the hole. At the end of it would be a cell. There I had been all winter. They had carried you to a table and laid you on it like a bag. They rummaged inside you. There was a grating like a stove. Their fingers had grown like tendrils. Men in armour stood on the stairs. Their swords stuck out like birds. From the iron bar across the tunnel I could lower myself into the hole. My legs became foreshortened as if going into water. I held myself by my back and elbows on either side. One side was soft, and the other was in darkness. I had to press outwards or else I would fall. My knees and wrists were fastened to iron rings. They had heated irons in the fire. Going down, there was a hiss of liquid. The tunnel led down to a cell. Beyond the cell was a grating. Beyond the grating was the sea. On the table, there had been the smell of burning: your body had been laid on a grid. Men in white coats stood over you. When they lowered hot irons, there was a hiss. I was in the cell, alone. Here I had been all winter. I was supported by knees and elbows. If I pressed too hard, my elbows would go through. There was nothing beneath me. The tunnel led down to a grating by the sea. Hands had come through the wall and held you. With one leg raised, they rummaged for an entrail. Drawing it out, through this, a body could breathe. They wound it on a windlass. The man like a bird had his beak against you: a worm drooped out on either side. Underneath the grid was a fire. My elbows and feet were pressed outwards against the walls: if I did not press hard enough I would fall; if I pressed too hard, I would go through. There was a wind which blew up the tunnel and fanned the flames. Your body lay while the men in masks bent over you. The shadows made shapes like blood against the walls. They were looking for a child, through which they might breathe. An oar had gone down into the water. When I had come into the castle I had fought to rescue you. My sword had flickered in the fire. I had fought with the men in suits of armour. Jumping, I had turned on the stairs. The breast under which you held the candle had burned. We had wrapped our cloaks around us and rushed across the draw-bridge. Hands had come out to help us. You lay on your back with one leg raised. I had been sitting in the cell all winter alone. I was facing a small window with iron bars. If I could move without seeming to, I could grow a shoot which would reach out through the grating. Beyond were reflections on water. There was a harbour with tall ships. We would come in from the sea. The oars had made whirlpools. From the back you had been split in two halves by an axe. You lay on a bed on your heels and shoulders. The tunnel fanned the flames. Men had flipped you. I could grow a tendril which would form a web to stretch through the grating. In my cell I watched shadows in the shapes of birds and animals. They had held you against the wall. If you pressed hard enough, you might go through. I had leaped up the stairs and fought with the statues in armour. Our swords had flickered like fire. Your body was a tunnel with an iron bar across the mouth. Putting a hand in, I had come across an entrail. Rummaging, I faced a small window with iron bars. If I could move without appearing to, I could reach out through the grating. Beyond was the harbour by the sea. I had rowed in and the oar had cut into the water. I was sitting in the cell alone. There was no floor beneath me so that the tunnel was like a fan. Flames came up. You were on the grating as if it were a bed. Men bent over you. Turning you inside out, I could find a shoot that was an entrail. There were mechanisms for doing this in the body and brain. Outside, the web would grow like stars. On the web crawled insects. By using my fingers I could mould the wall like clay. The insects

moved towards the window. The foliage was a trellis. I could
see you just beyond the grating: you were on hands and knees,
trying to reach me. You were dragging yourself along,
wounded. Light splashed on the stones. With blood, they had
made clay. You were trying to reach me through the grating.
Bending, I had put my head against your breast. My hands
were behind me against an iron ring in the stone. I had carried
you with your body over my neck. The tendrils had grown
through the grating and formed a web. On this we could
move. You had been on your back, and they had wound out
an entrail. By this we could breathe. Your two halves had gone
in different directions like an axe. There was a way through the
trellis into the water. You had crawled to the grating and your
hair had grown like spray. Your head made a hiss against the
seaweed. Crouched, I supported the universe. I had been on
the bed with my hands like irons beneath you. With an oar, we
went down into the water. The way through the grating led
down to the harbour. The line from the town to the harbour
was the sea. The other lines were by land from the harbour to
the cottage, and from the cottage to the walled town with a
tower. Here, we walked both under and over the sea. Going
down, my legs had become foreshortened; the water rose past
my back and elbows. You put your legs round my neck so that
I could breathe. Moving, I could see above me the surface of
the water. There was the place where we had wrapped our
cloaks round us and run across the drawbridge. I had fought
with men in armour. In an upstairs room you had been standing by a fire. Flames had blown up through the tunnel. Swords
had flickered as I had turned on the stairs. Under the water,
there was a taste of salt against the stone. Looking up, my
mouth fitted over the petals of a flower. Through this, like an
entrail, I could breathe. You were round my shoulders. We
had left the grating at the bottom of the tower. We were moving along the walls of the castle under the sea. I had looked

down: there had been a tunnel with a bar across the top. I had
tied a rope to the bar and lowered myself: I had been in a cell
all winter alone. Hands had come through the walls and held
me. The line led from the town to the harbour: this was under
the sea. Your legs were around my neck: your mouth against
mine. Like this, I could carry you and could breathe. I had
leaned over you; had put my head against your lap. My hair
spread over your thighs like weeds. I had been in a boat, rowing towards the harbour. I would climb out on to the quayside.
I was standing on your shoulders. With the oars in the water,
whirlpools followed the blades. From below, I saw your hair
spread on the surface. I was walking at the bottom of the
tower. Through the tunnel, or tower, I could breathe. My
mouth was pressed against your mouth. We were both above
and below the water. We were moving along the sea. When I
reached the harbour I would climb out on to the quayside.
Between us was the surface. If I turned it over, it resembled an
hourglass. I looked down and saw your hair like seaweed: I
looked up, and I saw your hair in the wind. I was approaching
the wall of the harbour. There was an iron ring in the stone.
The light on the water was like glass. I was both above and
below you. If I turned, I might breathe. On the map, there was
this line from the walled town to the harbour. We had moved
within the surface. We were two halves of an hourglass: turning, there was our reflection in the sea. Our hair was like tendrils. When I stood up the boat rocked. This was a diagram.
There was the harbour, the cottage, and the walled town by
the water. They formed a triangle. The triangle was on a wire.
The wire was what we balanced on. It passed through the apex
of the triangle at the cottage, and through the middle of the
base between the walled town and the harbour. This base was
both under and above the water. It span. I had climbed out on
to the quayside: hands had come through the walls and held
me. I had crawled through the grating at the bottom of the

tower. You were above me on my shoulders. I had rowed in on the sea. Holding all this in my hands, I could turn it. It was like an hourglass. The triangle formed two surfaces. We had moved along the lines of the triangle: the surfaces were on either side, forming two countries like a map. We had not seen the surfaces. One, which I held in my hand, was an enclosure with the shapes of birds and animals: there was a park, with an ornamental lake and yew trees. The air was clear. There were fountains: ladies and gentlemen walked on the grass. They made precise patterns. They wore coats like feathers: swords stuck out at the back. A man played a mandoline. You lay on your stomach, with one leg bent. You pulled at the grass. The earth, when I looked closely, was in the shape of mountains and valleys. On the grass were statues. Small boats rowed on the lake. The oars made whirlpools. There was a pink storm in the distance which made the air dark. Ladies and gentlemen lay on the grass. If we moved, the enclosure became unbalanced. It might tip. Cloaks rustled. Boats moved on the sea. You were on your front and kicked your leg back. You had been split up the back. If we moved away from each other, the enclosure might fall: if I moved towards you, our fists became pressed against stone. I could crawl to the edge of the enclosure. If I pushed my leg back, you held on. The earth was flat. It formed a triangle of which were two enclosures. I had walked under the water with your hair around my neck: rowing, I had dipped my oars into the sea. I reached the edge of one enclosure: it had tipped. Because it had tipped, I pushed my leg back. You held on. Underneath, was another dimension. It was in the shape of a triangle. There was barbed wire with a watchtower at each corner. Guards walked to and fro carrying guns. I looked round. The apex of the triangle was the cottage. The cottage was on a wire. The wire passed through the base of the triangle: this was halfway between the walled town and the harbour. These were two halves of an hourglass: one below and the other above the surface. We were at the base of the triangle where it passed through the wire. The triangle had two planes. Crawling to the edge, I had looked over. I had kicked my leg back so that I should not tip. Behind me, you lay by the ornamental lake in the sun. You kicked a leg back. Ladies and gentlemen walked on the grass. They wore the cloaks of birds and animals. I was looking over the edge of the enclosure. On the other side, the light was grey. There was the barbed wire with watchtowers at each corner. Guards walked up and down carrying guns. The enclosure was lit with arc lights. The shadows, from many directions, were grey. In the triangle were wooden huts like bathhouses. Footsteps went round making patterns. The patterns were formed out of mud. Men and women stood in the snow. They formed diagrams. They held their hands to their sides. They were like cutouts. They had stood like this all winter. Guards stood at the towers with guns. On the other side of the triangle was the ornamental lake with yew trees. Ladies and gentlemen walked on the grass. I was at the edge of the enclosure, which I held in my hands. The two surfaces were parallel: they were balanced on a wire. By moving, I could make them turn. I had stood up in the boat and the boat had rocked. I held it. The earth span in the same direction to which I moved: to balance it, I had to climb over the rim. There were the dark huts and barbed wire. I lay with one foot over the edge. The earth turned. I looked back and saw you clinging to my foot. Below you, the earth fell away. We were at the base of the triangle on the wire. On one side there was the green lawn with yew trees: on the other, the perimeter with guns. Men and women stood in the snow: they were naked. You hung from my foot like a pendulum. I had to pull you over the rim. Here people were imprisoned. I crawled because the earth had turned: the earth had turned because I crawled. There were arc lights on the surface. The light was grey. Looking back, I saw your face. It was terrified. Weeds, like hair, grew out of you. Tendrils had grown through the grating. We were on the perimeter of the surface on the wire. I had raised myself above the harbour. There were men and women naked in the cold. They grew roots. On the other side, beneath them, men and women walked in the sun. The guns of the guards stuck out from uniforms. The earth was a triangle on a wire. The three corners of the triangle were the cottage, the town, and the harbour by the sea. The base of the triangle was divided by the surface of water. This was both above and below us. The surfaces of the triangle were the lawn with the ornamental lake, and the enclosure with wooden huts like bathhouses. I held this in my hand. I had been rowing all day and was tired. In my hands, the world span. The earth, spinning, would be balanced. I remembered my journey. I had come to the harbour; I had tied the boat to an iron ring; I had looked above the quayside. Ladies and gentlemen walked on the grass. I had moved up the harbour past the row of white-washed houses. I had looked through a lighted window and had seen a child being born. Men and women were naked in the mud. I had moved up the valley. There was an ornamental lake with yew trees. This was above, and below, the buildings like bathhouses. The light, being overhead, made no shadow. There was the cottage in which we had sat all summer. I had gone down each day to the harbour to get food. You had waited by the fire. I held an instrument in my hand by which I might understand this. Every time I moved towards you you had to move towards me: blood ran on to the snow. This mingled with peacocks on the lawn. Every time I moved away from you you had to move away from me: men stood like prisoners in the mud. Holding this in my hand, I could make the triangle turn. Then, at some distance, we would be joined. With my hands behind my back I had gestured through the walls: tendrils had grown through and we had walked away hand in hand. Men and women were like particles within the compound. By spinning it, I might alter the patterns by which they moved. I could not see these. We had come to a walled town with a tower: I had run across a drawbridge. Blood had ran on to the snow. I had wrapped a cloak round me and had fought with swords. They had rummaged inside you like a suitcase. By spinning, I could make the triangle pierce like an arrow. It dug through my hand. You had been laid on a bed and men in masks had bent over you. Fire had blown up through a tunnel. They had drawn out an entrail: through this I could breathe. I had sat in a cell all winter. Arms had grown through and held me. My mind was a mechanism by which I might understand this. Men in white coats climbed on ladders. Looking up, I saw your face beneath. Spinning, we had moved both above and below the water. My mouth had been against your mouth; through this we could breathe. We had come to a garden with an ornamental lake and yew trees: underneath, were the rows of bath huts in a compound. I had put out a hand and touched the wire. The wire was alive and my fingers burned. There was your face, below me, with your hair in the wind. You were swinging on the rim: above or below you, was the desert. You held on to my foot: your face registered pain. If I swung, we might go over. The triangle turned. At the centre, in the imagination, there was rest. Around it, particles in groups made patterns. I was on the wire. Below me were crowds cheering. Looking down, I had the sensation of the world spinning. You were opposite, on the other side of the wire. The wire was between us like a pole. I had rowed into the harbour and reached the quayside. There were lights from the cottage in front; across the water was the walled town with a tower. The night was still. I sat on the harbour wall. I had the impression of figures having come from behind hills. They were trying to raise something from the sea. A rope was wound round a windlass. I held the model in my hands. I looked across towards you. You were sitting on the harbour wall. A body

was being brought up from the sea. The wire stretched forwards and backwards: around it was a triangle. Beyond a
lighted window a child was being born. A shadow had moved
parallel along the walls of houses. It came and sat opposite us
on the harbour wall. We formed a triangle. A body was being
raised from the sea. Figures pulled on ropes. I felt the world
turn. Like an arrow, around which was the triangle, the wire
went between us and the figure on the harbour wall; raising us
from the depths of the sea.

8

STEPPING OUT OF an aeroplane into Africa there is the light all around as if on top of a mountain and the heat in front like the smell of old socks. We had been flying all night and were tired. The Minister stood at the top of the steps and moved his lips quickly as politicians do before they face cameras either to get rid of spittle or to practise saying things different from what they believe.

The Minister was a small man with a long yellow face and a way of standing quite still while other people became deferential. In the aeroplane he had taken off his collar and rolled up his sleeves and had lain as if he were ill. He wore braces, and had long bony arms for sustenance to be dripped into.

We moved from the aeroplane down steps which swayed. I thought—Everything is collapsing now in Africa. The steps were of subtle British construction. At the bottom was a guard of honour drawn up: we stood with our hands behind our backs leaning into a wind. There was a national anthem blowing. I thought—Political life consists of rituals between one form of transport and another.

The guard of honour were black men in bunched khaki. Their bayonets went up past their noses. The butts of their rifles were by their groins. I thought—They are trees where lovers carve their initials.

The Minister walked up and down the lines of soldiers. He had bandy legs and a mouth tight shut to keep the wind out. I followed with two colleagues called Parkes and Ethel. Parkes had long hair and sideburns, and Ethel was from the Foreign Office. Inside my pale suit sweat began to run like rats.

At the side of the airport building were persons with flowered shirts. Some of them were men, with flowered bands round their trilbys. They were watching where we were standing in the sun. The Minister was led in front of a microphone:

he seemed to be saying he could not sing. The bowl was held against his mouth. Parkes and Ethel and myself waited. Heat rose through our legs and guts. I realised I was about to have diarrhoea.

I was twenty yards from the airport building. This was of glass and yellow concrete. Inside would be white pipes and tiles. The Minister was saying how glad he was to be in Africa. Inside me there was a rush of feet on cobbles. They were coming to arrest me. Between me and the airport building were the ladies in flowered hats: beyond them a line of cars. If I could start for the cars, I might find somewhere to disappear before I got there. The footsteps mysteriously came and went round a corner.

The Minister finished speaking. We were shaking hands. There was a bright blue air hostess like a button.

In the car I sat at the back beside the Minister: Parkes and Ethel were on small seats above our feet. I wondered what pioneers in Africa had done about diarrhoea; perhaps Rhodes had had diarrhoea when he had met Chief Lobengula. There was a return of fists hammering at my guts. I was a drop of oil, and spreading.

We were going past an African township. The houses, or huts, were in neat and similar rows. I wondered if they had lavatories. In the distance was a town with skyscrapers. The light in the sky was pink. The skyscrapers were pointless, because the space around was a desert.

The Governor lived in a large white house with two wings and a central portico. By the steps were sentries in bunched khaki. On either side were tubs of red flowers. The Minister had climbed out of the car and was being greeted by the Governor. The Governor was moving very slowly on crutches. I wondered if I could slip past him and look for a lavatory. His crutches took up most of the space between me and the door. Someone was about to play the national anthem.

I stood on one leg. There were photographers by the flowers. The Governor and the Minister were touching each other like oil. There was a small window beside the steps to the front door. This might be a lavatory. At the top of the steps was a large black man in a turban. In colonial life it is usual to present a front of unruffled calm. I thought—Like Gordon at Khartoum. I might pretend the revolution had started. The Governor was an iron-haired man in a white suit. Ethel suddenly rushed past him and was talking to the black man with a turban. I thought—He is asking for the lavatory.

For the next day or two my life became dominated by the lavatory; I was blown round Cape Horn, keeping a lookout for land yet pretending not too much to notice. The lavatory sat in my mind like a confessional. The Minister spent much of the time on his bed; he lay in his shirtsleeves and braces. He suffered from piles. The Governor stood downstairs with his leg in splints. He was teaching his dog to jump over his crutches.

We were working on proposals for a new constitution. This was of some interest at the time, but not now, because events overtook it. We sat in the Minister's room and listened for the sound of feet on cobbles. In the streets, Africans strolled or rode on bicycles. White men sat at the gates in flowered cars. Policemen waited. Journalists and photographers kicked their heels up and made jokes. I thought—Probably about lavatories.

There were six of us working in the house at the time: the Minister, the Governor, Parkes, Ethel, myself and the Governor's assistant. The Minister presided: Ethel made notes: Parkes rustled his papers. The Governor, or myself, dictated. The assistant sat with a pad on his knee. At the back of the house, on a lawn, was a tree with purple flowers. Here sometimes we could see the Governor's daughter.

By the evening most of us wanted to drink. Through the day we pretended we were not drinking. In the dining room there was a cupboard containing bottles. The cupboard was locked. The Governor carried the key on his watchchain. He sometimes swung the chain when he was encouraging his dog to jump over his crutches. In the evening he would give the key to the large black man with a turban. The black man would set out the bottles and glasses on a sideboard. We would pretend not to notice them, like the lavatory.

I had brought a bottle of whisky in my luggage. I kept this in my room in a cupboard that was unlocked. Once, I found that someone had locked the cupboard and left the key on my dressing table. I wondered if this had been the black man.

Politicians usually see only what they are meant to see; not because they choose to, but because they alter what they observe. I was the only one, I think, who went much out of the grounds of the house at this time, except to official functions. Once I went for a walk through suburban streets and I saw the thick lawns like matting hung in shops; men with large stomachs spraying hosepipes; women in the shape of trowels by their flower-beds. Cars were parked everywhere like gnomes and toadstools. There was a garage on a street corner where enormous black figures in goggles struggled with flames. They were Titans, forging a volcano.

In the garden at the back of the Governor's house was the tree with purple flowers where the Governor's daughter sometimes came. She rode a bicycle. She was a girl of fourteen; smooth as a chestnut. Because she was not allowed out of the grounds of the house she rode round and round the tree on her bicycle. She sometimes tried to do tricks; such as pulling up the handlebars and riding on one wheel like an acrobat. I had once been able to do this. She did not go fast enough to do it properly.

I used sometimes to work in the afternoons beneath the purple-flowering tree. The report I was writing had to do with the constitution. I sat with my pad on my knee and constructed a myth. I thought—This is at the mercy of my myth about myths. In the real world, there was the Governor's daughter. She wore pink shorts. The bicycle had a wicker-pattern seat. The marks of the wicker became imprinted on her behind. As with the lavatory or the drink cupboard, I pretended not too much to notice.

During dinner, after a long day, the Governor would say—Of course, we're a long way from the sea.

He stood at the sideboard giving us whisky. The back of his trousers were curiously flat. He spoke through a hatch to the black servants in the kitchen. His wife was away in England, looking at schools to which to send her daughter.

We, the men, held our glasses in our hands and watched the bubbles. They buzzed like bluebottles.

In the early hours devils still came to haunt me. I sat up in bed and listened; my heart thumped like poltergeists. Air pressure was pumped between my skull and my brain. If I lay down, my heart rushed in a body towards me. In a strange house, I could not get up to make tea.

At work I still made noises and gave opinions; but I had the impression, again, that it was not myself who was speaking; that there were recordings inside me to which my face mimed. I wondered that others did not notice this.

I thought—Perhaps we are all numb from the drink or pills we take against the devils making myths.

In the garden, underneath the tree, I tried to remember about good and evil. The wind from Africa blew seeds to the corners of the earth. A snake might come down and bite the behind of the Governor's daughter.

The large black man in a turban used to pass me in the passage. We stood aside for each other like Rhodes and Chief Lobengula. I thought—Perhaps I should offer him Bibles and whisky; in which messages might be secreted. He had scars on his face; where lovers had carved their initials.

In the lavatory, where I still sometimes went, there were

bags of lavender spread out as if in some cabalistic ritual. I wondered if the black man had arranged them for me.

The day was approaching when I was due to visit Ndoula in the desert. I did not know if the Minister would come with me. If he wanted to, he would: if he didn't, he would be ill. It depended on what expediency was required. There might be something practical to be done, or publicity for Ndoula, or publicity for the people who were keeping him in the desert. On the other hand it might be useful to stay away. The Minister sat up in bed and put out his antennae. He switched his wireless off, which was pouring out information.

I stood at the window and looked at the purple tree. I did not know whether or not I wanted to be on my own to visit Ndoula. I could not put this into words: if I tried, what I wanted might be ineffective. People hoped for clear objectives; but these achieved a dream. What was effective was some style by which ambiguity operated. The Minister patted his stomach. He said "Dust still under the counter!" I did not think he would be coming to visit Ndoula. I sometimes caught him watching me: as if he glimpsed something through a lighted window.

The day I was going to visit Ndoula was very hot; the trees in the streets were wicks of burning candles. The Minister said he was ill: I was to be escorted by the Governor's assistant, who was called George. George was a tall young man with shadows under his eyes. We waited for cars beneath the portico.

The road led out through an African township. The rows of huts were neatly in squares. I did not want to talk much to George. In silence, I could worry about what I was doing.

I said "How are the camps guarded?"

"You mean, what arrangements have been made for the camps to be guarded?"

George put his head down close to mine, trying to understand me.

In the desert there were small bushes that seemed to float and suck up sustenance from stones. Telephone poles propped wires. George held on to a strap at the side of the car. I thought —As if he were being beaten.

He said "I haven't quite twigged what exactly it is you're doing."

In the front seat were the deep grooves of policemen's necks. I felt in my pockets for my dark glasses, handkerchief, aspirins. I thought—I may need these necessities; like those of Egyptians when they were buried.

I said "I'm doing a report."

"What on?"

"Conditions."

I wondered if Father Whatnot would be praying.

The road swerved round potholes. A hundred years ago pioneers had come this way and had had to eat their horses.

The road disappeared and we drove along tyre-marks.

I tried to imagine the prison camp. There would be low wooden huts surrounded by wire: perhaps a watchtower at each corner. If a prisoner escaped, he would come to the desert.

I thought—In any decision speculation is impossible: you either do it or you don't—

—I would either give Ndoula Father Whatnot's message, or I wouldn't.

George said "What about London?"

"What?"

"These sex shows. What are they?"

I thought—What decides you, is everything you have ever been or has been done for you.

There was a blur on the horizon. We were driving to it at an angle. Our dust made a smokescreen. I thought I should make it clear to George about seeing Ndoula on my own. There might be microphones; closed-circuit television. I did not

know about these things. They were fairyland. The blue became defined as wooden huts with a tower. The tower held
water, like an explosion.

I said "I want to see Ndoula on my own."

He said "Surely."

Across the entrance to the camp was a fanciful wooden ar-
chitrave. It was painted like the gateway to a Chinese pagoda.
A dragon writhed up each side and met at the top.

The gates were opened by soldiers with guns. They wore
khaki. Their faces were pink. They wore red-and-white check
bands round their hats.

The dragon was roughly painted and had cracked teeth.

In the compound the heat shimmered like water. I was
wearing a white suit. I stood on concrete.

A line of blacks with buckets moved in the distance.

A man in khaki stood in front of me and saluted. Round his
hat were red-and-white check squares. A stick stuck out from
beneath his armpit like a bird. We went towards a hut with
white posts and red-scrubbed flowers. I did not breathe too
deep or the heat might cut me. He said "What about a drink?"

He showed me into a corridor with a lavatory. There were
pipes and white tiles. I had an impression of people screaming.

In a room with easy chairs and a fan spinning I asked for
water. I thought this was right. There were men with red hairs
on their arms: their mothers might have burned them. Someone came in with a bundle of letters. He said "Excuse me."
The car which had brought me had also brought their letters.

On a notice board was a timetable. The timetable was on
yellow paper. The notice board was of cork. The windows had
metal frames.

I unbuttoned my jacket. Spiders ran inside.

We went across a compound with my hands behind my
back. In the distance was the line of black men carrying buckets. Beyond them were blue and green hills.

The Commandant said "Those aren't ours you know!"
"Who?"

"This fence isn't to keep ours in, but to keep the others out!"

I had to ask about numbers, conditions, programmes. It would not be myself speaking. There were seven trucks by a goalpost. The goalposts were of white piping. The trucks had red-and-white squares.

We came round a corner and there were men sitting on the ground. They were in a group, or crescent, with a teacher at the centre. The teacher was drawing in the dust as if it were a blackboard. When he saw me he stopped. He had a sad, furious face. I noticed—They have no shoes.

The man with the hatband shouted. The group struggled to its feet.

I said "No!" They settled down again. The soles of their feet were white.

I said "What are they doing?"

We stood, I in my white suit, the Commandant beside me. Behind us were soldiers. We were watching the prisoners, who were squatting in the dust. In the distance were blue and green hills. The sun was overhead on my shoulders.

The Commandant said "What are they doing?"

I did not hear what was said. The teacher drew in the dust; the dust got into their eyes. They wiped them. The men on the ground had their backs to us. Their white feet stuck out. Our ancestors had passed this way; had sown seeds in the desert.

I wanted to say—Don't you know what they are learning?

I was taken round a laundry, bakehouse, mess room. Such and such a weight of flour was needed to boil so many thousand potatoes. Looking back, I saw the prisoners as if saying their rosaries.

I said "Ndoula's here?"

The Commandant said "You want to see Ndoula?"

There was a redbrick building set apart. It had a strand of barbed wire round it; and in the enclosure, as if for Christmas, a single tree. The tree grew in a tub. The tub was painted white. Above it were clouds. They were stationary like observation balloons. I thought—Or cherubs.

I said "Can we sit underneath that tree?"

The Commandant laughed. He gave orders. I wondered if microphones could be hung in it like apples.

Once, up in the hills, the Africans had offered friendship to the pioneers. They had thought the pioneers might be like gods. But god had looked down on a beautiful world. He had leaned from his observation balloon with a machine gun.

I was watching the redbrick building. It was like a lavatory. There were soldiers just inside. They were jamming the entrance as if at halftime at a football match. Someone brought out a chair and carried it to the tree.

I could not work this out. History was going in a certain direction. This was right, because it was the way history was going. But to be on the side of history some people, some time, had to be against it. Only like this could it go where it was going. But I was not concerned with this. I was concerned with what was right: which was, or was not, to do with the way in which history was going.

The soldiers stirred at the entrance to the building. A black man, who was Ndoula, was led out to the tree. George and the Commandant were still with me. The sun was overhead. We were thirty yards from the tree.

Ndoula arrived there. He was a small man with a large head and a white shirt. He was a figure in mythology. I thought that I might faint: then I would be carried back to the car. But I was used to this; having been through it so often with Natalie. I wondered if the soldiers would bring another chair for Ndoula. Or for myself. You waited for a time; then walked forwards.

Ndoula stood a short distance from the tree. You had to get everything quiet, so you could hear. There was a strand of barbed wire between myself and the tree. I stepped over it. George and the Commandant stayed behind. I was in the compound on the far side of the wire. I said "Can we have another chair?" A soldier listened. I looked at the blue and distant hills. I wondered if there were tribesmen. The soldier went off to get a chair. I said to Ndoula "Won't you sit down?" I did not look at him. I thought—There are mechanisms for doing this in the body and brain. The soldier came back carrying a chair. I smiled. The soldier had pale lips. I wondered if in any fighting he would be killed. I arranged the chair so that it was at an angle to the other. I said to the soldier "Thank you." I waited. I wondered if Ndoula would show interest. I looked at the distant hills. The soldier went away. I began to sit down. Ndoula was holding the back of his chair. I took off and wiped my dark glasses. Ndoula wore sandals. He had splayed feet. We were like two spectators at a cricket match. I said "This place is like a university." Ndoula sat down. He frowned. I thought— But he will know I want him to be rescued? I said "Do you have any complaints?" This sounded absurd. His legs were bony. He might have been undernourished as a child. I wondered if he would not speak to me. This would make things easier. I had had a great deal of practice at this with Natalie. I said "You're not kept in that building all the time are you?" He said "What building?" Sweat ran down inside my shirt. I contracted my chest. I was a refrigerator. He said "Oh, no." Then—"University?" I said "A lot of revolutionaries have used prison like a university." I did not expect him to answer. I was on my own, with the boat rocking. I said "They meet other people like themselves." I thought—I will be all right now I am talking. I said "A revolution often at first doesn't know what it's doing." I tipped my chair back. There was a soldier watching in a red-and-white hat. I thought—I am mad: I will

be put in a building like a bathhouse. I felt in my pockets for a
piece of paper to write something down. I could say—Do you
want any books? papers? In my pocket I found my wallet, the
case for my dark glasses, my handkerchief, my aspirins. Ndoula
said "I should like to be allowed books and papers: to have
some contact with my people." I thought—Well, there we are
now. I could not find a pencil. I wondered if I should ask—
Haven't you got a pencil? It might have fallen through the
lining of my jacket. I said "People talk about violence or non-
violence but this isn't the point; you need authority." He said
"What is authority?" I was sure I had come out with a pencil. I
looked towards the distant hills. I did not see how rescuers
could reach the prison camp. He said "I have always said I
disapproved of violence." I said "Yes." I suddenly found my
pencil. I said "But do you?" I had forgotten what I had been
going to write down. From here to the hills were hundreds of
miles of fields-of-fire. I said "Books, paper, writing materials."
The point of my pencil broke. I thought—But revolutions
only succeed after so many thousands dead. The young soldier
with the red-and-white hat had come to the wire again: I
could shout—Do you want to be shot? I said "Even if you got
power, there would be violence." Ndoula said "Of a different
sort." I thought—I have got sunstroke: I am handing over the
keys of the kingdom of heaven. The soldier went away again. I
wanted to get back to the Governor's house and have a drink.
I had tried to analyse how a person could make up his mind:
there were movements for doing this in the body and the
brain. They would either be strong enough or they wouldn't.
Men sat inside me facing dials. He said "You cannot take away
our choice." He was a small man with the large head of a wise
old man or monkey. He had gentle, angry eyes. I said "You
know Father Watkins? Whatnot—" I thought—I have now
eaten the piece of paper: let me tear it into bits and put it down
the lavatory. I said "A priest with a long thin nose." Ndoula

stared at me. I thought—He will not answer: will even despise me: perhaps he is right. The sky seemed split above my head; like a spear, or a shaft of annunciation. We were sitting with our hands on our knees. Beyond us were distant hills. We were beneath a Christmas tree. I said "He says he'll try to get books and papers through to you at the very end of the first week in December." I thought—Ndoula is a good man: he will know that the sun has confused me. I could now retire from public life. I thought I should look more closely at Ndoula. He was a man with yellow eyes and teeth like plaster. His feet were dusty. They were pressed against the earth. They were like electrodes. I wanted to go. I wondered if the Commandant would give me a cup of tea. I had my hands on my knees. I wondered if there was anything more I could say. I said "You see that?" In another few minutes people might notice. I had been asking questions about conditions in the desert. Ndoula had asked for books and papers. He was being harshly treated. I said "The trouble is you have to do everything on your own, or else it's not your achievement." I was pleased I had remembered this. I had been ready to get up. We were a white man and a black man in the desert. There had been a certain transposition of empire. Ants were biting at my legs. I swatted them. I said "Or perhaps, by doing nothing, you may beat everyone." I thought—I do not believe this; but I have to say it. Then—What are my motives? He said "We just want justice." I thought—Oh yes, justice. I stood up. The soldier came towards us. I patted my clothes. I had my wallet and my spectacles and my aspirins. Ndoula stood too. I held out my hand. He took it. I suddenly feared I might not have done enough. But the message would be whatever it was. He suddenly put his two hands round mine and was bowing over them. He was a small neat man like china. The soldier stood by us. He was a pink-faced boy with pale lips. I thought—My enemy. I was standing on one leg: with the other I was rubbing where the ants had bitten me. I thought—But I love everyone: even my enemies. I walked away. The boy came with me. I thought—But I have not even said good-bye! I stepped over the wire. George and the Commandant were waiting. I thought—Perhaps after all no one will come for Ndoula.

When I got back to the Governor's house I found it empty except for what appeared to be carpenters and removals men. It was as if the revolution had begun and the Governor and the rest were being put in their coffins. They would be exhumed years later as bullet marks in the woodwork. I went to the dining room and knelt down in front of the drinks cupboard. It was locked. There was no sign of the black man with the turban. I went out on to the lawn. There were men cutting down foliage and hanging it above a stage. I thought I might borrow their axe to break into the drinks cupboard. I could explain—My own whisky, like my job, is finished.

On the lawn was the Governor's daughter. She had her bicycle. I said "Do you know where I could get a drink of whisky?"

She said "Oh are you thirsty, you poor man?"

I wondered what would happen to the Governor's daughter. She would go to England to a public school. There they would make imprints on her, like the wicker seat on her behind. She came with me to the dining room. She squatted down by the drinks cupboard. Her shorts were pulled down from her waist like a drain.

She said "It's locked."

"Yes. Do you know where the key is?"

She went ahead of me up the stairs towards the bedrooms. I thought I should try to love the Governor's daughter. In the coming revolution, we could lie in the dust side by side.

Her father's bedroom had a single bed. There was a locker beside it. She knelt down. From the locker she took a bottle of whisky.

We sat on the bed side by side. She said "Do you need a glass?"

"No."

"Are you going to get drunk?"

"Yes."

She put a hand on my arm. I wiped the bottle. Her shorts were pulled up between her thighs like a knife.

She said "Will you promise, please promise, to get drunk tonight?"

"Yes. Do you want some whisky?"

"No."

I drank.

She said "Please, please, get drunk tonight at the party!"

I said "Oh that's what it is! A party!"

I thought I should go and have a bath. I thought I should help the Governor's daughter. She was all alone in the world, with just an imprint from her bicycle.

I said "How much longer are you going to stay in this place?"

"Where?"

"Here."

"Oh I don't know."

I took another drink. Whisky, like flies, ran inside me.

I thought—On her father's bed; celebrating the revolution.

She said "Can you take me with you?"

"Where?"

"To London."

I swatted the flies. I said "I don't know." I thought—I will consider this in my bath.

There was the lavatory where I had spent so much time with its delicately laid-out paper. This, and all such innocence, belonged to a different century. Now we were in an age of experience. I sat on the bath and watched the water which made bubbles and whirlpools. It would overflow and sweep away the country. I would jump in the flood and rescue the

Governor's daughter. Hanging on by my toes, we would swing above a waterfall. I would be thanked by her father, and a grateful country.

I lay in the bath with the whisky propped beside me. The water in the bath was full of steam. The steam was in my head from the whisky. I was running across a no-man's-land with barbed wire.

I must have gone to sleep, because the water in the bath was cold. The whisky had mysteriously evaporated.

Outside it had become dark.

There were noises of people assembling for a party.

I remembered the party was being given for local dignitaries to meet the delegation of the Minister.

I could not get out of the bath. I had frozen and become a mammoth beneath an ice cap. A vacuum was left around me. If I moved, the cold would come in and I would fall apart like paper.

Or I might rise up, dripping, and appear at the party naked. Long hair would flow from my limbs.

I moved a leg. There was a ripple. An earthquake occurred in Peru. Men and women ran screaming.

There was the sound of a military dance band.

I watched myself: solid and steaming.

When I did appear at the party I was dressed in my white suit. I had spent a long time wondering whether or not to put on black trousers. A platform had been set up at the end of the lawn. There was the band conducted by a sergeant major. Soldiers blew and scraped music. Above the platform were coloured lights. There were a few Africans in dark suits; African women flamboyant as a department store. I realised how much I had missed the sight of African women. I went to the bar to get a drink. The man in the turban was serving. I thought—I am on a battlefield on one elbow with a hand out. He gave me a glass. I took it gratefully. It was neat whisky.

Further down the table I saw George talking to the Governor. The Governor would have discovered the bottle had gone from beside his bed. I hoped he would feel guilty.

I thought I should go and inspect the dance floor. The platform had been placed at one end of a tennis court. The conductor was serving and might knock over skittles. A man with a cornet had the ball stuck in his throat. The purple-flowering tree was like a net. George came up and said "Can I ask you something?"

I said "Yes."

He said "What do you think of this country?"

African women were by the dance floor. They were waiting to be asked to dance. They wore extravagant headdresses like generals. They had thin necks. They were beautiful. No one spoke to them. I could say to George—You do not see how people might be like gods! I wanted to be above the gathering so that I could observe it. There were patterns of cells and molecules. You looked through a microscope and what you observed was altered by that which observed. He said "You think we're all going to be murdered in our beds?" I could say—At least, you won't be in anyone else's bed. I thought this witty. I looked around for the Governor's daughter.

There were a few couples dancing. They held their arms high; skating on banana skins. There was wire round them so they could not fall off. I thought—To go dancing with one of the African women would be too easy.

I said "Not in an African woman's bed." George moved away.

A red-haired man was talking to the Minister. He would be talking about Ndoula. He had large hands. He had worked on his farm, day and night, for thirty years. I should have more consideration for these people. They had come to this country as pioneers and had had to eat their horses. The wind had blown red dust in their eyes. Families clung to their dinner jackets.

The Minister was approaching. He held the red-haired man by the arm. I said "How do you do." He said "How do you do." The Minister said "He saw Ndoula." The red-haired man said "Yes." He turned to one side and picked his teeth. He held a cigarette cupped inwards in his palm. The Minister said "How did you find him?" I said "All right." There was one African woman dancing with one white man on the tennis court: this was to show solidarity. She looked over her shoulder as if she, or he, were leading a poodle. I said "He wants books and papers." The red-haired man said "What for, can he read?" I could say—What would you do, wipe your arse with them?

I wanted to find some way to end the evening. I did not want to be rude. Ropes were being lowered into a harbour. One day, but not now, I might have to come back and fight. The Minister had moved away. The Governor's daughter was standing by the dance floor. I saw Father Whatnot approaching.

I had not expected Father Whatnot. He wore a white cloak. It trailed behind him like a bird. Looking so pleased, he floated forever above his ocean. He put a hand on my arm. I said "I didn't expect you!" He squeezed me. He said "I expected you!" I thought—We are in love!

The red-haired man moved away. I wondered if he were a policeman. I said to Father Whatnot "I'm so glad!" He said "So am I!" He wore sandals. His feet were dusty. His pale eyes glittered. I said "Can you give me asylum?" He looked curious; then said "Yes." I said "Where?" Then—"I'm retiring." I thought—He is like Abraham; watching his child.

I ran a hand through my hair. I found I was still holding my glass of whisky. It poured down my neck. I brushed myself. I said "I'm setting myself on fire!" He doubled up with laughter. I said "I want to go somewhere and think for a while."

I should have to try to make sense of this party. The party was taking place on the Governor's lawn. The house was lit up like a backdrop to a fire. One or two Africans had been invited to the party to give it tone: they stood around demurely. I thought—I must get away or I will die. White men stood at the bar like wrestlers: white women had almost disappeared in the heat. They were pale and desultory. There was a group of them at a table by a swimming pool. They were separate from the men, who were by the bar. I thought—It is because there is no contact that they will die: Ndoula can help, if he gets out of the desert? A phrase came into my head—What this country needs—. I looked round for George, who had asked the question. I went to the bar for another drink.

There I found the red-haired man: he was watching me. I thought—Now, perhaps, we can go out and fight. The man with the turban gave me another enormous whisky. He smiled. I thought—That is the first time he has smiled: perhaps he is passing me a message. The dance floor was a small construction slightly raised off the tennis court. It was about the size of a boxing ring. The red-haired man said "I want to tell you I don't like your tone." I could say—My tone! But I had given a lot of thought to this: I had decided my gesture should be witty. He said "Will you come outside?" I could say— Where there aren't any ladies? I began to laugh. The Governor's daughter came up to me. She said "Oh when are you going to get drunk?" I said "I am." The red-haired man had his hands in his pockets, his thumbs pointing forwards. I said to the Governor's daughter "Can I borrow your bicycle?" She said "You want to borrow my bicycle?" I said "Yes." She stared at me. She went off towards the house. I said to the man with red hair "What this country needs—" I looked at the stars. You could see their patterns clearly. All the men and women had left the dance floor: they were in their corners, in their separate compartments. The Governor's daughter came back with her bicycle. I said "What this country needs, is a trick cyclist." I took the bicycle. It was pink, with its soft wicker seat. It should have had fixed pedals, then my trick would be easier; you could push the pedals backwards as well as forwards. I wheeled the bicycle on to the dance floor. You got the front wheel up and balanced on the back one by the pedals. It was like being on a tightrope. I put a leg over the seat. I became fascinated by the purely technical problem. The dance floor was small. The music had stopped. The red-haired man had followed me. I suddenly had forgotten how to ride a bicycle. I shot forwards. You have to go fast or you fall over. I jerked on the handlebars; the front wheel came up. I stayed there for a time. I seemed to knock against the red-haired man. A group of ladies went screaming. They seemed to be running in the face of an earthquake. I pedalled fast. I was pleased. I was heading for the swimming pool.

9

M Y LOVE,
  This is a marvellous place on the side of a hill looking out over blue and green plains to distant mountains. Somewhere to the south is the valley where human life is supposed to have begun—a crack in the earth after miles of flatness where consciousness dribbled into a crucible.

This is a low white house with lawns and fruit trees. An old man walks up and down all day mowing grass. I was met at the airstrip by Miss Cecilia, an Irishwoman. We drove fifty miles over potholes. No one asks you questions here. The people seem to have suffered some wound. Life's upturned them, and they're on a raft working out the rules.

I walk up and down on the lawn. The trees have tall pale trunks and leaves like feathers. There is a slight noise of wind all day. Sometimes it isn't the wind, but the sound of cattle munching.

I think I'll stay here for a while. Father Whatnot got me here. I was slightly ill at first, but now am better.

I want to understand something about success and failure. When you know good sometimes comes out of evil, what do you do?

In the enormous plains to the south of here where animals munch there is no such thing as goodness—herds move across plains and it takes all day to munch—only occasionally do they move in leaps when a predator gets them. But even a predator is lazy. He puts his hand on your shoulder like a village policeman. After which you settle down again; with just one or two of your number missing.

In this place people move about quietly with some knowledge of good and evil but as if in gym shoes, with a corpse upstairs. I don't understand this yet. The house is run by five or six women: the people for whom they run it are exhausted missionaries.

In the valley where human life is supposed to have begun what happened, people think, was that some monkey who had formerly been peaceable—munching, that is, like factory machinery—picked up the thighbone of a deer and hit another monkey over the head with it: and so became human. By destruction, that is, he got power; and self-reflection. For the thighbone stuck up out of the other monkey's head like a flute.

The people who move around so quietly here as if a god were dying upstairs do so out of guilt, but also knowing they've got what they wanted. It was kind, after all, for the old man to die. There has been some liberation.

But what would it be like to be a god—because this is what man is, also, after he has hit the other monkey? He stands at the monkey's grave with two fingers raised like Christ Pantocrator. And perhaps makes a rude noise, to get himself comfortable. But he doesn't seem to know this yet. He thinks he's still one of the boys on the plain munching: with just one or two million of his number missing every now and then from being hit on the head by a thighbone. But what if he knew that out of destruction came creation? There would be some different machinery.

Life is very ordered here. There are little paper bags on the trees to protect the fruit from predators.

Give my love to the children.

Very much love,

My darling,

I'm sorry I haven't written before. I've been somewhat ill, but now am better. I'm at this place where I'm supposed to be convalescing.

It is very beautiful here, high up on the side of a hill. The landscape seems carved out of the inside of a sphere by one of those craftsmen in ivory.

I have a little hut on the edge of a lawn. I live like a hermit. If there were a lion, I think I would make friends with it.

I want to find out something about how we understand rather than what. I mean—we receive impressions and construct patterns; the patterns are mechanisms of our minds that are there. But what are the mechanisms? We see life as comic or tragic; these patterns are primitive; they arise from our being half monkey and half god. About such a predicament there is something comic or tragic. But to see it only as this is also despairing, because tragedy and comedy are comments on a situation and not efforts to do anything about it.

Here there's some recognition of this: life moves in a pattern which isn't looked at closely but is not comic nor tragic; people tread purposefully as if there were an old man dying upstairs. Only, no one goes to look at him.

Somewhere to the south of here is the crack in the earth where human life is supposed to have begun. In myth, an animal disobeyed the rule of not wanting to know about himself; and so became like god. But he also became confused, because the act of evil had landed him in good; that is, becoming like god. And he has been confused ever since; not only because of the knowledge, but because of this interdependence of good and evil. For his mind is not made to accept this. He thinks—I should still be an animal munching innocently on plains; because this is how I was constructed. So what does he do? There is a further myth which is still hardly noticed: which is to do with a choice not between, but to recognise the interdependence of good and evil. This choice is practical; and perhaps possible.

Our minds are logical. We have to say—A thing cannot be, and not be, at the same time. But experience doesn't demonstrate this.

If this were recognised, we might even be able to choose good rather than evil.

I was trying to write something of this when I came to Africa. I felt the top of my head coming off. I was neither comic nor tragic; I was impossible. So I rode a bicycle into a swimming pool. Did you hear about this? It had to be dragged out of the depths.

I do hope you are well. I think of you much of the time.

Very much love,

Dear Father Whatnot,

Thank you for telling me of this place. It is good. I flew here in a single-engined plane and was met by Miss Cecilia in a Land Rover. We drove the thirty miles over potholes. At one point the road had been washed away and we had to push. I found myself giggling. Perhaps it is this—your being children —that makes you like members of a worldwide conspiracy.

I wanted to talk to you about the difference between what I think is your attitude and mine: you try to come to terms with life by renunciation (I know these words are paradoxical) rather than by affirmation (I know this is ridiculous). We neither of us think that by a social heave we can all get over the hill. People who imagine this have a sort of innocence, I think, like the deer that munch on these huge plains; they dream of a past or future heaven, where men in cloth caps work on harps. And the predators get them. But you and I (forgive me) know that there's a predicament here not due to lack of knowledge, but which seems to increase with the increase of it; an ambiguity at the heart, as in an atom. You can't pinpoint what's going on in an atom not because you don't know enough but because of the nature of observation: the act of observing orders the thing observed. And it's like this with being human. We don't know what we want because when we get it we don't want it. So what do we do?

Your answer, it seems to me, is to stop wanting. You say— granted the more we struggle the more we increase confusion:

we are peaceable and live like animals, murder and die like gods: therefore our understanding, and actions, must be limited: we must do murder only to our hearts or genitals; become locked up like animals in kennels. Then there is less chance of catastrophe. The iron may enter the soul, but it will form a cohesion there. And this is logical. But there's that scene in Job—Job! you see my paranoia!—where he has been sitting on his dungheap for some time and has been trying to be logical: and he complains to God—Look, God, either I'm a good man and I shouldn't be on a dungheap or I'm not and I should; which is it? And God just says, in effect—Rubbish! Now this is important. What you don't seem to have noticed (you—you of all people) is that at the moment when man got knowledge—when he struck his brother, that is, or disobeyed God's commandments—at this moment he also got something else—which was, that his knowledge of good and evil was not of them apart in opposition but together in opposition; they were always like this and it was only his brain that would separate them. But it was his brain that had observed this. So at this moment he knew that good can come out of evil—that if you want to know about life you have to get yourself strung up or be thrown out of the garden; if you want to be like God you have to disobey him—but also his mind, which had started working because of this, had to deny it: because his brain was logical. Thus he was split. And no wonder, with his skull caved in by a thighbone! And it is almost impossible to talk about this, because language has been mostly logical.

But God, when Job confronted him, said—Who cares about logic? You're on a dungheap; stop moaning! Contemplate the Leviathan!

This is shocking. But after a time, Job got all that he wanted.

Perhaps it is true that to those that have shall be given, and vice versa, or whatnot. Do you believe this? And those that have not should not be pitied, or else they will stay forever on their dungheap. Job prospered because God told him—Rubbish!—and Job both accepted and did not accept this. At least, he listened. I think the world is full of such evidence; to which no one listens.

The fact of knowledge implies there is something like a god; to make observation possible. There is a relation, that is, between the observer and the thing observed. This relation is distinct but not separate.

I'd like to find a language for this—for the contemplation of Leviathan on my dungheap. I suggested some sort of affirmation—and asked you to forgive this. But I should like to say—Perhaps you don't only have to have faith in order to love (this being a discipline) but have to love in order to have faith—this being a discipline. For this will soon enough sit you on a dungheap. And then you may get everything back again; out of the manure, lilies. This is not logical. If you want to be humbled, that is, you don't have to go to the desert; a successful life will do it for you. Perhaps that is why I've come here. Certainly, in the dark, you see the prevalence of angels! As anyone who has been in love will tell you. This is a mystery. So here I am. All right, I love the Leviathan!

With very best wishes,

My love,

There is a couple staying here who, every time I make a joke, sit with their hands on their knees and wait as if for a cup of tea to be raised to their lips by levitation. They are missionaries, in unknown territory.

I am better now. Perhaps one should be ill more often. There is a rhythm about this; like sleeping and waking.

I sit on the lawn on a wicker chair by a wooden table. There is a tree with lilies which hang upside-down.

I feel like a crusader in the Middle Ages. Someone who gets

himself imprisoned so that he can send messages to you, my wife, who stays at home.

There is a huge mountain to the south of here which Africans never climbed because they thought a god sat on top. And they did not want to ask him awkward questions. But white men have been to the top; and they call it a dead volcano.

One night when I was in the Governor's house I had a sort of vision—I was tired—of our life together as a pattern apart from history: we were in a house, like the cottage, and I was in the corridors as a sort of devil; some dark and hostile monkey; and you were in the rooms as something pure. And I had to hurt you, because that was my nature; and you had to suffer, for us to learn. This became an almost physical hallucination—I woke up shouting—and I wanted to start moving out of bed, on foot, to tell you—what? that I was sorry. And that the monkey is a poor stunted creature; and his victims flourish.

I think that if the whole of creation is sick, perhaps I came out sick in sympathy with it. I went on a gluttony strike—for the universe. People's prayers are for the hungry: what happens to the over-indulgent and full?

I'm trying to write a story that will describe some of this—occurrences in function rather than in time—or as if time were spatial, so that one could move to and fro in it by looking. This is difficult: we see a moment or a pattern, not both: one cuts out the other. But if we do not know, perhaps from some third point, the moment and the pattern at once, then each seems meaningless. Because, on its own, each is an abstraction, not an experience. The experience is both. But our minds are not constructed for this: which is why, perhaps, we make myths—such as that of the man here dying upstairs. But we do not understand myths. Writing a story is an effort at a view from a third point; it tries to bring together reflection and action; to get the pattern in a moment and the moment as change; perhaps—a man resurrecting. Everything, that is, seen according neither to some absolute nor to itself but to change. But this would be timeless; in the present, because in comprehension. I wish I could write this.

Every now and then the old man, or young man, leaps out of bed upstairs and puts his hand around your throat, laughing.

My love to yourself, and the children.

My darling,

You are becoming one of those figures in Egyptian frescoes or Mayan sculptures—a girl with contemptuous lips and a body like a cupboard within which veils are hung—a look as if you not only wanted men's heads on a platter but would complain if you hadn't got an egg spoon.

I miss you. I think of you much of the time.

I wanted to say something of the last few years—not as things happened, because this I can't know, but not simply as a construction either; rather in some consciousness of what a construction is; which is how things happen. Perhaps this is why I moved to and fro all the time: writing, as my life, should contain some irony. Most writing has a limitation—which is, that only a certain type of person writes. Writing, to be good, has to be done in solitude: so our recorded vision of the world —for this is what good writing is—is conditioned by solitude. But much of life is not to do with solitude; and this goes unrecorded. So there is a peculiar split between our experience and our accustomed vision: which is what we have not become accustomed to.

In solitude a person writes comedies or tragedies: he looks down on the world and, being lonely, has some fear of it and hostility. He is a pessimist. By spiting life, he protects himself.

Experience is the present; but when you sit down to write, the present is different. So what do you write? The present is neither comic nor tragic: it is a state of mind, an attitude. It is confronted by choices. But the choices are not so much between this and that, but to do with the recognition that there are choices.

There should be some style which would convey this—both a person reflecting and his actions. Life isn't a pattern we know at the time; we know it because we are moving. But, looking back, we see the pattern we have made. But still we are moving. So we can learn. By recognising the predicament, that is, we might even deal with it. Recognising two forms of recognition at once, there would be a sort of knowledge—of freedom. This would be optimistic.

Do you remember how when we first met you used to come to that awful hotel and you were contemptuous and tragic and I was comic and shifty; and none of this mattered: I mean none of it matters now although, God knows, we suffered at the time: and other people suffered: but what mattered was something in quite a different area—I can't explain—but we almost knew this at the time, or how could we have continued? Something, that is, kept us going. To our destruction and salvation. And now here we are, and this is what matters. I just don't know how to write it. Certainly, it would be ironic.

Darling are you going for long walks? Are you sitting up straight and eating your pudding? If you take your hurt out on other people, other people will take their hurt out on you. Good. Then, out of sadness, there may grow exotic blooms like angels. There are dungheaps anyway: one might as well flourish. I think if everyone did what they wanted, perhaps other people might use this to get what they want. Discipline would be in limitation—through exhaustion. It's hard enough, goodness knows. You see, I think the world is good. What makes people helpless, is the effort to assume for another person. Like this you assume power; and that the world is bad. You force it. And this doesn't work. I'm tired. I'm sitting up late in the dark. Beetles bang against my lamp. They crawl around with one wing broken. They are pencils on my Ouija board. You are my Muse. Natalie Natalia.

Very much love,

Dear Father Whatnot,

You remember my telling you about this person called Natalia? Well, there was one summer when her husband was suing for divorce: this was causing a good deal of pain; also comedy; there was no other way; the lawyers were nurturing the business like godfathers. Well, we went abroad together, Natalia and I; drove through vineyards and stopped at inns with trout-pools; sat across tables with check cloths and jugs of wine: we were happier than we had ever been before in our lives—we kept on saying this—we are happier than we have ever been before in our lives: and we arrived at our destination which was a chalet by a lake with a garden and palm trees and grass like a cloud; and we sat across a table with a chequered cloth and wine jugs; and there was a moon in a path to the water through palm trees; and happiness was something we could hold in our hands and turn; and I thought—What can we do now, when we are happier than we have ever been before in our lives? For life is to keep moving. And I thought —I am like Faust, who was damned because he found a moment so beautiful that he asked it to stop. And I thought— Who can save me? what voice from a cloud? And at that moment Natalia said "You know, when I get home, I won't go through with the divorce." And I think then I was hurt more than I have ever been hurt before in my life: because she would go back to her husband, and had saved me. And I went up to the bathroom to be sick. And I hated Natalia because I had been so much hurt; and Natalia lay on the bed and did not comfort me. She was hating herself, too, and being hurt, because she had saved us: she had not said Stop. And I was not comforting her. Yet even then there was something quite

184

different happening: pain, like previously the pleasure, was not quite the point. But I did not know what to do about it.

I could not explain to Natalia—You have betrayed me; I wanted this; because of this we are in pain; how else could we have had such pleasure and been saved? And if she did not feel guilt, how could salvation be lasting? I knew no words: I wanted to take her by the throat and strangle her. She wanted me to do this; then there would be tragedy or farce. So we would know where we were, and be at peace. Or dead. This is what all lovers dream of. Could I say—Love is a totality, to do with growth and change: we are mothers, as well as children, bleeding over a basin or in bed. I stared at the porcelain. Natalia was on the bed with her neat child's face. I thought— I might explain, but it will not comfort her: an explanation only helps when looking back. I thought—I am being too wise; a god would act. I felt like a god; with so much joy and suffering. I thought—All this will be helpful for our children and our children's children: they are absolved by our examples. I went back into the bedroom. I was still thinking—What can I do? I had a pride—What else is love, if it does not give freedom? With such happiness, there must be something to do.

I sat on the bed. I looked down on Natalia. She was like the earth, imprisoned with violence. I thought—What does a child want who has betrayed its love? She had only done, after all, what love required. Which I had not had the knowledge to do, not being feminine. I thought I should be brave with her. This was man's prerogative. She had this child's hard face. It was blocked with blood like a devil. I thought—Free her. Then— But I must not condescend.

She was lying on her front. I pulled down the bedclothes. I thought—I will raise a hand like Christ Pantocrator. I had, after all, been responsible for love and suffering. She said "What are you doing?" After a time she said "Stop!"

I thought—At least, for a god, it is neither pain nor pleasure.

She said "That hurt!"

Then we went on with our marvellous holiday. And she went back to her husband.

Yours very sincerely,

My love,

Yes, I saw Ndoula. He was all right.

You sound very distant.

I have sent the children postcards. I do think of you, all the time.

Here I have to sew on my own buttons. Last night I got a needle and thread and pierced the cloth and my thumb at the same time and was like Jove being hit by a thunderbolt.

My room has green walls, a wooden floor, a blue bedstead. It is four paces from the door to the wall and four paces back again. There is a mark like a moth on the lampshade where the bulb has burned it.

I think everyone has this terrible need to hurt and be hurt. This is not only evil. Children, perhaps, only flourish at the expense of hurting—their hurting us, and our hurting them. Otherwise they don't grow. We can't arrange this. But it happens. And wears us out.

I have a feeling like a clapper in a bell. When I move my head it gives me warning of a thunderstorm.

I don't think only of myself! What else do I know?

Perhaps all moralistic statements should be a taking back with one hand what has been given by the other. Then the other person can do as he likes. Parables in the Bible are like this: so are prophets. They are all crazy. People can do what they like.

I wish you were here. For a weekend. We could rush into the gooseberry bushes. Roll in the poisoned ivy.

So many good people pack it in after forty. As if this were some sanctity! I want to shout—Where's the resurrection?

I know what you mean when you say I think so much of myself.

This place is quiet. There are no seasons. Enormous events go on elsewhere. The house is a factory for a secret product. The people aren't beautiful, but their product seems to be beauty. This is a mystery. I want to waylay them in the passage and ask—Where's the beauty? But they would smile; and go about their business.

At first I wanted to tell them—You are like people in war; there are enough real wars; do you have to make up your own? But I think perhaps all wars, like love, are indivisible.

I went for a walk with Miss Cecilia. We stood by a waterfall which splashed through the palm trees. We took off our gumboots and paddled. We were like children.

Their conversation is a code of which they themselves have lost the key; but still they transmit messages. They are the stars which may be extinct but which are still shining.

Perhaps their double vision is like binoculars.

Father Whatnot is expected here in a week or two. I will talk to him.

I do hope you are well. Give my love to the children.

My darling,

Writers have written about free will but not described it—not only its effects, but its experience. Writers, in cutting themselves off, describe life as determined: or describe themselves alone, which is the same. Freedom, the experience of it, is the ability to move between the two. We live this, but can't describe it. The mechanisms of description are to do with what is pinned down. Perhaps I could get some style for all this; which could be used, even if not simply to do with description. I need a style that is saying two things at the same time: both to move between, and—to acknowledge my behaviour! Novelists once used a so-called God's-eye view not to describe their freedom but to explain their lack of sense of it. To describe one's freedom one would have to imagine oneself a god: being faced with infinite possibilities. This itself is a choice: then the chosen, whatever it is, happens. But it would be one's own. The refusal to recognise possibilities would be the prevention of choice. Perhaps, yes, this would be a description.

Darling, my mind can't deal with this. I'm two people, in parallels, at once—the thing that is writing and the thing it is writing about; the person here and the person in England; who wants to see you and who does not want to and keeps away. My story is of people who love and stay apart and come together: love is freedom. This is not easy. She is the wife of a Conservative M.P. She is sometimes difficult. He is perhaps insane! Like this, they move towards some understanding. Perhaps she should be an artist: yes, like you. Then she would see things growing in her hands. But the hurting nearly defeats them. What are you doing now? Working? Hating me? What would we have done in hell or heaven?

We have planned nothing and have got what we wanted, haven't we?

With such dedication!

Very much love,

Dear Father Whatnot,

My wife Elizabeth and I married when we were young. We were in love. We wanted to live full lives of our own. We could do this if we were together. That is, each could use the other for their advantage. What else is loving?

This is all right until the object has been achieved—you are on your own. This is a triumph: but what need have you of another? There is no marriage in heaven.

But if that which has enabled you to be yourself is another, how can you be yourself if you are not?

In a good marriage, this ambiguity continues.

Sometimes, when your ear is to the ground, you hear the stream running back to the sea. This tells you that love is all right—you have trusted. But it is far below the surface; and you are flat on the ground.

When I first told my wife about Natalie (I did this because I thought I should no longer be seeing Natalia—the innocence of love is not to think it will last forever but to think that it will not) when I first told my wife about Natalie she did not say, as she might have done, anything—she was feeling angry and also planning, I hope, how this might be to her advantage. It was I who had hurt her; why shouldn't she? And when I saw Natalia again she hated it; but did not try to stop me. Because where then would be her advantage? This was natural. If I were guilty she could go her own way, which she could not if I were not; because then she would be guilty.

She would rather do anything, I think, my love Elizabeth, than suffer drought: because she is to do with growth, and the stream going back to the sea. And she did go her own way. And made use of me. And of her sorrow. And of mine. And good luck to her! Perhaps we both suffered because she wouldn't lay down and die. I so admire this.

There was this time when Natalia's husband was suing for divorce and there was difficulty not only with Elizabeth but with the children—and we were having lunch somewhere abroad, Elizabeth and I; facing each other across some red-and-white chequered cloth (you see, patterns are repeated): and the table was at the side of the road with the cars going past like bullets—images have a life of their own after all in the unconscious—and we had not slept much the previous night because we had been using each other and were tired: and devils had come in: and I had intended to say that I might be going off with Natalia—to the hotel by a lake I think—but it was difficult to say this when I was opposite Elizabeth; because we had had such a good life together, after all, had done so much for each other to our own advantage. And I was waiting for Elizabeth to say some word and to make me stay with her: even if this meant some death, as she knew it would. And there were tears in me like bullets. And I thought—We must give up: must have one thing or the other: I can no longer bear going between, in freedom. And Elizabeth said "All right go off with Natalie; and come back when you want to." And I thought— So it is all right: she has hurt and saved us. And I thought I would cry, because I was so lonely. And the world was good. And I did not think I would ever leave Elizabeth. But I could not explain. Women have an instinct where men, with knowledge, only have courage. I thought—But I cannot bear this. She said "What's wrong?" I shook my head. I thought—I cannot stay here: and I know what will happen if I go to Natalie. Perhaps in the end, like Elizabeth, I will have to go somewhere on my own; to comprehend it.

Your very sincerely,

October 30th

Waste. Things are born, come to fruition, die; in proliferation. This is necessity. A million seeds are blown; one lodges. Winged insects fall like snow in the evenings; you tread on them; they struggle, more beautiful than diamonds. We say each human being must be saved; yet step on bodies, use tear gas against children. We chase each sperm to put it in a test tube; produce—impotence.

What if we saw that in human generation as in any other there is waste—that bodies are driven to the fire where there is wailing. We might have dignity. But we can't say this; only know. The men on street corners; children hit by buses. We know, but can't choose. We can only choose to lie down on street corners ourselves: which is a different dignity.

Some small part of us however might still be walking up and down in the empty garden like God; sick to death at so much misery. So he would have to get a job in a prison camp in the desert; become two persons, to have more dignity.

I walk up and down. I whirl my arms. This the wind: this the windmill. Some seeds, like a sail, might blow to fruition.

My love,

Thank you for your letter. When I come home I'll make it up.

I did see a doctor. He said I was all right.

I think I'll go and climb the mountain to the south of here. Perhaps I'll talk to God at the summit. You are said to get frostbite and sunstroke at the same time—a familiar predicament.

Father Whatnot came: he was no good. This place is a hospital; with a production line for wounded.

Somewhere to the south of here the Chinese are training freedom fighters. They, and we here, sit round the golden calf. Dancing is supposed to be frivolous.

I am writing a lot. Forgive me. I feel as if I have little time. One day I will be brought home on a gun carriage. With plumes nodding.

You are good at patching up wounded. I'm not.

With very much love,

Dear Father Whatnot,

How can you be humble—even sitting in a bowl of rose leaves and drawing the thorns up through your arse—if what comes out has the beautiful scent of angels? I'm trying to write like this, you see—to make myself humble! I've been reading your books here—they're in code: you're sitting on the key!— and what they say is, that salvation doesn't come by effort but expectation—so how can you be humble? You're all proud; in your black cloaks like broomsticks. The world would humble you for a small consideration. If you let it. Which is why I make jokes the whole time, so that something may go up the wrong way from my bowl of rose leaves. And maintain a small airline to the surface; as if I were a three-day fakir.

Why are there so few married saints? They would have to be made holy by their inclinations, which is difficult. Success perhaps would come at night; with a catch of swollen fishes. I once said to Natalia—I am a man hoist with my own petard! She said—You make a magnificent specimen! Saint Augustine said—Love God and do as you like. Saint Paul said—God loves a sinner. I was once on my way to Natalie and I thought—I may yet fall down a coalhole! And I did. That is, I was caught by her lodger. Then once I had not seen Natalia for months and I was helping an old lady across the road—and so on—do you think one should not say this? Sin is doing what you like: anything else is artificial. If you help an old lady, at least someone may get helped in Australia. Don't you trust this? Shouldn't one be a saint? Miracles were the proof of God; you were only told not to speak of them. But you did: for the instruction was only to guard God's humility. But to do what you like is still difficult. You have to practise for years. And all the waste! Bits get chipped off. I wish I knew someone who trusted life—thought it was good—tried—and was not defeated. Went to the salt mines, but after a short while was back again. With everything a hundredfold. Because how else are we salted? You say, don't you, in your mumbo jumbo, that man has been taken up by God: well, why don't you believe this? What would it mean? A voice in the mine shaft—Are you there? Yes! Are you all right? Yes! But more. For every now and then you would be the person sent down with the beer and sausages; and coming back with the empties, for your twopence.

Yours sincerely,

Darling Madeleine,

Long tide no sea, as the geologist said in the Sahara.

The desert, as a matter of fact, is within a few thousand miles of where I am; having come here to collect some specimens.

And the old bottles, which are my brain, are somehow holding new wine; which could be a miracle.

How are the old folks at home?

Do you know this story?

Once upon a time there were two trappers in a hut all winter in Alaska. They made an arrangement whereby one of them should do the cooking until the other one found the food too disgusting; then, the other would take over. Well, one had been cooking for a very long time and had got fed up because the other one never complained: so he thought he would serve up something truly terrible. So he made a pie out of moose turds. Well, the other one sat in front of the pie and took a mouthful: for a moment he almost spat: then he said "Moose turd pie! But good!" So the first one had to go on cooking.

I think this is a story about God and Man. Perhaps I will call my book—Moose Turd Pie.

Much love,

Dear Tom,

Do you think you could go round to my flat and see if there are any letters? You can get into the hall by ringing the doorbell downstairs (where there lives, like the lady of Australia, someone who paints herself like a dahlia) and, if there are any letters, could you possibly forward them here; where I am supposed to be having a nervous breakdown.

Actually, I am very well, but don't tell anyone.

I'm trying to write a parable; which, one thinks, means something different from what it says. But it doesn't. What it says is inexplicable.

Also, it is a commentary on the political situation. Why do politicians have to split into groups and abuse each other like children? Because of such is the kingdom of heaven?

Outside my window there's a marabou stork who walks up and down all day. It mows the lawn. Its hands are folded as if in prayer.

I hope you are flourishing. Don't forget my letters.

Love,

Dear Father Whatnot,

I am sorry I disappoint you.

Perhaps I write in code to get past the censor. Have you thought of this? That old man upstairs.

You gave me a choice: one switch in the computer. You couldn't have known my choice: but this was yours.

Yes, I passed on your message. I imagined I knew what it was about.

In all life it may be necessary to present a formal façade: this can protect tenderness.

For instance, everything could have two or three meanings: so a person's mind could leap.

Sometimes, yes, we would get stuck on each other's backs like frogs. To the world, this would be obscenity.

All right, I am two or three persons. You should know about this situation.

Africans might bring about a revolution simply by expecting nothing else; by saying—Life is wonderful!

Whatever did happen to that body by the way? Did it get out of the tomb (or jail) free?

The point of a censor is, that everyone can fill in their blank spaces.

You flatter God. You do a travelogue of a bloodred sun above a landscape. But it is true—there are people running!

You shouldn't be ashamed of your instruments of torture.

They are symbols of sensuality. Natalie, when she suffered, seemed to be torn apart by horses. Her legs went in different directions. She too thought the clock should be stuck at twenty-five past six. Like that crack in the temple. But the stone was rolled aside.

If you never pray for the healthy, do you wonder the world is sick?

As we are not computers, we need new programming.

I leave my clues; my trail of gunpowder. I'm trying to write like Saint Paul. I love Saint Paul. He tied himself in knots; only to break out, with one great leap, from the world's serial.

Best wishes,

Darling,

You never write. I suppose you never will.

Fresh flowers are brought in each day. There is a piece of muslin over the milk. So flies, when they get in, cannot get out; they have to drink it all up to reach the bottom.

I don't want you any different. Perhaps you can only be happy when I am sad. And I the same. Thus, we drink. It's a glorious life. Hung in the fresh air all day! Back in the cupboard at night! Counting all those sheep. And the goats marching.

There are a lot of things I don't tell you. And which you don't tell me. You would find it easier to be told—so you could object.

Stand on one leg then. Take hold of the other. Pull it. Slowly! Now move out of the casement window. Old saints, when they wanted to beat the devil, farted at him. Lure him down to the basement with promises of delight. Give him blackcurrant juice and take away his money!

Then, he might not trouble you.

I thought I saw Edward in the town here the other day. Is this possible?

Much love,

To the Editor of the National Sunday Newspaper.

Dear Sir,

If a country wants national regeneration, it should arrange to be defeated.

Yours, etc.

November 15th

I was born into a rich family. My grandfather made paper in Newfoundland. He sold it on street corners as a boy. He came over to England and sat next to the Prince of Wales. In those days you sat next to the Prince of Wales as you might at a cinema. He put his hand up your reticule.

My grandmother had blood like the same people had horses. She followed hounds. The huntsman caressed her with a sanitary towel.

There are photographs of my grandparents in summer dressed in winter clothes like asbestos. Around them are the hundreds of dead birds killed in the fire.

My father was born with a silver hook in his mouth. He used it to buy his own aeroplane to fight in the war. He wore a cloche hat and a pistol. He had to lean so far out to shoot round the propeller that someone winged him with a machine gun.

My mother, in a horse-drawn ambulance, was waiting underneath. She picked him up and dressed him.

My family were all politicians. On Saint Valentine's Day they posed with the Mafia. Around them, like dead birds, were their hundreds of constituents in the fire.

I was a serious boy. I wore a cloche hat. I heard them laughing from the lavatory. When you pulled the chain, a snake was apt to jump out.

Sometimes they dressed in medals and walked on the tops of trenches. I wondered if they were mad, or only pretending.

My father carried a sword stick. His other leg had been shot off. One day he swam with his face too close to the sun and sank, in full armour.

My mother lay in bed and drank sal volatile. She whitened her face with ashes. She did not like to be close to her child, for fear of contamination.

There was another war by this time. I took out my father's old pistols. By putting one bullet in and spinning the cylinder, I could do quite well.

The seat in Parliament was being kept warm for me. You don't believe eggs like this hatch, but they do.

I thought—This will be my bargain against the devil: if things become too horrible, I will say stop.

I have wondered whether to make my hero a politician. Politicians are almost untouchable.

About environment, or background, this is all that should be known; where we start from.

The rest is up to us.

To the Editor of the National Sunday Newspaper.
Dear Ned,
    No, I don't expect you to print my letters.
Yours,

My love,
    I'm sorry I haven't written. I go to climb this mountain tomorrow.

I hope you are all well.

I feel I am sitting on a tree and sawing off its branches. Soon, I will fall. Then I will come home. I will try to know something not only of the tree but the fruit—perhaps my children. To our children we should be nothing—we have created them. They must be on their own. Looking back, life is a straight line without variations: this is where we are. Looking forward there is profusion; creation. I should like to see myself through the eyes of my children—in which I would be nothing, but as much in the way as a god. On a rocky pass. Or standing on a lawn and looking in through a window.

At the beginning there is a journey; my hero moves across a plain. He imagines heaven and hell. We see people in terms of need; as did Odysseus or Dante.

When he returns he would be in disguise perhaps; the better to look through a window. He would walk up a valley—and stand on the lawn. The window would be lighted. Do you remember the wall I built last summer? The dark-haired stranger would not be his wife. She would be a young girl, with her skirt up round her waist. She would be making love. Perhaps to his son.

His wife would be in bed upstairs.

On the lawn, he would be dancing.

                    With very much love,

November 30th

The following fragments, discarded, will be footprints to the bottom of the mountain.

"All you can think about is your beastly little illness!"

He: "I've been ill for nine months!"
She: "What an interesting period!"

If you want a person to be free, be kind: if loving, unfeeling.

You lacerate yourself to get power, fail: lacerate others, succeed: so—continue self-laceration.

I thought—I will be responsible because I do not want to see her again.

I was on my hands and knees scrubbing the floor. She said "It is obvious you are in love with someone else!"

Elizabeth: "Do you want us to be happy like Joe and Margaret Gregory?"

The taste of Natalie—shit, that makes things grow. Of Natalia—spittle, that cauterises.

What is myth? what is reality? on a journey.

In reality you do not go round and round. You climb.

Encampment of Freedom Fighters at Marudi

You turn off the Marudi–Tanka road. The encampment is surrounded by barbed wire. The wire is not to keep intruders out but to keep the freedom fighters in. The gateway is like the entrance to a Chinese pagoda. There are five thousand Chinamen in the Sahara but because they are yellow no one knows they are there. Recently one or two tanks have become operational. They hold water. Please wind up the windows and keep your children in the car. Do not feed the animals. Pedestrians are dangerous. In case of breakdown, remain seated until the whole machinery has come to a halt.

Events that are supposed to be important—pain, infidelity, all forms of political manoeuvre—are seen as peripheral to a central effort of which they are symptoms, like sweat. This effort is the construction of a certain style in which a man can trust what is happening; and thus can affect it, when reasonably he is dead. What happens is the quiet walk in the garden; his meetings with one or two women. This is living. His own part in it would be tiny; but he would not imagine it anything else.

December 6th

You stand in a small courtyard with climbing roses and bougainvillaea. Above and beyond you is the mountain. My loves! My darling! The sun is a drop that runs down your face and stings. You move off through banana and maize plantations; porters carry your luggage with iron bands round their heads. They support the universe. The earth is red with cracks where rivers parch it. The mountain is out of sight within the level of clouds. You move towards heaven. Your body is two feet walking. There is an association between your body and brain. The outside is cold: your breath keeps a furnace inside you. You walk all day through a forest of lichen. You come to a cottage with a rose patch. Here is someone like the fair-haired girl whom you have left behind. She has got there before you. You sit on a rustic bench; not quite alone.

The next morning you are out of the forest and on to the plateau. Your porters are not with you: they have gone round behind hills. They carry your food and blankets. Energy is transmuted by the sun. Ghosts stand at the foot of the mountain; you still cannot see it. You meet climbers coming down: they blush; are garlanded. You have nothing to say. The path goes up over small chasms. You eat sandwiches in order to sit by a stream. Your legs have sackcloth for protection: your arms to keep whiteness from the sun. You do not talk because there is no medium through which sound travels. You arrive at an encampment halfway up the mountain. There are clouds below you. Fingers reach up for a sign.

In the evening the mountain becomes visible. You sit on your bench and drink tea. When you blow on it, the clouds break. You stamp your foot against the cold. The ice becomes milky. Porters, or angels, bring your food. They are dressed in sackcloth. They give you spoons, so you cannot do yourselves injury.

At night you lie on a wooden bunk with your eyes curled. You cannot climb quickly because the air is thin. You are sleeping in a cell; not quite alone. You have a stake driven through your heart. The stake is what you have left behind: those who love you. If you move too quickly you put your knees and elbows into the cold. The stillness of a fire, inside, makes a vacuum. Through this no sound can pass.

In the morning there is ice and your body goes milky. As you walk there are stokers working rhythmically inside. At the highest stream on the mountain a deer has died; its skin is dried paper. The valleys are paper; crossing them you are a ladybird escaping from fire. Above the mist you now see the mountain clearly: it is a dead volcano covered with snow. The plain you are walking on is lava. It ran down in a flood towards the sea. You do not get any closer or further away: you are on a slope keeping level. In the clear air there appears to be no one walking beside you. On the top of the world you are a pointer giving direction. You have no shadow, because the light is all around. The last hut shines in the distance: it is a star, made of tin. The shepherds have gone round the other side of the hill. The path is a thread tied to a needle: it runs back to the sea. To climb out of a maze you ignore the walls around you. You are in a flat plain between mountains. You cannot remember clearly where you began. There was a courtyard with fountains. Ladies and gentlemen lay on the grass. The mountain does not get any closer nor further away. It is the end of the thread at the centre. The porters, or angels, are at the hut ahead of you: they have laid out food and clothes. They are hung with sackcloth to keep them warm. You stand in the sun which freezes. There is a patch of earth on which to stamp. Around is snow turned to iron. On a plate is an apple which will make you sick. You cannot eat at such an altitude. You lie in bed to keep warm. Your head and shoulders are in the cold. Somewhere ahead of you is the girl you have left behind. She has pink hair which melts the snow. The angels gamble at your feet. They have your possessions.

In the middle of the night you are woken; you have not slept. It has been too cold. They have come to get you. You are ready to go up the last stage of the mountain. You say—My loved ones! You leave behind your shape on the bunk; a body to which you will return. The angels do not climb; they stay to guard your possessions. You are already dressed; you are at the foot of the last summit. You are no longer characters; you are diagrams cut in the snow. There is a lamp which goes ahead of you. One behind the other, you are a body which is carried: you move slowly or you will not reach the tomb. The air is thin and your head failing; tendons stretch from your neck to your heart and lungs. You follow the lamp; are an earthworm; take small steps so you do not appear to be moving. You stamp, and nails are driven into the snow. Your feet are turned outwards to the slope of the mountain. If you fall forwards you put a hand a short distance from your face. At your front and back are guides; these are now gods, not angels. They are there to catch you. After every few steps you rest; lean on your stick to get your lungs. At your feet is Orion's Belt; the clouds are cathedrals. Your hands are folded over the top of your stick so it will not go through. The stick is a spear; your forehead on your hands. The shaft runs back to the sea. There is a cave where your ancestors have sat. Your heart is a drum giving warning. You want to go on. Others wait for the dawn: they scratch their names in dust there. Icicles make tin music. At this altitude breath is powder. The dawn has started. Below, the sun struggles. Fingers come out from the clouds. The sky is solid; black and red lava. The clouds are lips: the sun is the head of a baby. Do not worry, loved ones! You take note, for the first time, of the other groups around you; each has a guide in order not to fall. The guide has a woolly cap and gumboots. He carries a pole by which he balances. His acolytes hang on.

Some are on their knees or curled up vomiting. It is difficult to be well at such a high altitude. You are spread about as if in purgatory. The dawn has risen. You have to be thinking of yourself: others remain as if they were praying. At every step you slide back two. Your guide is there to help you. One climber has no stick; he is like a skater on the rim of the world. At such speed he might go over. To the slope of the mountain he appears horizontal: but he is vertical, the same as you. Your guide waits; at every step he smiles; you move on two. In one group is the girl with fair hair and cream-coloured skin; she lies face down, vomiting. She leaves marks like flowers. She covers them like a dog. The white light is all around you. You see only the slope and your feet in a line; there is no line behind you. You lean towards earth. There are yellow marks like intestines. She was curled up like a dog. You stop every few paces because your lungs are outside being eaten. The dog breathes you. Being yourself, you do not watch the people on either side. You see them clearly: there is just enough air to breathe. God is a man in a woollen cap and gumboots. He carries a stick. Other people turn back. There is only yourself, curled, with your hands and feet like the sky. You hold on with your fingers and toes. You are near the top of the mountain. One or two others join you. They are strangers, whom you have touched in the course of your life—the still-open head of a child, a dying man in Australia. They are on their hands and knees, like the sky. The top is a crater. Once, it was a volcano. You do not remember how you got here. You have been doing this all the time. Sometimes your lungs were outside you in the snow. Sometimes you watched the dawn come up like a furnace. This took centuries. At the other side of the crater is a world of ice. There are huge shapes of rocks and empires. The light is solid, because of ice. No one goes there. This is the highest point of the mountain. Crawling, you have climbed from the sea. You have grown from flippers. You hear the bees. The heat around you is like insects. There is a pole with a tattered flag. You sit with your woollen cap and gumboots. You have come to the point where you have to return. You put a finger against the sky. It flashes. There is nothing to stay for. Only a journey here and back. You sit on ice. In the mist, you see nothing. That was what it was like, my darlings! In the cold. And heat. Remember it. Being so gentle! You begin to slide. You wish you had stayed a little longer at the top. Your footprints are like blood. You will not remember this clearly. Your heart is outside on the snow like roses. You remember the dawn. There are rocks that might dismember you. As you slide, you burn; the snow is like water. God, because he is indulgent, follows you: he has only warned you not to hurt yourself. You pass the people you were with on the way up—the girl with pale hair and sick like roses, the man with his arms out over the rim of the world. In another age you might have helped them. But not now. They are themselves. You have been there. You are sliding down. On your back with your arms out. They will do it on their own. Having come this far. I hope you succeed, my loved ones. At the silver hut there are your angels: they have gambled and kept your clothes. You notice the daylight: the sun is black-and-white against rocks. You take off your sackcloth. You are wearing a jacket, two jerseys, a waistcoat, and two vests. Take care, my loved ones. The porters will start behind and end ahead of you. What you have achieved is to be able to go down. You cannot rest at such a high altitude. The angels still wear their sackcloth. You are in your shirtsleeves. You have been to the top. You see the whole world spread out beneath you. I wanted to say this—I climbed a mountain! It was something on its own; and is related. I feel very well. I will come back now. Once upon a time I stood in a courtyard with roses and bougainvillaea. Five days and sixty miles—a part of my life. Coming down, I am one of the red-faced men from the mountain. As we pass others, we blush. I will not remember this well. I will make a description. A girl lay curled up and was sick in the snow: a wild-faced man with his arms out went over the rim of the world. These figures occurred on my journey; they were themselves: I was myself. I should think of others now. I wanted to do something on my own: or with words. I climbed a mountain. These things happened; which I can neither possess nor impart. There is a map: this is how to do it. There are mechanisms in the body and brain. God stays with you as you move down through the ricefields. Crossing the lava, coming back through the banana plantations, you have to settle up. He waits for you. You come to him. He touches his cap. It seems he reminds you—

These are your children; and your children's children.

III

Natalia

10

I WAS IN THE sitting room with Catherine. I thought I saw someone watching us through the window. The curtains were undrawn. The window looked out at the front of the cottage on to a lawn and a wheatfield. There was no one else in the cottage. My mother and father were away.

I said "There's someone at the window!"

I put my thumbs in my ears and ran to the window and made a roaring noise.

Catherine was lying on the sofa.

There did not seem to be anybody on the lawn.

Catherine and I had come to the cottage the day before. We had hitchhiked from London and walked through the wheatfields. We had both been working for the CRPP—or Committee for the Release of Political Prisoners. An action group had been set up to collect signatures for a petition. There was to be a march and demonstration at the office of the High Commissioner. Opinion was split about whether or not we should try to break in. Some thought that violence would give publicity: others that violence was bad news anyway.

Catherine was on the sofa with her legs tucked up. She said "But what's the point?"

"The point of what?"

"Going to Africa."

Catherine and I had been working in the printing room of the CRPP. They were doing posters which I carried in bundles to a sports car. The sports car was driven by a man in a white fur hat. I had laughed.

Catherine said "You have to act through responsible society."

I said "What responsible society?"

Hitchhiking, we had stood a long time at the side of the road. Then I had hidden behind a hoarding and Catherine stood alone. A lorry stopped. The driver had wanted to fight me.

When we got to the cottage it was dark and we had a meal and sat in the sitting room. I tried to get Catherine to cook. I said "Just like a woman!"

She said "Just because you expect them to do everything!"

There was one spare room with two single beds in it and my own room with a single bed. My mother's room had a double bed. In London, at the CRPP, we had all slept on the floor.

Catherine and I argued about Central Africa. I did not think this did any good.

She said "Why not an invasion?"

"But you don't like violence."

"I didn't say I didn't like violence! What about the petition?"

"Honestly, I think some people just like arguing."

At the office there had been a red-haired boy who had been sent to stir up a spirit of aggression. He was called Pete. I used to copy him, nodding my head and shouting in dialect.

Catherine said "Invasion would be by a constitutionally responsible government."

I said "What does that mean?"

At the cottage, we were not used to one another. I thought it would take some time and then there would be a click and it would be all right. This had happened before.

"What are you thinking?"

"Nothing."

"You must be thinking something."

I wanted to get her to laugh. That was when I ran to the window with my hands in my ears.

"Was there anyone?"

"No."

"Who could it be?"

"The police. We've got a load of dynamite here."

At the CRPP I used to wait for Catherine in the corridor outside the printing room. She came out sometimes with the boy with red hair. I used to say—He is pathetic!

I said "The point is, it doesn't work. If you invade a country you just have to sit there till it's time to have to go out again."

"According to you, nothing would work."

"Well what does?"

"What?"

"There can't be a perfect society."

I sometimes found myself saying things like my father. I only did this when he was not there.

I didn't think I should go on too much about the boy with red hair. It would be better to ignore him.

I walked on the lawn outside the window. The wheatfield was black. I tried to remember the stars. There was Orion's Belt on the horizon. We had lived in the cottage since I was a child. I had spent every holiday there, except sometimes when we had gone abroad.

Catherine stayed on the sofa.

I said "Disgusting!"

"What?"

"Lying around all day."

She had a patch on the side of her jeans that was splitting. I had said—You do it on purpose!

She had said—What for?

"What do you want to do tonight?"

"In what way?"

"Do you want to go for a walk or something?"

I could have said—Come on, we'll go upstairs.

"I'm all right."

"You can't stay downstairs."

"Why not?"

"You can't."

Catherine was supposed to be having a baby. I thought it was right I should take some care of her.

"Do you feel well?"

"Fine."

I thought that in the morning I could go and get food from the village. I could walk through the wheatfields.

I was not certain how long my mother would be away. She was in London.

Catherine said "I don't see why there can't be a constitutionally responsible society. All societies are constitutional or else they wouldn't exist.

I said "You're saying two different things."

"I'm not."

Catherine had a round face and lower lip that jutted out. I sometimes found things easier with her when we were angry. She pushed me away.

I said "Agitator!"

I thought I could put her in the spare room and sleep on the other bed.

I said "Oh well let's stay here then!"

She said "Don't go away!"

I had been thinking about going out to Africa. There were people I knew there with whom I could stay. I could see for myself what was happening. Or get some work in a hospital.

As soon as I moved away she wanted me to come back. Then she became watchful.

By the following night we might have got more used to each other. I put my head on her stomach.

I said "How old is it?"

"What?"

"I can hear it miaowing!"

I thought I could go with her up to the bedroom and sit on the edge of the bed. She had only brought a handbag and a coat.

"I'll carry you."

"Don't you dare!"

"You should be in a harem!"

"Men always say that!"

She walked up the stairs ahead of me. I stumbled, and leaned against her. There should be some way of doing this by luck, like gambling.

"Where'm I sleeping?"

"Here."

"Have you a toothbrush?"

"Yes."

The only toothbrush I could find was my father's. It was splayed like a fountain.

"Isn't he having some sort of breakdown?"

"Who?"

"Your father."

"I don't think so."

I sat on the bath. She bent over the basin.

I wished there were some quick way of getting out to Africa. I would have to find out about transport.

She said "Don't watch."

"Who wants to watch?"

She was doing this in some sort of aggression. I thought— But it doesn't work.

We had both just taken our university entrance exams and had nine months with nothing to do.

I thought—But she's having this baby.

"Who do you think's going to do the invading then?"

"Of course the army does the invading."

"Would you join the army then?"

I wanted her to say—How can I! I'm a girl.

"That's not the point."

"Why not?"

"It's personal."

I said "Killing's personal."

Then—"What's that?"

There was an extraordinary mark on my hand. I seemed to have burned it on the towel rail.

She said "Are you all right?"

I said "We could go abroad."

She said "I don't want to go abroad."

The mark on my hand was in the shape of Africa.

I said "What are you going to do then?"

"About what?"

"The baby."

"Such as?"

I thought—Or we might go back to London. The demonstration was planned for the following Sunday.

She went into the bedroom. She was wearing pants. I thought—Like a boxer.

She said "When was this bed last slept in?"

"Last night, by a tramp."

"It's damp."

"Let me feel."

"Don't do that!"

"I call that dry."

She kicked me. I held on. After a time, she became compliant.

"Do you feel sick?"

"No."

"Perhaps we should go back to London."

The last time we had been on a demonstration was outside the American Embassy. There had been a crowd trying to provoke the police. The police were behaving calmly. The red-haired boy, Catherine's friend, had lit a newspaper and had held it under a horse.

I had said "Don't you care about horses?"

We were lying on the bed. I could do nothing when

Catherine was so watchful.

I said "All English girls care about are horses."

She pushed me in the ribs.

There was a boy in London who was supposed to be making homemade bombs. He worked as a cook in a cafeteria.

I wondered if I should go to the cellar and get a bottle of wine. If I took one bottle from each row, it might not be noticed.

She said "I suppose you know a lot of foreign girls then."

Her stomach was peculiarly flat. I wanted to turn her over. I could say—Is that comfortable?

At the last demonstration the boy with red hair had torn out a piece of railing at the edge of the square. It had pulled earth up with it. Catherine had helped him.

She said "When are your father and mother coming back?"

"I don't know."

"Do they often go away separately?"

When the police had tried to push the crowd back the boy with red hair had put his hands over his ears and had gone limp. The police had lifted him by his arms and legs as if they were taking his clothes off.

"Why are you laughing?"

"It's funny."

"Look. I'm tired. I really must go to sleep."

"All right go to sleep then."

I lay beside her on the outside of the bedclothes. I used my arm as a pillow.

If you thought about things too much perhaps you made them more difficult.

I woke up in the middle of the night very cold. I was still on the top of the bedclothes. She was asleep. I had a headache. I climbed into bed beside her.

I could feel where she was breathing. I did not want her to wake.

I did not think there was much point in making love unless you thought of marrying. People made such a fuss of this.

Once Catherine and I had gone dancing in a club and a boy had come up and asked her to dance. I had told him to go away. Some of his friends had come up and a fight had started. I had not fought back; after a time they had gone away. I had said—They were pathetic!

That was the first time Catherine had stayed with me.

When she slept, she was peculiarly soft and warm.

There was something hard in her, being pregnant.

I thought that in the morning we would get food from the village. We would walk hand in hand.

I did not think I would sleep. But when I woke, it was morning.

"Come on! The sun's scorching!"

"What time?"

She came awake slowly, stretching and licking her lips.

"You've got your clothes on!"

I lay on top of her. I still had a headache. I had drunk too much the night before.

"Get off!"

"Look, they're coming!"

"Who?"

"The police!"

I thought it was better not to do too much because of the baby.

She said "Come on, I've got to do my exercises."

"You don't need exercises."

"You should do some. You weigh a ton!"

I dangled my head towards the floor. She climbed out of bed and hugged her arms round her. She went on tiptoe to the door.

From upside-down she seemed a giant.

She opened the door and took hold of the two knobs. She lowered and raised herself on her haunches.

"What good does that do?"

"Strengthens the muscles."

"What muscles?"

"I suppose you think women shouldn't have any muscles."

I had rolled on to the floor. I dragged myself along on my elbows. I lay on my back.

"Ow!"

"Serves you right."

"You've broken my nose!"

She sat on the floor. I thought—That was amazing.

"What was that?"

"What?"

"I thought I heard someone."

Later that morning, we went across the fields to the village. It had snowed in the night. The trees were heavy. Our feet made a booming sound. It was very cold. I hadn't got shoes or socks, so I walked in my sandals.

"What do you want to do in Africa?"

"If enough people joined together they could do something."

"Such as?"

"Well, walk between the firing lines or something."

"But there aren't firing lines."

"I know. Then all the easier."

The light was extraordinarily clear. The trees seemed carved out of the sky. I did a funny walk. I could say—My feet are going to drop off.

"Why don't you wear socks?"

"Self-laceration, probably."

In the village we bought bread and eggs and paraffin. When we got back I tried to thaw my feet out on a stove.

"Oughtn't you to see a doctor?"

"Oughtn't you to see a doctor!"

We cooked a large piece of meat for breakfast. I poked at it every now and then. Afterwards, I thought we should try to tidy the cottage. There were an enormous number of plates and glasses on the floor.

"But what does your father think?"

"About what?"

"Africa."

"Oh, he thinks there has to be some sort of fighting some-where, so it might as well be there, I think."

"That's terribly cynical."

"Yes isn't it."

She sat cross-legged with her feet up on her thighs. She pulled her stomach in. She took a deep breath and held it.

I carried some washing-up through to the kitchen. I thought—This goes on forever.

It was terribly late. It was already almost teatime.

I might walk across the fields to the pub. But then what would we do in the evening.

There was the peculiar mark of the burn on my hand. I wondered if it were a portent.

I was standing in bare feet on the tiles of the kitchen. One of my toes hurt badly. I felt as if I were on hot coals.

I could go and stay in my father's flat in London.

Catherine did not seem to be doing anything. She was on the sofa in the sitting room.

I said "You are hopeless!"

"Why?"

Or I could look for a job of work.

The telephone rang. I went into the hall, I said "Hullo?" I thought I could say—I am the fire brigade.

The telephone clicked. There was the dialling tone.

I had once overheard a woman talking to my father. She had said—I'm going to kill myself. There was one telephone in the hall, and an extension upstairs in the bedroom.

I was still in the hall when the telephone rang again. A voice said "Hullo?" It was my mother.

"Oh hullo!"

"Are you all right?"

"Oh, fine."

Catherine had come out of the sitting room and was going upstairs. I wondered if she would be getting her things together.

"Is Catherine there?"

"Yes."

"I mean what's she doing?"

"What?"

I thought—I am acting stupid.

Catherine couldn't get out of the house without going through the passage past me.

I said "Oh! She hasn't been very well. She's upstairs I think. Resting."

"Do Joe and Margaret know?"

"I don't know. Shall I ask her?"

My voice sounded childish.

My mother said "I do think she ought to tell them. I mean, how long are you going to stay there?"

"Oh. I don't know. Two or three days probably. Or tomorrow."

There was a pain at the top of my head. I thought—This stops me saying what I want to.

My mother said "She's only seventeen!"

"I know."

I thought I should try. I said "There's this demonstration in London on Sunday."

There was a silence.

My mother said "But you're all right?"

"Yes."

"Well I'll see you then."

"Good-bye."

I went out into the garden on to the lawn. The cold seemed

soothing for my feet. I wished I had thought of something better. I didn't know what Catherine was doing.

She was lying on the bed upstairs. She seemed to have been crying.

I said "What's wrong?"

She had taken her shirt and trousers off.

I said "How long ago did you see the doctor?"

"Two weeks."

"And what did he say?"

As soon as I sat with her she became active again. She pushed herself up on her elbows.

I said "You can stay here. I'll ask my mother."

I thought I could go alone to the demonstration on Sunday. Catherine could stay. I would talk to the boy with red hair.

I said "Or you can do anything. Why worry?"

She said "Give me a handkerchief can you?"

The telephone downstairs began ringing again. I thought I would not answer it.

She said "He says he'll be dead by the time he's thirty."

I said "Who?"

"Peter."

Peter was the name of her friend with red hair.

I said "Well that's stupid!"

She said "One thing he isn't is stupid."

By the time I got downstairs, the telephone had stopped ringing.

I sat down by the telephone and looked at numbers in the book.

I wondered if I could go down to the pub. Catherine would not hear me go. I could say—But I've been here all the time!

People seemed to have to have some need, or drive, to keep them going.

Last summer I had worked on the land. This was in a remote island in Scotland.

It was almost time for supper, I could make a cup of tea.

Catherine came down and said "Do you know the times of trains to London?"

I said "You're not going to London."

"I am."

"There's not a train."

"There is."

She was in her underclothes. She was carrying her trousers, which she seemed to have been washing.

I said "Just because I said he was stupid! Honestly."

She went into the sitting room and lay face down on the sofa.

I said "You've got to make up your mind."

She crossed her ankles.

I said "You're not a bloody computer!"

She said "Computers make their minds up all the time."

I thought—When she is with Peter, she treats him like a baby.

I wondered if I should beat her.

She said "Have you got some music?"

"Yes. What would you like?"

"Vivaldi."

I said "Vivaldi! Vivaldi!"

Outside it had become quite dark. I put a record on. I lay with her on the sofa.

When I was holding her, she began to cry. I said "It's all right! All right!" I stroked her.

I was on the very edge of the sofa. It was like a knife-edge.

I said "We're now in a constitutionally perfect society."

There was a moon on the lawn outside. I forgot there might be something looking through the window.

I said "What does Peter mean when he says he's going to die by thirty?"

I thought suddenly—This time, it is going to be all right.

She had her back to me. I had not been expecting this to happen.

She said "All right! Go away! Leave me!"

I said "I'm not going to leave you."

She turned and took hold of my face. She looked into my eyes.

I thought—But I must not stop.

Her face was blotched with tears.

I said "Do you want to get married?"

She said "What?"

I said "Because we can."

Her eyes went to and fro between mine.

I thought—I can always get out of this.

She said "Do you mean that?"

"Yes."

Her face was large and soft.

I thought—So it is happening now. Thank God.

It was much the same as I had imagined it. I was a knife on the edge of the sofa. It was a flame.

Afterwards I thought—Well, everything is possible now.

She pushed me. She said "There is someone!"

I said "Where?" I wondered—What made it possible?

She said "A burglar!"

I said "A burglar." I raised myself. I looked at the window.

I thought—Perhaps because I both cared and didn't care.

I said "Shall we ask him in for a cup of tea or something?"

I looked round for a weapon. I found the handle of the Hoover.

I jumped up. I said "Me entertainee burglar!"

As I lifted the handle of the Hoover it became detached from the head and dust poured out of the bag on to the floor.

I left her on the sofa. I tiptoed to the door and looked through the keyhole.

There was a light on in the hall. I was sure there had not been a light before.

I said "I say! Dash it!"

I was holding the handle of the Hoover from which the bag hung. It poured dust out.

The door began to open.

I felt terrified.

A figure came in. I did not know who it was. It was in the dark, with the light behind it. I recognised my father.

"Oh hullo!"

"Hullo."

"It's you."

"How are you?"

"I thought you were in Africa!"

I raised my hand to my head with the bag of the Hoover in it and the dust went over me.

I said "Oh goodness!" I laughed.

My father looked towards the window. Catherine was pulling on her trousers.

There were piles of plates and cups on the floor. It was as if we had been having an orgy.

"Hullo Catherine!"

"Oh hullo!"

"How are you?"

"Very well thanks."

"Don't move."

Catherine was looking for her sandals.

He said "Mum's not here?"

"No."

"Where is she? London?"

Catherine said "No."

Every time I moved I made more dust. I said "Did you have a good time in Africa?"

"Yes, marvellous."

"What did you do?"

"Climbed this mountain."

I did not know why Catherine had said my mother was not in London.

My father said "You have porters, you know, and everything. I've just come down. It's the highest mountain in Africa."

Catherine was trying to clear up the plates on the floor. The patch was peeling off her behind.

I thought—It was like going into marshmallows.

He said "I rang from the station."

I said "Oh, I was upstairs. By the time I got down it had stopped ringing."

I thought—Why were we upstairs?

He went into the kitchen. He looked at the piles of washing-up. I thought we had done it.

I thought—All right, I can marry Catherine.

He said "And what have you been doing?"

I said "Oh. There's this big demonstration in London. On Sunday. We're marching to the office of the High Commissioner."

He said "What about?"

I said "Ndoula."

Catherine had followed us into the kitchen. She was trying to attract my attention.

I said "How did he escape?"

My father was standing in the doorway. He had the light behind him.

He said "Ndoula's escaped?"

I said "Yes, didn't you know? It's been in all the papers."

He said "I've been travelling."

He went back into the sitting room. He knelt down by the television and turned it on. He thumped it.

I said "Oh that seems broken. It was broken before we got here."

He put both hands on the television and leaned on it.

He said "What happened about Ndoula?"

I said "There was some sort of raid."

He was unscrewing the back of the television with his thumbnail. It might electrocute him.

I tried to mend the Hoover. Until I did this, I could not get up the dust that it had spilled on the floor.

I said "Did you see Ndoula?"

"Yes."

"What was he like?"

"Fine."

Catherine had come up to me again and was making faces. I couldn't understand what she was saying.

My father got the back of the television off and was fiddling inside it.

I couldn't see how the bits of the Hoover fitted together.

I said to Catherine "What?"

My father jerked his hand away and swore. He crawled round to the front of the television.

I said "Did you see the freedom fighters?"

"Yes."

"What were they like?"

"What one expected."

Catherine was baring her teeth at me. She looked like a cat. I said to myself—All right!

The sound of the television was coming on. There was cowboy music.

We watched a scene in which men in Robin Hood hats seemed to be shooting one another with bows and arrows.

I said "Hey pardner!"

He said "Were you in the last demonstration?"

"Yes."

"What were the police like?"

"Wonderful."

Catherine said "I don't think you can call people wonderful who—"

My father turned the sound of the television down. He sat back on his heels.

He said "You can defeat anything by being wonderful."

Catherine was cross-legged on the floor. She was pulling pieces out of the rug beneath her.

The telephone rang. My father said "I suppose I better answer it."

I climbed out of the window on to the lawn. I did not want to stay with Catherine. The moon made the grass black. The snow had melted. The sitting room was lit up with extraordinary brilliance.

My father was going upstairs to the bedroom. The woman's voice that I had once overheard on the telephone had shaken like a fountain.

Catherine's head was on a level with the seat of the sofa. Anyone could have seen us through the window.

The news had come on television and was about Central Africa. There were soldiers with guns round a hut.

I went back through the window to Catherine. I put my hand on her knee. I thought—Perhaps there will be a war, and I will be all right.

Catherine was looking at the carpet.

My father came back and said "What's happening?"

I said "Oh, reprisals."

He sat with his arms along the sides of a chair. He watched the television.

I said "Will it make any difference?"

"Yes. No one knows quite what."

I could not remember what Catherine and I had done all weekend. We had been only once to the village.

I said "Oh yes. Catherine and I are thinking of getting married."

He said "Are you? Congratulations!"

Catherine was in an odd position on the carpet like a wounded bull. She had her legs dragged behind her.

He said "Well, we must celebrate."

Catherine said nothing.

He said "Champagne!"

He was in the chair with his arms pressed along the sides. He did not move. He said "When did you decide this?" He touched Catherine on the head.

The television changed to a picture of a man with a long sad face being interviewed.

I said "I know him!"

Catherine stayed with her head down.

There was the sound of a car arriving at the back of the cottage. The headlights swung round the trees on the lawn.

I said "Who's that?"

We stayed where we were.

A car door slammed. Footsteps came to the door.

I thought—I must get out of this.

My father looked at a corner of the ceiling.

I wanted to put my hand to my head and say—This is mad!

My mother's voice said "Are you coming?"

I went to the door. Someone, at least, should do something.

I found my mother in the hall. She was sorting a pile of letters. She said "Have you had a nice time?"

"Yes."

"Is Catherine still here?"

"Yes."

She was putting letters from the top of the pile to the bottom. She was not opening them. There were some in my father's handwriting from Africa.

She said "Joe's in the car."

I couldn't think who Joe was.

My mother had left the door open. The house was freezing.

In the sitting room my father seemed to have disappeared.

I said "Oh Joe Gregory!"

My mother said "Have you had supper yet?"

"No."

"Hullo Catherine."

"Hullo."

"Have you had a nice time?"

My mother was holding a postcard with a picture of a mountain. She put it to the bottom of the pile.

I said "Is that the mountain?"

She said "Catherine, are you any good at getting your father out of the car?"

Catherine said "My father's in the car?"

"Yes."

She said "What's he doing there?"

She went to the door. She said "Poppa!"

I thought I might go out on the lawn. I seemed always to be doing this.

My mother went into the kitchen. She said "Goodness how tidy!"

My father must have tidied it while we were watching television. I could not remember this.

My mother took some eggs out of the refrigerator. She broke them into a bowl.

My father had appeared in the hall and was looking at the pile of unopened letters.

Catherine came in from the drive. She said "What's wrong with Poppa?"

My mother said "We've just come down from London."

My father had come into the sitting room.

My mother said "I didn't know you were back."

He said "I've just arrived."

He came up and kissed her. She turned her cheek.

Catherine said "Do you want me to get him out or shall I take him?"

I put my hands to my head: I said "Oh God!"

I heard my mother saying "And what are you going to do Catherine? Are you going to a university?"

I thought I might walk over the fields and get a hitchhike to London.

I went out to the back drive and looked at Joe Gregory. He was sitting in the passenger seat of his car. He did not seem to be sleeping. He was staring through the windscreen. I bent down so that my face was on a level with his. He was making small movements with his lips.

I thought—We are in an aquarium.

My father had come out and was on the other side of the car. We could see each other past Joe Gregory through the windows. I thought—He has come to find me.

I said "What's he doing?"

"I don't know."

"Is he drunk?"

"He seems to be eating."

I became doubled up with laughter. I put my knuckles into my mouth. My father leaned on a mudguard.

We went together round the house. We walked on the lawn. We passed the courtyard we had been building in the summer.

He said "Is Catherine having a baby?"

"I think so."

"You don't have to marry her you know."

"No."

He said "I'll talk to Joe and Margaret."

I had a feeling such as I had had once or twice before in my life—that there was an aeroplane flying miles overhead and it was a toss-up whether or not it dropped a bomb.

He said "Don't do anything for any reason other than that it seems right in itself."

I said "No, of course not."

Catherine and my mother seemed to have gone to the car on the drive. We could hear their voices.

My mother was saying "But can you really drive?"

Catherine was saying "Yes really."

My father and I walked round the house. The trees above us were like hands in the cold blowing.

Catherine had opened the door of the car. Joe Gregory nearly fell out. He put an arm around her hips. He said "Fatty!"

I could say—Are you going?

My mother said "Do be careful!"

My father stayed in the shadows.

I thought I should go and lie down on the grass. I would look at the stars. Perhaps I would sleep there.

I heard Catherine calling. Then my mother. I stayed on the lawn.

The grass was wet. There was a tree in which I had hidden as a child.

There was the noise of the Gregorys' car starting up: a grinding of gears.

My mother and my father appeared in the sitting room. The scene, through the window, was brightly lit. My mother lay on the sofa. My father stood with his hands in his pockets, talking.

I lay on the grass. I could say—Catherine! Catherine!

I could rush after her and join her in London.

I did not think I would see her much now.

Orion's Belt was low on the horizon. The sword at his side was dripping.

My mother and father went on talking.

I must have fallen asleep. I was woken by what I thought was the sound of a scream.

There was just a light on in my mother's bedroom. The sitting room was dark. My feet were painful. Snow was falling again. In a dream, I had imagined a finger from the sky pointing.

11

ARRIVING HOME AFTER a time abroad you are like an angel fallen on an earth that has forgotten God existed. From the station I took a taxi. I did not know who would be at the cottage. I went on to the lawn and looked through the sitting room window. I saw Adam with his girl-friend. They were on the sofa.

In the hall were piles of letters like the droppings from an elephant. I picked through them, hoping for diamonds.

There were a dozen from my bank manager: a telegram from Ned Symon: a card from Yseult saying would I get in touch with her urgently.

In this strange world I did not think I would see again Natalia's dark blue paper, childish writing, the characters spaced out like flowers on Mount Parnassus.

The hall of the cottage had wallpaper with urns and scrolls; a hard oak chair where you sit by the telephone. I hoped the telephone might ring. I would appreciate the company of a dragon in the rocky landscape.

Adam was moving about in the drawing room. I thought I should go to the door before he found me.

He was carrying what seemed to be a truncheon.

"Oh hullo!"

"Hullo."

"You're back!"

"Yes."

Catherine was a big girl with an opening in her jeans. Her skin was like putty.

I said "Is Mum in London? Is she coming?"

In the sitting room there was a faded elegance of sofa, footstool, marble, tapestry: which we had laid out, Elizabeth and I, and which had flourished and in the course of time withered.

I should begin sorting my letters. This would fill in time; making piles on the floor before transferring them to the wastepaper basket.

"How did the exams go?"

"Oh all right."

"You'll be going there next year?"

"Yes."

Adam had a sort of youth, beauty, about him, like a chestnut with the white still showing.

He said "Where were you staying in Africa?"

"In a sort of rest house, on a hill. You could look over hundreds of miles of plains."

I smoothed my letters. There were handouts from Greece, Nigeria, Burma, Cyprus. My bank was insistent about my overdraft.

Catherine said "A sort of monastery?"

"Sort of."

She said "I couldn't bear that!" She shivered.

I wondered if she would be kind to Adam; look after him when he was ill.

I said "They take care of you."

"Who?"

"The people who run this house."

Adam said "But were you ill?"

I could say—I fell into a swimming pool. I hurt my arm.

I said "Not really."

Ned Symon wanted me to get in touch with him about my articles on Central Africa. Yseult said there was trouble with the Local Association.

I said "Were you at the last demonstration?"

Adam said "Oh that was a fiasco!"

Catherine said "I don't think you can say that about something that has had such an obvious—"

I had written so many letters; Natalie had not written to me.

I thought—It is for the best: I am free.

There was a letter from Tom Savile which began—"I am going to ask you something that I know you won't like—"

I wondered if people could still go to prison for debt. I should be taken care of.

Adam said "But what'll happen in Africa?"

"Who knows."

"Will Ndoula's escape make any difference?"

I said "Ndoula's people have an interest in staying alive."

I wondered if Catherine would say—You mean other people don't then?

There was another letter from Ned Symon saying he was sure I would understand if my articles—

Catherine said "Do you mean they won't fight?"

I said "There's more room in Africa. You're high up. You can breathe."

Catherine said "But the economic conditions are appalling."

There were magazines at the bottom of my pile with articles about Africa. Africans were fighting one another: children were starving.

I wondered, if I rang up Yseult, if she would know what was happening.

Adam said "Did you climb that mountain?"

I said "Yes. I've just come down."

One of the articles said that the British and the Russians and the Chinese were all sending arms to Africa.

Adam and Catherine were whispering.

Catherine said "But can't we send in troops?"

I thought—At the end of the world there will be people asking—Can't we send in troops?

I said "You can't force people."

I thought—I was walking through the trees one day and I saw Adam and Catherine in the garden.

I said "Even if you knew what was for their good. Do you think your parents, for instance, should force you?"

Adam looked embarrassed.

Catherine said "That's different."

"Why?"

"It's personal."

Adam said "As a matter of fact, I'm thinking of going out there."

I could say—But Adam, I've just come!

I had once said—Don't!

It was as if we were walking up a stony hill towards a thicket. There was a ram caught in a bush.

I said "Why?"

"We don't know what's really going on."

He was red in the face. I thought—Of course, he will have to do everything for himself.

He said "I just think people should know, that's all. Instead of always talking about it."

I said "Well don't get killed."

I thought—Catherine should stop him.

Then—But women don't.

I wished Elizabeth were at home.

There were photographs in the magazines of the fighting. Children stood with their hands over their stomachs. Soldiers held bayonets.

It was a cold night. I could go out into the garden. I would wait for Elizabeth underneath the trees.

He said "But are you saying one can do absolutely nothing?"

I could say—You think I have not done anything? Yes: all right.

He said "What are you saying then?"

I thought—But of course, he will have to challenge me.

I said "I'm not saying anything."

I thought—This is an odd technique.

Catherine was a big girl with a rent in her jeans. I thought—Perhaps I should fight her; or stay at home and look after her on my dungheap.

There were extraordinary piles of crockery and glasses on the floor. Someone seemed to have emptied a dustbin.

The telephone rang.

I could be like Buddha, craftily smiling; or Mohammed, rolling his eyeballs.

Adam and Catherine were whispering. I thought—If he married her, he would not defeat me.

I went into the hall. There was silence at the end of the telephone. I said "Hullo?" There was a cold dead weight. A line from my heart went down to the depths of the sea.

I thought if I bent over the telephone steeply enough I could send a message and say—Don't worry my darling! Everything is all right!

The world was lying in the dark with its head down by the floor.

I repeated "Hullo?"

There was a click and then the dialling tone.

I did not quite want to ring up Yseult, for news.

I could explain to Adam—With all the suffering in the world, how can one of us, you or I, not hurt the other?

I sat by the telephone. I felt as if I had been put in a corner of the hall and forgotten. Someone might trip over me and curse.

Adam opened the sitting room door and looked out and said "Oh yes. Catherine and I are thinking of getting married."

I said "Congratulations!"

I thought—Now I have something to do.

"When did you decide this?"

"Just now."

"Catherine!" I went into the sitting room. She was pulling bits of rug from the floor.

"Don't get up!"

I put my head on her head.

"We must celebrate! Champagne!"

I thought—If I am nice enough, something proper will occur.

We should have a meal together. We could sit round a table. What was proper would be recognised by a mixture of orderliness and pain.

I said "Let's have a meal! Let's do the kitchen!"

There were huge piles of utensils in the sink. A lamp was lying on the floor.

I thought—Natalia on the telephone might have been seeing if I were back?

I could say—Catherine, what are you doing now? Are you going to a university?

I was standing in the kitchen by the window. In the sitting room on the television there was someone talking about Ndoula.

There was the sound of a car on the drive. The lights swung across the ceiling and the trees.

Because I so much wanted to see Elizabeth, and could not wait, I went out of the kitchen on to the back drive. The cold had made a dew. There were my footsteps where I had gone round to the sitting room window.

Elizabeth was talking to someone in the car. She said "Aren't you coming?"

I stayed where I was.

I thought—I will be like this: standing in the cold, underneath a tree.

Elizabeth's footsteps went to the back door. I watched her moving like a frieze past my courtyard.

I thought—I am in the position of a sculptor or a god.

I went to the car. There was someone in the front seat staring through the windscreen. I recognised Joe Gregory.

I said "Joe?"

I thought—Perhaps he has been defeated by her.

I looked at Joe through the windscreen.

I thought—Catherine would be no good for Adam: she, like Joe, is a victim.

Joe moved his lips as if he were eating.

I thought I should go back to the cottage. Since she had been with Joe, things would be easier with Elizabeth.

Elizabeth and Adam were talking in the hall.

I could ask—Where's Sophie?

Elizabeth said "Oh you're back."

I said "Yes."

She looked uneasy.

I had forgotten how strong she was: a Jacob who would have no difficulty in taking on the angel with one hand holding the ladder.

She said "Did you have a good time?"

When I leaned to kiss her I looked over the edge of a precipice to a valley.

I said "Yes."

She moved away.

I wanted to cry for a moment, as so often before—But I've been ill! I've just got back!

They were all in the sitting room. Elizabeth was leafing through her letters.

I said "Where's Sophie?"

"Staying with friends."

"Why's Joe in the car?"

Elizabeth moved into the kitchen. Once, like this, I would have rung up Natalia. I would have gone to the call box in the village. There would have been a silence: I would have said—Are you all right? Natalia would have said—No. I would have said—What can I do? She would have said—Nothing. I would have said—Can I see you?

Or she would have said—Thank God! Thank God!—and I might or might not have seen her.

I thought—But neither would have made any difference between good and evil.

I thought I might go out again and walk in the garden.

When I had been in Africa there had been four paces from the wall to the door and four paces back again. I had been quite cheerful.

Father Whatnot had visited me. Like a great white bird he had alighted on the grass and we had listened to the munching of cattle. He had said—You are putting yourself outside human experience.

He had a way of making his arms disappear inside his cloak like a vulture.

I had thought—One day he will defeat himself.

I said "Oh hullo Catherine are you going now?"

She had appeared at the door in her overcoat.

"Yes I think so."

"But we'll be seeing you again then?"

She was a pretty girl, with a lower lip slightly protruding.

They all went out on the drive. I could hear their voices.

I thought I should take the opportunity to ring up Yseult. There was no answer for a long time; and then Yseult said "I'm afraid I can't speak now."

I said "Yseult, have you got someone with you?"

I sat by the telephone. There was a figure being raised from the depths of the sea. The breaking strain of the wire, and the weight of the object, were roughly equal; so that any movement meant that the wire might break. But if there was no movement the object remained in the sea. It was necessary to get some weight added to oneself and the object equally.

I went into the garden and found Adam. I said "Do be careful about going out to Africa."

He said "Yes."

I said "Good works can be both proper and destructive."

I thought—Natalie was an instrument by which exact weight could be placed upon oneself.

We were walking round elm trees. The sky was damp.

He said "I see that."

There was a light on in Elizabeth's bedroom.

I remembered—Events that are supposed to be important—pain, infidelity, all forms of political manoeuvre—are seen as peripheral to a central effort—

Adam said "Oh well, I think I'll go in now."

I said "Yes do."

"Good night."

"Good night."

I went up to Elizabeth's bedroom. She was at her dressing table. I said "Well, they've gone!"

She had her back to me. She was looking into a mirror.

I said "Joe and Catherine. Did they get off all right?"

She put ointment on her face so that steam seemed to condense there.

I sat on the bed. I folded my hands above my knees.

She began to undress. Her body was white like a huntress.

I could say—Well, what about you and Joe Gregory?

I was a wax image; on the edge of steam.

I said "Tell me."

She said "I sometimes wonder if you think I'm human."

Running through trees, the breath of her dogs would burn me.

She said "You never asked about the children. You never wrote."

"I did."

"Not to them. All you wrote about was yourself. That's all you think of; ever."

She walked between the dressing table and a cupboard. A bowstring caught against her breast.

I thought—If this is savage enough I will not mind.

She said "Who else did you write to?"

I thought—Could I have used the wrong envelopes?

She said "And why are you stopping Adam marrying Catherine?"

I said "Am I?"

"You try to charm him. You don't stand up to Adam."

I thought—How does she know all this?

She said "Don't you know Catherine's pregnant?"

A patch on her body was red; as if it had been slightly burned without sweating.

She said "If you do anything with Catherine I do think it will be despicable."

I said "What can I do with Catherine?"

She said "You know you flirt with her."

The devil which had approached, and which had formerly made me want to hit myself or go to the bathroom to be sick, became frozen, falling to hell.

She said "And why don't you tell Adam he can't go to Africa?"

I said "Why shouldn't he go to Africa?"

She said "Do you want to be rid of him?"

I thought—She is meaning, do you want him killed?

There was a wire drawn through me by which I was turned on a spit.

She said "You're a fool. Don't you think things are different now?"

I waited.

"You leave me alone here week after week—"

"But you wanted—"

"Put it all on to me!"

Her breath was a bellows fanning flames.

She said "You take no responsibility. You're riddled with self-pity—"

I thought—The gold we have laid up is now tapped and has become dynamite.

I said "What are you trying to say?"

She shouted "What do you think I'm trying to say?"

I pushed my hands palm upwards on the bed.

She said "I'm sorry, but I can't take it anymore."

I thought—But when it was true, you could.

She said "Will you give me money?"

I said "Yes."

I thought I could go now. I could walk down the stairs quietly. I might not be seen.

I said "Well, I think we've had a marvellous life together."

I went out on to the lawn. The weight in my head, which had also been in the sky, had cleared slightly. I walked through the frost. I thought—But there are such galaxies exploding!

At the bottom of the garden was a wooden shed. It was a joke—a beam and a rope there.

It was true one never quite imagined another person's pain. Blood blocked your heart; air holes crammed; mouths opened lonely against porcelain. She might have known this; night after night.

In the shed was a scythe with a rusted blade. This symbolised castration, or the passing of the years.

I sat in a corner. I thought I would spend the night here.

I wondered—If we cannot remember suffering, is it right to suffer then?

There was a garden mower which had bright blades. I could put my fingers into them.

I wrapped myself in sacking. I had not slept the night before. I had been travelling for several nights, and was tired.

It was very cold. On a shelf there was a candle. I could hold it underneath me to keep me warm.

I had been used to sleeping like this on the mountain. I had lain in thin air. Sacking, as if on potatoes, had preserved me.

Or I could sit on the scythe: the mower would scatter me in patterns.

Trees brushed against the roof. Cows made blowing sounds.

I wanted to ask Father Whatnot again—Whatever did happen to that body?

The sacking was gritty against my tongue. The earth hurt like truncheons.

I wondered—Did he rub against the stone like Aladdin?

By some accident with the rope, or the scythe, my children might be fatherless and free.

I thought—Take care my darlings! I will watch over you!

Against the cold earth trapped men scratched their initials: above my head hung icicles.

I was walking through wheatfields. I called—Good dog! Good dog! The rabbits ran out. The stubble burned. The seagulls got them.

I must have been dreaming.

I thought—Did I make this fair world out of chaos?

You do not know the moment between sleeping and waking. Enough sleep is necessary for the proper working of the brain: too much, and the devils do not come out at you. They sit quietly working in your brain.

I heard a voice running through the morning calling "Daddy! Daddy!"

Perhaps I was still dreaming.

I had lain here all night. An icicle had gone through my temple.

"Daddy!"

"Darling!"

"Daddy, where are you?"

In the toolshed, darling, among the flowers and bees.

"Daddy!"

"Yes?"

"I can't find you!"

All in one piece, darling. In good condition like potatoes.

"Daddy! Daddy!"

"Sophie!"

"What are you doing?"

My trousers fastened. My shroud *en déshabillé*. Arranged for artistic satisfaction.

Sophie stood in the doorway. There was light behind her. With her gold head, my one true angel.

"Daddy, what are you doing?"

Thinking of myself, darling; among the pots and dungheaps.

"Are you drunk?"

"No!"

"What are you doing then?"

"Waking."

I kissed her.

An acorn; a nut; somehow fallen from my old branches.

"When did you get home?"

"Last night."

"But have you slept here?"

"Yes."

"That's funny!"

Nothing hard, bitter. Peeled like a mushroom.

"And where have you been darling?"

"Staying with friends."

"You are grown up!"

A hand like a shaft of light coming down from her gold head.

"But I want to sleep here too!"

"You can't."

"Why not?"

Because I hope to be coming in, soon, darling.

"Come and sit here anyway."

And then I can hang up my old head, a bull's eye; my heart, a football; my genitals, onions.

"Daddy! Daddy! Can I go to Africa!"

"No!"

"But Adam's going!"

We held on to each other tight. Sophie had a way of passionately wanting everything in the world, which made her shimmer.

"I wouldn't get in the way! I'd be quiet!"

We were side by side in the sacking. Her head was against my shoulder. I thought—Perhaps they stayed like this for some short time before they went out into the garden.

She said "Tell me a story!"

"Now?"

"Go on!"

"What about?"

"Anything."

"I can't."

"Why not?"

"I'm tired."

She made a fist like a cloud and hammered at me.

I said "Once upon a time there was a person who was in two places at once."

"Two places at once?"

"Yes."

"But that's impossible!"

She turned to me. Her delicate breath, under a microscope, was the wing of a bee.

"He lived in a cottage with a garden like this—"

"Like this?"

"Yes."

"Gosh! And where else was he?"

"Underground."

"Why?"

"Because he was growing."

She made a noise like a wolf. She said "I'm frightened!"

"One day, he decided he should try to make the two parts of him come together—"

"Go on! Go on!"

"I am."

"You're not!"

"I'm trying!"

I had been listening for any sound from the garden.

"So he put a hand down below the earth—"

"How could he?"

"And another into the sky—"

"This is stupid!"

"And became a tree—"

"Gosh!"

"With roots and branches."

"Roots and branches!"

"Which was what he was all the time."

"All the time?"

"Yes. So he sat in his branches—"

There was a voice calling from the garden. "Sophie!"

Sophie said "Oh finish the story!"

I said "That's all."

"All?"

"Yes. He could sit in his branches."

"But that isn't a story!"

"It is."

"Sophie, where are you?"

"Mummy! Mummy!"

Elizabeth would be walking across the lawn. She would carry the sun like a lantern.

"Mummy!"

"Where—"

"Listen!"

Elizabeth stood in the doorway. I thought—We will appear to be with cattle and donkeys.

Sophie said "Once upon a time there was a person who was a tree he could sit in—"

"What on earth are you doing?"

"Resting."

"But why here?"

Sophie and I were holding on to each other.

"Mummy, mummy, you're not listening!"

"Oh just a minute Sophie!"

"Daddy's telling me a story!"

"I didn't know where you were."

"I've just got back. I've been in Africa."

"Oh ha ha!"

I said "Perhaps someone at last can get into bed the right side this morning."

I thought—That's witty.

She looked round the hut, sacking, scythe, mower.

She said "Yes, well, come in and have a lovely breakfast!"

12

COMING UP TO London after a time abroad you have the impression of a show mysteriously put on for your benefit—a vision of hell for warning and correction —scenery slotted to form an exercise yard of a prison; buses in side streets waiting for signals like tanks; too many people for them all to be human. I stood at a street corner and was a spy in the country of the damned; I should tread carefully so that I should not hurt the victims. It was Christmastime and there were gigantic crowns floating in the sky; these were for the benefit of the toys that went round streets and in and out of tunnels: they did not notice the watchers at corners. To the toys, these would be just agents of generation and destruction. I had a vision of a time here I had lived in but had not quite believed; when people could put their hands down and pick up pieces.

I thought I should visit my old friend Tom Savile. He might be on an assignment such as myself. We would not talk of this: our codes, or communications, did not include such a system. It was a day like a last day on earth, with sirens ringing.

In the Underground the bright dolls' eyes rolled in time to music; hands lay quietly on racks and could be taken down and looked at. I thought—I will never know who is on my side and who is not: perhaps everyone, and the rest is illusion.

I stood outside Tom's door. His head and shoulders appeared at the window. I thought—He is halfway to resurrection.

"Hullo!"

"Hullo!"

"It's me!"

"I didn't expect you."

Cars moved up and down carefully. They were seeing whom they could pick up or run over. Tom threw down his keys. They landed. I hoped they had been defused. I climbed Tom's long staircase. Here he might have sat all autumn.

"How are you?"

"Fine."

"You got your letters?"

"Thanks."

Tom was dressed in a neat tweed jacket and tight black trousers. He smoked a cigar.

I thought—Perhaps he will give me some sign, like a password.

He said "Do you know what I've been doing?"

"No."

"Do you want to hear?"

"Yes."

He walked up and down. He puffed. He said "I've been made secretary of PONSA."

As he moved, his jacket stuck out at the back like a bird. I thought—We have our memories.

He said "Do you know what PONSA is?"

"No."

"PONSA is an association formed to analyse the crack-up in Western society, and to suggest what might be salvaged from the holocaust."

I said "What is this holocaust?"

He said "That we don't know. But whatever it is, it will come."

I sat down. I said "But what are the symptoms?"

"One, a complete denial of the female principle. Two, the use of energy to produce as a process, waste; rather than, in a circuit, feedback."

I said "I agree."

He said "You know about feedback?"

He blew on his cigar. I thought—Perhaps anyone who is a good agent is double.

He said "The amazing thing is, I've been asked to be the secretary."

I said "But that's good."

He said "The trouble with you is, you don't believe in society."

I thought—Perhaps after all it is because we are on different assignments, that we cannot communicate.

I said "What was the thing I wouldn't like you wanted to ask me?"

"What?"

"You said in your letter—"

"Oh yes." He stood with one hand like Napoleon. I thought —Through his cigar, he may send strange music through the universe. He said "Will you take back Madeleine's clothes?"

"Madeleine's clothes?"

"Yes. I can't do it myself."

I thought—We should go out, Tom, you and I, and have a meal together.

I said "How is she?"

"I don't know."

"You don't see her?"

"I think, as a matter of fact, she is a corrupt human being."

I could say—But Tom, so are we all.

I said "Would you like some lunch?"

"Oh that would be pleasant!"

"Where shall we go?"

"Have you got any money?"

I had begun to worry about money. I had enough for a few weeks.

Tom took from a cupboard a small leather hat. He stroked it. He said "Do you like my hat?"

"Yes."

I thought—My job is to keep people alive: to tell them all is well with them.

We went out into the street. I carried the parcel of Madeleine's clothes. Tom carried his hat. There was a wind blowing. Leaves blew like bodies for the fire.

I said "I don't think there can be a perfect society."

He said "I know you don't."

I said "There is good and evil. But the fight's elsewhere."

Tom raised his eyes and held his hat on his chest as if he were in front of a memorial.

He said "But we're conditioned by society."

I said "But we can change."

I looked round at street corners. I had begun to wonder if someone might be following me.

Tom said "Can I ask you something?"

"Yes."

"Did you have an affair with Madeleine?"

I said "No." Then—"Would it have mattered if I had?"

Tom laughed. He said "You're a funny fellow!"

I thought—But it's almost true.

We went into a restaurant. Tom put his hat on a chair. He shouted "Don't sit on it!"

I read the menu. I was still worrying about money. Elizabeth now had enough; and the children.

Tom said "I sometimes think if I died no one would ever notice."

I said "I would."

"Would you?"

He blushed.

We were two men sitting in a restaurant. By shovelling food in we created warmth. The warmth was transmitted round our bodies. Time passed in the street outside. Cars lined up for a funeral.

I thought—Perhaps I won't see much more of Tom.

Tom said "I think I'll go away soon. To Africa."

I said "Everyone's going to Africa."

When Tom laughed his face became wrinkled as if he were taking a bite of an apple. Black pips showed between his teeth.

I said "I mean, of course one fights for the good; but success depends on what one is, which is a bit of everything."

Tom said "I agree."

I thought—Some part of me will always be sitting in this restaurant with Tom—in Africa, or as secretary of PONSA.

I asked for the bill.

He said "Before I go, I'd like to give you something."

I said "What?"

"My hat."

I said "That's extraordinarily kind!"

He held it cupped like an acorn. He said "I'm extraordinarily fond of this hat."

I thought I should be moving on to see Joe and Margaret Gregory. I would get news there of Catherine.

He said "You will wear it!"

I said "I promise. Thank you!"

I held it in front of me as if I were at a memorial. I thought —This is some sign.

"Good-bye then."

"Good-bye!"

In the streets, from the tops of buses, civilisation was on its back. Its legs were in the air. You could lean over it on the grass and feel life crawling.

Bells of ambulances rushed past, taking policemen to a fire.

Being Christmas, the crowds were pressed like weeds against a weir. I thought—Roman soldiers will soon clear them.

Joe and Margaret Gregory lived in a tall street where young men in sports cars drove up and down farting. The airlessness was compact.

Margaret opened the door.

"Oh hullo."

"Hullo. Did Joe get back all right?"

"Joe get back all right?"

Margaret was a big girl with an apron to wipe her hands on. It was tied by a cord round her back.

"I wondered if there was anything I could do."

"About what?"

"Catherine."

"Well come in."

"Thanks."

"What sort of things?"

"Help."

"How?"

"I don't know."

Margaret moved around the kitchen. I didn't know if I should mention Catherine's having a baby. Margaret went to and fro between the stove and the larder. She lifted her apron to lift saucepans. I thought—She will always be in a kitchen; carrying food from one side of an exercise yard to the other.

She said "She's having a baby."

"I know."

"She told you?"

"Yes. Adam and she thought of marrying."

Margaret was pulling at her skirt; this made it tight at her bottom, as if her skirt were coming off.

I said "I don't know if they should."

"Why not?"

"Would you like them to?"

She said "More than anything else in the world."

She put her face over steam. It seemed to reflect her. I thought—She should have had more of what she likes in the world.

She said "You know Adam's not the father?"

I could say—No, I didn't know that.

I said "What'll you do then?"

252

"About what?"

"The baby."

"Look after it I suppose."

I said "That's wonderful!"

She might have been crying. There was condensation on her face. Years ago, when we were young, Margaret and I had made love. We had been on stony ground, and it had withered.

She said "Have you eaten?"

"Yes."

I wondered if I should eat again to please her. I already had indigestion from the meal with Tom.

She said "Would you like some coffee?"

When she stood over me it was as if she had tried to absorb some sorrow in her womb and keep it there.

I said "Margaret sit down!"

She said "Shall we lie down?"

I wasn't sure if I had heard this.

I put a hand round her skirt.

She said "Oh it's all such hell!"

I put my head against her. I thought—I could lean against her stove, and burn, and then she could comfort me.

We could be seen from the street outside. The kitchen was in the basement of the house. I was embracing Margaret. She was a tall house with people moving inside her. Against my cheek was her kitchen.

I said "Where's Joe?"

"Upstairs with Sylvia."

"Sylvia?"

I tried to give warmth to Margaret. Inside her was profusion; leaves and acorns fell.

Margaret said "Sylvia's had a complete nervous breakdown."

I said "Here?"

"Yes."

"Shall I go and see her?"

"Do."

I pulled myself away. I thought—After all, I am a removals man: halfway up Margaret's stairs is a sofa; on her first floor a bed.

The last time I had seen Sylvia she had been sitting in her pink-and-white boudoir. She had said—Watch out! Natalie and Edward are dangerous.

Climbing the stairs of Joe and Margaret's house I thought —I will remember this journey: from the station to Tom; from Tom to the restaurant; from the restaurant through the streets to where I am climbing the stairs of Margaret's tall house. This is a map of someone's last day on earth; or to buried treasure.

At the top of the staircase was a nurse. She was a strong woman in a blue cap. Her legs were astride the staircase like a colossus. I aimed between them in my bright ship.

I said "Good evening."

The nurse said "I was pushed!"

In the bedroom Sylvia was sitting up in bed. She wore a white nightcap. She was looking at the screen of a television set on which there was nothing but flickering lights. The light was thrown against Sylvia's white face. I thought—She is being tortured.

"Sylvia—"

In her deep male voice she said "Get the man can't you?"

I sat on the bed. This was in the spare room of Joe and Margaret's house. Sylvia seemed to have been taken from somewhere where she really was, and put in this place like a cutout.

I said "Is it broken?"

"Where's that devil?"

Sylvia leaned so far towards the television that she overbalanced and could not get up. I pulled at her.

She said "Can you see my arse?" She giggled.

We held on to each other. Her arms were bony.

I said "How long have you been here?"

The nurse rushed into the room with her legs apart as if on horses. She said "I heard you!"

Sylvia could not balance. Her nightgown was up round her waist. When I let go, she toppled.

The nurse hit at her pillows.

Sylvia said "Can I have my bomb?"

The nurse said "You've had your bomb!"

I said "Who's her doctor?"

We watched the blank screen of the television. The light was like bullets. My arm was around Sylvia's shoulder. I thought—Waiting for shadows, we will be always in this room.

I said "The man's coming to mend it?"

She said "He doesn't come."

I wanted to ask the nurse—What do they give her? What do they do to her?

I thought perhaps Sylvia's brain was damaged, so the shadows would be permanent.

Joe Gregory came in. He said "Can't even have a decent pee!"

Joe looked tired. I was holding Sylvia. I thought I might, with my head down, send little shocks of sympathy or something up Sylvia's long neck until they reached her brain.

Joe said "What did the old devil do? Whack you?"

The nurse stood with her legs apart.

I said "Hullo Joe."

He said "Gentlemen friends!"

Joe settled on the other side of the bed. He took hold of Sylvia.

I let go. Sylvia lurched towards the television. She said "Get the man can't you?"

The television went on flickering.

Joe said to the nurse "Has she had her bomb?"

Joe put Sylvia's head underneath his bosom. He cradled her as if she were a child. He said "Now what's that arse doing?"

I thought—I should go: they do this better than me: they are on a life raft, working out the rules.

Joe said "Up the puddletoes!"

On this ocean there were huge birds, albatrosses, which never landed but which laid eggs on the sea; in the hope that they would land on flotsam, and float like rotten bodies till they hatched out in Atlantis.

The room smelt of sick. There was a white metal lamp above white porcelain. I thought—I remember this.

I said "Good-bye Joe."

I went downstairs to Margaret. I said "Who are the puddletoes?"

She said "A game they used to play as children."

Margaret was by the washing-up. I stood behind her. Outside the wind blew. I thought—There should be a better way of leaving people: one minute you are there, and the next you are a puff of cloud.

Margaret said "That woman won't even do the washing-up!"

I left Margaret and walked across the park. I would think of our children and our children's children. I was carrying the parcel of Madeleine's clothes. Also Tom's hat, which was too small for me. I was eating a lump of sugar which I had taken from Margaret's kitchen. The leaves blew like scraps of bread. Cars queued up in the cold. People sat with their arms out. The ground was an anthill of which I had knocked off the top. I looked for a white egg. It was almost dark, though afternoon. I was coming to the pond around which men flew kites on windy days. The wind was a hurricane. There was a man there now, tied to an umbilicus. The cord was invisible going up into the sky. He held it to his stomach. He was being dragged

towards the pond. I thought I knew him. He was having a tug
of war with the sky. He turned and stared at me. I could not
remember who he was.

"Hullo!"

"Hullo there!"

"Fancy you here!"

"Don't go!"

"I'm not."

In the dark, he had a grey face and thick hair. He might be
the man I was always meeting in the park. He might be a detective, or an old friend of Elizabeth's.

He said "You saw Ndoula?"

"Yes."

"I'd like to talk to you."

He was being dragged towards the pond. The reel he held to
his stomach was like a fishing rod. I thought—Perhaps he has
been hooked by God.

He said "Could we meet at my club?"

"Yes."

"The Athenaeum."

He seemed to have come to the end of his line. He would
either lose his kite or go into the pond.

He said "Have they got on to you yet?"

"No."

He shouted "I want to thank you!"

I did not want to stay. He had one foot in the pond.

I went on down to the road south of the park. The cars were
pressed against each other for warmth. Or for the few crumbs
that might fall. Taillights wagged. I remembered—In human
life, as in any other, there is waste.

I thought—With the experience of free will there has to be
an idea of God: without this, there is only cause and effect.

I passed a machine for consuming litter. Beside a similar one,
in another age, I had tried to lift Natalia.

257

In the road outside my flat a car was parked. I thought it might be waiting for me.

"Mr. Greville sir!"

"Yes?"

It was the man with pale trousers and the green felt hat. He had his hands in his pockets. He seemed to be dancing.

I thought—On a dark night, in a coalhole, I might still have known him.

I was pleased. He seemed to be trying to pull himself up by his trousers.

"Can I speak to you?"

"Of course!"

People asked me this and then were silent. I was becoming accustomed to so many coincidences.

"Are you well sir? And how are your family?"

This could go on for a long time. In Africa, it was politeness.

We were out in the cold. The man had a fine-drawn voice as if a hook were pulling it.

I said "Won't you come in?"

"No Mr. Greville sir!"

He closed his eyes.

I thought—He sees me as if I were a confessional.

"I should like to say, Mr. Greville, how extraordinarily grateful—"

"Oh that's—"

"Just a moment!"

He gasped. He put his head in his hands. I thought—He is a one-man-band with his elbows stuck.

I wondered—Does God read a magazine in the confessional?

"I should like to express, sir, on behalf of myself and others—"

He was squeezing himself out like toothpaste. If I stopped breathing, time might go faster.

He was such a sad man, with his long thin body and acorn head.

"We are having a small party tonight sir. Would you come?"

"I'd like to. Where?"

He rubbed his hands. He laughed. He said "Seven-thirty. Athenaeum."

"Athenaeum?"

"A small drinking club. Soho."

He seemed to be miming a song. The sound came and went. There was something wrong with his connections.

He said "I was so sorry about Father!"

I did not understand.

I thought—We will always be facing each other like this; on a doorstep, not knowing whether to dance or to cry.

He said "Thank you!"

He tiptoed away.

In my flat there was airlessness as if the carpets and furniture had used up the oxygen. I opened all the windows to keep things alive. I walked from room to room. Here I had once been happy and sad. The stove, the gramophone, the table at which we had sat—these were no longer alive. I thought—We have moved to somewhere different.

I had picked up a morning paper in the hall. There was a civil war in Africa. A child lay with nutcracker legs.

I thought I would wait quietly for a while before going on. I could look both inward and out, like a Gothic statue.

Before altars, and blank screens, people had forgotten how to pray: they waited for an announcement in front of the blank screens, switching themselves off and on.

I sat in the dark. I wondered—Doesn't anyone think that we might kill ourselves?

Natalie had had a suitcase like a removals van.

I thought I should go on again.

Walking through streets, sitting in buses, I thought—How much longer will I be moving? There will be an explosion, or I will be renewed. I came to the building like a battleship; above it, was the starred sky unseen. The lights of the battleship blazed. The Abbey was a toad. Only its thorax moved, to show it was breathing.

I felt my hair, my skin, my teeth should stand on end. There was the courtyard where I had been so many times before; the keepers in knee-breeches; the men passing and re-passing with their thumbs in their pockets pointing forwards.

"Good evening! Good evening!"

In the artificial light I did not duck. I had hoped I would seem invisible.

Through a door I said "Yseult!"

"Ah!"

"My oldest friend!"

"Hullo."

In this room I now had no desk. I was a genie out of my bottle. Yseult, with her wick trimmed, sat on top of a bushel.

"I've come to pick up my things."

"They're all in that drawer."

"And how have you been?"

"Oh I complain you know!"

I could scarcely remember in what guise I had once been in this room. I thought—As a child; or Aladdin without his treasure.

Yseult said "Sorry I couldn't talk much on the telephone the other night. I was with someone as a matter of fact."

She blushed.

I said "Yseult!"

I thought—Children run through the streets singing; winged insects fall; in celebration, we are gathered for the bonfire.

I said "It suits you!"

She said "Are you coming to the committee?"

"Yes."

"They've fairly got it in for you!"

She banged on her typewriter.

Going down stairs, along a corridor, I began to think—I am not being judged; I am the judge; everyone is about their business. I followed Yseult. In the committee room, underground, the people who had chosen themselves were gathered; some of them seemed ready for the fire. I thought this so often now; with their skins so fragile against snow. The room was dismal. It was like a deep shelter of which the top surface was a fungus. I did not think anyone would greet me. I thought— It is because they are sad they spend no time alone. The Chairman said "Shall we begin?" He pinched his trousers. He was anxious to move from one appointment to another.

Leaves drifted to their seats. One or two had greeted me. I thought—I will sit bright-eyed on the ceiling. But they would not ask me again. The Chairman said "Shall we take six?" Someone said "Why not?" The Chairman said "After which, anyone who wants to can go." At the other side of the table there was Edward Jones, Natalia's husband. I wondered if he might have been in Africa; there had been a man who looked like him climbing the mountain. He had gone sideways, not carrying a stick, over the rim of the world. I smiled. I thought —Perhaps he is glad to see me. He had a sticking plaster at his throat. The Chairman was talking. I pushed away my pencil, my paper, my blotter, my mind. I thought—I will not need these. Or I could practise my drawing of the harbour and the sea. It was in the shape of a triangle with an arrow sticking through it. Like a sacred heart. It would spin. It came together in my hands. The Chairman was saying "I think we should hear—" The pressure in my head seemed to have cleared. It had been with me for some days. I thought—What does it mean that I am here with Edward Jones? The Chairman said "Tony?" They were referring to me. I shook my head. He said

"Nothing?" I thought—I have explained all this: I have been
ill: I fell into a swimming pool: what more have I to say? We
were generals in war: my feet underneath the table were by the
parcel of Madeleine's clothes. I thought—Like a bomb. The
Chairman said "Well, we can't force you." I wondered if the
ventilation holes were blocked. We were in a committee room
which was hung underground like a bell. I was in the middle of
the table holding my diagram. I was opposite Edward Jones. I
could send out a pigeon: receive it back, with two fingers
raised. I said "I've said I'm clearing out. Resigning." The
Chairman said "Shall we get on then?"

I did not know if I should leave. I was preventing them
forming new hostilities. I had not meant to be unkind. I looked
at Edward Jones. He had this plaster at his throat. Perhaps she
had tried to kill him. The committee had moved on to the next
item on the agenda. This was on the subject of the war in
Africa. Children were dying. About this, they could talk about
what to do. The Chairman said "Edward?" Then—"You're
going out there tonight?" Edward looked at me. He smiled. I
thought—It might have been some emanation that I saw in
Africa. He said "Tony?" I thought—We will always be looking across this body of Natalia. I said "Yes?" He said "You've
just come from there haven't you?" My hand was shaking. I
thought—This is not fear; but to get one's blood to the right
heat to survive. I said "Nothing we say here will make much
difference." The Chairman said "Do you want us to do nothing then?" I could say—People are always asking this! I looked
at Edward. I said "They must do what they choose." He said
"We can pick up some pieces." I said "Yes, but they're their
pieces." I wanted to pick up my papers and go. There was my
drawing like a seesaw. The Chairman said "But which side is
right?" Edward said "That's not the question."

I stared at him. I thought—We have learned then. Edward
was looking at his watch: he had his hands ready on the arms of

his chair. The Chairman suddenly stood up and said "Good heavens! I adjourn." He picked up his papers and walked out. No one except Edward had quite been looking at me. I had my feet by the parcel of Madeleine's clothes. I thought—So it is all right: I can now go and find Madeleine. Someone came up and put his hand on my shoulder: with the other, he shook me by the hand. His face was bright red. I thought—He is one of the people I both know and do not know. People nodded to me and smiled as I went out. I thought—So after all, I am seen to be carrying wine and water. I looked for a telephone box to ring up Madeleine. Edward Jones had disappeared. I began to have an imaginary conversation with Adam. I would say— You see, what we do has an effect on quite a different level. He would say—But do you know? In the call box, there was a smell of almonds. With gas there should be no smell. I said "Hullo, Madeleine?" She said "Hullo!" Then—"Just a minute." I thought—Perhaps both Elizabeth and Adam will go to Africa; there they will help suffering children. Madeleine said "Hullo there!" I said "I've got your clothes." She said "Are you wearing them?" This seemed quite witty. She was whispering to someone at the other end of the line. I began to imagine a conversation with Elizabeth. I would say—But it's you who've always thought you could do something in Africa! Madeleine said "Meet you in the pub then." I said "Now?" She said "Yes." I said "All right."

Walking towards Trafalgar Square, to a pub where I had sometimes met Madeleine, I thought—It's a way of getting people out of the house; they have to be rid of their parents and children. In the days when I had been with Natalie I used to say—I do it for the kiddies! The evening was so beautiful. Ice blew in the fountains. The water sprayed outwards like a bell. I could explain—Each drop is a million unborn children. Madeleine was a smooth-cheeked girl with a skirt of soft leather. You buried nuts in her like a squirrel. You could not grow an oak tree in a drawing room. There we might have stayed all winter. I wondered—Why is it, in God, there is no female principle? I thought—But relationship itself is female. I thought this quite clever. I went into the pub. There was a man there whom I recognised. He was the doctor I had met at Sylvia's party. He had a small squashed face like an apple. I thought I could ask him about Sylvia. He said "What have you been doing, getting rid of the priestcraft?" I did not understand this. His face twitched; I thought—There is a worm in him trying to get out. I thought I should buy him a drink. I did not have much money. I said "I saw Sylvia, what's wrong? is she on drugs?" I did not think he would answer. He was wearing a thick woollen jersey and corduroy trousers. I said "Would you like a drink?" He said "Yes, double whisky." I thought—I still have my flat and the contents. I went to the bar. I was still plagued by the indigestion from the meal I had eaten with Tom. Madeleine, or Marlene, appeared in the pub. She was wearing her short leather skirt. She saw the doctor and bared her teeth at him. She was prettier than I remembered her. Elizabeth had once said—But is Marlene white or black? I had said—White. Elizabeth had said—I always thought she was black. I could have said—You see, I do not notice the difference. I fetched drinks to the doctor and to Madeleine. I said "I've brought your clothes." The doctor took his drink and moved away. Madeleine watched him with her teeth bared. I had this idea of time, or god, in which enormous areas were simply waste. Then, being fallow, things could grow. I said "Are you with that doctor?" She said "Yes, is it awful?" She put her head on my shoulder. She had such blue eyes and smooth brown cheeks: she was untouched, like a film star. She said "It is nice seeing you!" I said "It's nice seeing you too!" She was looking at me imploringly. I was trying to hand her the parcel of clothes: it was in between us like a bomb. She said "I'm so sorry." I said "What about?" She said "Father."

I thought—It can't be my own father who has died. I said "Father who?" She said "What?" I said "Father Whatnot?" I put the parcel down on the floor; then it would not matter if it went off. She said "He's been killed, didn't you know?" I said "No." She said "By some Africans." The doctor had come back and put his arm round her shoulder. I wondered if he was evil. I thought—Father Whatnot was the only good man I have ever known. I could say—Which Africans? But this would be to betray him: with his broomstick, and his great black cloak. The doctor said "Perhaps we'll see you sometime at Sylvia's." I pushed my parcel over towards Marlene. I thought—She will always be like this, someone's arm round her shoulder, being fed with food through bars of cages. I began looking for Tom's small hat. It was like a flannel in my pocket. I said "Well, I must go now." Marlene said "Must you?" She bared her teeth. She was underneath the doctor's arm like a parasol. I thought—I scatter my blessings. I went out of the pub. It was a windy night. People held on to their hats. Father Whatnot had said—All life is a preparation for death. I had said—I don't believe that. I wanted to say—You should see me now, because I loved you. He had not understood about me and Natalia. Natalie and I had been happy. When you are happy, there is nothing else to do. You stand beaming like a skeleton. On the roof, with two fingers raised. I thought —And you, Father Whatnot, you loved your Christ, your black-eyed beauty! I was walking through streets on my way to the black man's party. The pavements were littered with the blown-up bodies of women. They would be presented, like those of animals, to the fire. Crowds rubbed their legs together like insects. I thought—The world is screwed up and cast into a handkerchief. There were stone steps down to a basement: a notice—*Athenaeum*. I thought—All this will end in impotence. I went down the steps. There was a door with a grille in it. An eye looked through: the black man said "Mr. Greville sir!"

I could not remember his name. I had thought it right to come here. I could explain—These are the catacombs. I was led into a room where there was a celebration for conspirators: candles, dust, and a record playing Mozart. My friend wore a black-and-grey-striped jacket; dark red trousers. He said "Let me introduce you." There were ten or twelve: they shook me by the hand. I thought—I am an undertaker having a reunion with his clients. They said "Most pleased to meet you." I said "I'm glad." They were like the candles: the blackness unguarded at their heart. My friend said "What can I get you?" I was grateful because I had hardly any money. With red velvet on the walls, and tinsel, the room seemed prepared for the fire. Above, in the streets, were the cries of women; they were being offered to Roman soldiers. My friend said "Well, Mr. Greville, and what do you think will happen now?" They were seated in a half-circle round me; I thought—I am a teacher drawing in the dust. I said "It'll take time." I thought—I will never be able to talk about this. They waited. Beyond were the blue and green hills. I could say—Good can come out of evil: or vice versa: but this is not the point. And perhaps should be secret. I wondered if I could ask them how Father Whatnot had died. But he, again, would not have liked this. I said "You want a language." Their yellow eyes, in darkness, looked inside. I wondered what had been taught in the dust of Africa. In the room there was one very beautiful girl; her body like an S; her head an armpit. I thought—They might give her to me if I were not on a journey; then I could settle down. They had turned off Mozart the better to hear me. I could say—Turn it on! I have only children's riddles. They said "But what will the government do?" The fact was, there were too many people. We were in a mine shaft: the air was running out. I suddenly realised I should be saying good-bye to my wife and family. I had only come here to pay my respects. I said "You'll be all right!" I thought—I will be the prodigal father coming back to give comfort to his son. I was drinking what appeared to be fruit juice: I thought—My last chance to be victualled. Pips floated on the surface: I thought—They will breed. I said "I must go now." They said "Must you?" They did not want me to stay. After all, it was not easy. I thought—In this room we will always be like this; not knowing whether to go or stay, while war and famine roam overhead. I finished my drink. I thought—The beautiful girl might have stopped me. They came with me to the door. I thought—They'll remember my glass coffin; the bones and tooth and wooden splinter. I thought I should try to run all the way to my flat; to see if my legs would carry me. It was a fine night. Placards and papers announced there was a cease-fire in Africa; teams of relief were being sent out there. I had once said to Elizabeth—If you do go, you will be just one more mouth to feed. She had said— Do you believe that? With her long straight legs like those of a colossus. I had said—No. No one knew what was happening in Africa: stories, like history, became myth. So people went there. Like my children. I ran, on and off, to my flat. The sky was above me like a finger. I became elated. The streets were full of people. There were migrations. I wondered how Father Whatnot had died. Skidding over the world, perhaps, with his arms out on his broomstick. There were crowns floating in the air. Outside my flat a car was parked. Two men were sitting in the front. When one saw me he got out. He said "Mr. Greville sir!" He was white. I thought—This is some transmutation. I said "Not now!" I ran up the steps. In my flat was a scene of extraordinary activity. Elizabeth was talking on the telephone. She had spread her claims around her in the sitting room. She seemed to have struck, as usual, gold. There were boxes and haversacks and overcoats. I could not remember what the flat had looked like before. I had been here only a few hours ago. The bedroom was full of half-packed suitcases. Elizabeth said "Just a minute!" She was writing on her knee, holding the telephone. She said "And linen." I said "Are you really going to Africa?" I stood by the bed. There was a small box of plaster and lint. I thought—You can't bandage a continent! Or perhaps you could, with a few loaves and fishes. Elizabeth was waving a piece of paper. I took it. She looked very well: her hair a long halo. The piece of paper said—Will you ring Mr. Symon very urgent. Elizabeth said into the telephone "And where do we land?" Sophie came in eating an ice cream. I said "And where are you going?" She said "Staying with friends." I said "Of course, you're so grown-up now." Every time I tried to sit down there was a box or a bottle of medicine. I thought —So I will be alone again. Elizabeth put the receiver down. I said "Who was that?" She said "WANA." I said "Who is Wana?" She said "It's all been done through them." She strode about amongst her equipment. She put her cheek down for me to kiss. She was soft as roses. She said "I'm sorry I couldn't let you know." I had forgotten how warm she was. I thought— But where is Adam? I sat by the telephone. I thought—If Elizabeth, as well as Adam, go to Africa, this then is the female principle? I thought this clever. I dialled a number on the telephone. Ned Symon's secretary said "Oh Mr. Greville sir!" She seemed in a state of extraordinary excitement. She said "Oh we've been trying to get you everywhere!" I thought—If Natalia's dead, there will be no point in these preparations. The secretary said "Just a moment!" I thought—I will be an old man forever on a cloud. The secretary kept on saying: "Just a moment!" I thought of Africa: the blue and red flowers: concrete carried like bodies on a stretcher. I thought—When Sophie grows up she will go off too: I will have freed, for this, all my children. I suddenly could not bear it. I said "I'll ring back later." The secretary shouted "Oh no Mr. Greville sir!" I put the receiver down. I turned to Elizabeth: she was busy among her cases. I said "You're the only person I like." She said "You're the only person I like too." She glowed. I thought—She will come back; if only for her daughter. Everything came back, transmuted or translucent, on the curve of the universe. I watched her. I thought—This is the point. There was a sudden thundering on the stairs: someone fell and seemed to remain prostrate. Sophie ran to the head of the stairs: she shouted "Adam!" He appeared extraordinarily energetic; his gold hair in a nimbus. He said "Oh hullo!" I said "Hullo." Sophie said "Mummy's going to Africa!" He said "I'm going to Africa!" Elizabeth said "But not to the same place." She greeted him, carrying her bottles. I thought—They are the two halves of an hourglass. Then—A father should perhaps not know what the other half is doing: then, he can enable them to do it. I said to Adam "And who are you going with?" He said "Crupps." I said "Crupps?" He said "The CRPP." He was carrying an enormous haversack. He swung it like Sisyphus. He said "Do you think that's all right?" I said "Yes, that's all right." I thought—How good of him to ask me! The telephone rang. I picked it up. Ned Symon said "I've found you!" I thought—I must wait till Elizabeth and Adam have gone. He said "About those articles!" He was passionately whispering. I put my hand over the mouthpiece. He said "How soon can you let me have the story?" Elizabeth and Adam were finishing their packing. I said "When does the plane go?" Elizabeth said "Tonight." Ned Symon, on the telephone, said "Tony! Tony!" I took my hand away: I said "Sorry, my wife and son are just off to Africa." He said in a low voice "Look, I can advance you—" He mentioned a sum that seemed astronomic. I thought—Well, that will see me into my hermitage in the desert. Elizabeth and Adam were picking up their bags; they were festooned like Christmas trees. Ned Symon said "Tony! Tony!" I wondered if the price would go up. I said "What sort of thing?" He said "Autobiographical." I thought—Well it will be that, won't it. Elizabeth said "We must go." I said to Ned Symon "I can't talk now." Ned Symon said "Tony! Tony!"

Then—"Don't talk to anyone else!" I said to Elizabeth "I'm coming!" Ned Symon put the price up. I said "Good heavens!" I said to Elizabeth "Wait!" I put the receiver down.

When I helped Elizabeth and Adam to carry their luggage downstairs we were all like Christmas trees; with Sophie at the top, a crowning angel. In the street I was careful; the car with the two men in it seemed to have gone. I thought—They may only be asleep; like apostles or sentries in the desert. Elizabeth had hired a car to take her to the airport. Sophie sat on my knee; Adam sat in front with the driver. Elizabeth held her box of medicines on her lap. I said "You will be careful." She said "I know you want me killed." I shouted "I've just said I don't!" As we moved off, a car passed us and pulled up by the flat: I thought—So they've been only telephoning or drinking. I said "You are lucky." She said "Why?" I said "To be going to the sun." The lights from the street flashed on and off. I thought—Perhaps the feminine principle is to be in two places at once: if so, I too am feminine. The car moved like an electrical impulse along a viaduct. I said to Elizabeth "How soon will you be back?" Sophie shouted "She's coming back tomorrow!" Elizabeth said "No not tomorrow." I said "Soon." I thought—If our children were not in the car we might make some sentimental demonstration, such as hold hands or weep: perhaps the world is tough because of what cannot be done in front of children. I put my hand on her knee. We approached the airport. I said "Don't get near anything ridiculous like fighting." I thought—They are like aristocrats in the old days, going off for a winter campaign in their yacht. Then—But what of Adam? At the airport there were yellow lights and a vacuum. I thought—Here people take off for the moon. Elizabeth was arranging the packages on her Christmas tree. I thought—Nowadays women and children go: men, who have fought, watch them. I said to Adam "You won't go near the fighting?" He said "I don't suppose so." I thought—So he will take over, being wise and beautiful. They stood side by side in front of a counter. They both looked so young. Elizabeth had her hair scraped back. I thought—They are brother and sister: this is the potency of myths. I was standing hand in hand with Sophie. I wanted to say—Look after one another won't you? Elizabeth said "Look after her, won't you?" I said "Yes." We were on the rocky pass; the scene had to seem to be eternal. I looked round the airport building: there did not appear to be anyone else I knew. I did not see Edward Jones, Natalia's husband. I thought—I have created this: freed them. I thought I might cry; then there would be another flood for Noah. Elizabeth and Adam were my bright angels. I said "Time for a cup of coffee?" We went past the coffee counter. It was extraordinary how Elizabeth was not sad. She said "You'll see that Sophie gets to her friends?" I said "Yes." We arrived at the barrier. Sophie and I stood like widows. Elizabeth stooped for me to kiss. She said "And take care of yourself." I said "I will." She leaned down to hug Sophie. Their two heads were like gold. I said to Adam "And if you get into trouble, let me know and I'll send a gunboat." We laughed. I thought—Or an angel: but anyway he wouldn't want me to. This scene had to be somewhat ridiculous. There was this bright light all around. We were on a cloud. I was sure this was how it happened—in some waiting room, halfway between heaven and hell. They went through the barrier. I waved. I thought—They are on their way round the world and back to Eden.

I said to Sophie "Shall we go and watch?"

"Where?"

"On the roof."

We climbed the stairs. No one seemed to be following me. The roof was frozen. I thought—We are a mosaic, Sophie and I, on a ceiling. Below us was the mass of the airport buildings. Hell was solidity or solidarity; locked and broken. I thought— And to be an individual is to be on a wire; within oneself and on a roof. Planes were lined up like a bomb rack. Sophie said "But which is theirs?" I said "I don't know." Planes crawled on the earth. Sophie said "But you must know." I said "Why?" Sophie said "You know everything." She was pulling me along the roof top. I thought—Also nothing. I said "There!" She said "Where?" We glimpsed Elizabeth and Adam as if through clouds. I thought—A miracle. Sophie said "It is!" I thought—Now, good-bye my loved ones! They were climbing into a bus. Sophie said "You see?" There had been a time just after Elizabeth and I had been married when we had gone to live in a farmhouse by the sea: Adam had been born there. I had watched his head appear between her legs like the earth. Sophie said "Look!" There were a few stars visible. I wanted to say—I might have done better my darlings! But I hadn't. I said to Sophie "Shall we go?" She said "Oh no!" There was snow falling. In the cottage, when they had been young, I had nursed them both one winter. They had lain side by side. Sophie had been born later. When her head had appeared it had been like the sun. Sophie said "But they might be killed!" I said "They won't be." Sophie said "But how do you know?" I said "You said, I know everything." There was an aeroplane taking off; its lights flashed fire. I thought—You hold them by the legs and hit them; cut them off like a wound. Then, when they are older, a world holds together. This is hope. The aeroplane crawled into the sky. Sophie said "There now!" I said "Yes, let's go."

Coming down the corridors to the waiting car I wondered if anyone would have caught up with me: there was no one by the barrier. I said to Sophie "Have you got your address?" She said "Yes." We climbed into the car. We sat side by side. I held her hand. I thought—I am old now. I wished that I had said good-bye just once more: told Elizabeth how much she meant to me. But I had done this. And my son, Adam. I said to Sophie "Do you like staying with your friends?" Sophie said "I love it." I said "That's good then." We approached the town again with the lights like snow. The car turned into a side street. I said "Is it here?" Sophie said "Yes." I looked out of the back window and there was another car following me. I said "I'll just drop you and then I must go." Sophie said "Good-bye then." I said "Good-bye my loved one!" I kissed her. I said "I'll telephone." There was a mother and a small girl waiting on the steps of a house. The mother was pretty. I waved to her. Sophie ran out of the car and up the steps. I thought— Thus life is normal. I said to the driver "Can you go back to where we started please?" The car behind was still following me. I wondered where I could stay tonight: in what magic hedgerow. There was a crowd round the door of my flat. I had half expected this. I had no money to pay the driver. When the car pulled up some cameras flashed. People called out "Mr. Greville sir!" I was on the backseat, searching my pockets. I thought—I am like the black man whose bullets are buttons. There was another car parked between me and the flat: a man was winding down the window. I recognised Ned Symon. He beckoned. I said "Can you lend me some money?" He opened the door of his car and I tried to open the door of mine but we were like two trains in a tunnel. Some men had got out of the car that had been following me and were running. Ned Symon pulled at me. I got into his car. He said "I've got the cheque." I said "Good." He mentioned again a figure that seemed astronomic. I sat beside him in his car. One of his men was paying my driver. I took the cheque. He held out a piece of paper for me to sign. I thought—In blood, because it is so ridiculous. Then—But the children of darkness have to learn from the children of light. I signed the piece of paper. I thought I might put—The Unjust Steward. I folded the cheque into my pocket. I said "As a matter of fact, it's almost written." He said "Marvellous!" There were men peering through the windows of the car; they were gesticulating and saying "Mr. Greville!"

More cameras went off. I said "It may not be what you want."
He said "But you were with Father Watson?" I said "Yes." I
thought—I always thought it was Watkins. He said "Well
then." There seemed to be some fighting outside the car: men
were trying to prevent other men from reaching it. I said "I
must go now." He said "Don't let them near you!" I said
"No." I thought—Now everything is buttoned up and com-
pleted. He shouted "Where will you be?" I might say—In a
field, with my thousands of pieces of silver. I could explain—
But this is funny!

It was nearly midnight. I thought I would have to run
through streets again. I was used to this. Men pressed round me
working flashlights. A man with what seemed to be a machine
for spraying insects held a microphone under my chin. I could
explain—Now, you see, all opposites are reconciled. I ran
rather slowly in the middle of the street towards a main road.
The pack lolloped after me. We arrived among the traffic:
there they became stuck like mud against a weir. I thought—
So this is not too serious. I slowed to a walk. I thought—Roman soldiers with rakes will come to clear them. I was on my
own. I was heading south. I took deep breaths. I thought that if
I passed a bank I would drop Ned Symon's cheque through a
letterbox, to make it safe. At each corner there were coloured
lights for Christmas. I was walking through a maze. I had the
thread, which ran back to the sea. I could say—Do you see it?
She would say—Nothing. We had broken patterns; shattered
mirrors; I did not know what would follow. I had argued, to
Father Whatnot—Life is better than death. It was cold, with
the dead souls for Christmas. Once I had used to visit Natalia in
the afternoons; as Prince Charming, with my white frills and
ankles. I created these myths out of unconsciousness—or
knowledge of order. I had been working very hard and was
tired. I thought—If it happens this time I will believe; which I
do anyway. As I was passing a rubbish bin I saw on an evening

paper a huge picture of Father Whatnot; beside him, one of Ndoula. I thought—I will be joining them soon; as someone wanted or on an altar. I would go into hiding. I was glad Elizabeth and Adam had gone to Africa. I would say—Tread carefully, my loved ones. They would move between bodies with temperature charts and candles; trail their bandages across minefields. I came to crossroads: I could go this way or that. Either way, now, I would not meet my son at a crossroads. Nor my wife. So we would live. This was the way I often went. I could say—Take me in, my sweet one, out of the cold. Or I could come down from the ceiling. Having, like Job, lost all my principles and servants. And getting them all back again. She would stand in front of a figure formed of clay and spittle: would be sticking wings in it. I would ask—Are you well, my angel? For what did God do when there was all that fuss at the inn? Sit at home with his wife and family? Still, there was not enough darkness. For rest. With your feet by the fire. I went past the entrance to the mews where I had so often gone. I thought—Mews, muse, let me hear your music. There was a light on just in the basement. I had been on these steps before. It was after midnight. I thought—I may have to jump the last few yards. And perhaps she will not be surprised. You disassociate yourself from yourself, if you have courage. I looked through the basement window. The room had changed. I thought—This is the place where all opposites come together. There was a wooden door. I knocked. I thought—I am the plague or salvation. There was the sound of a bolt being drawn. She opened the door. She was different from what I remembered: older, and with more space in her: no less beautiful. I thought—I can live then. I said "Can I come in?" Her eyes went to and fro. I thought—She is not deciding: if I stand long enough, she will believe. In her face was some hatred of man, God, history; a woman's prerogative. Also love for the creator of her children. Between these, she existed. She stood back.

The basement had been converted into one huge room like a granary: here she worked. And here, in times of famine, rich men would grow richer while perhaps the poor starved. I thought—For a while, I can stay here. At the far end of the room, on a platform, were two large spheres made of clay. They were hollow, on wires. Inside one was the figure of a man walking forwards; inside the other, a child. The bones and veins showed through. I said "Did you do this?" Her hands were covered with clay. She held them close to her sides. I thought—So she cannot embrace me. I smiled. Her face was darker and more animal. I thought—She has been gnawed at by rats: they have broken their teeth on her. I said "You're looking very well." In the presence of Natalie there was this impression of effluence, or effulgence, like light in darkness. I thought—I am here for life; energy; for the earth and sun. The construction on the platform was like genitals: life moved inside it and around. I said "That's good." The room was a cave, with a stream running back all winter. I said "How are you?" She said "All right." Her voice contained love of man, God, history; also hatred, for the torturer of her children. I said "You got my letters?" In the room, in one corner, was a bed; in another, a stove which burned. She said "Yes." Between her legs, in the blackness, a sun might appear and disappear. She began scraping the clay off her hands. She held a finger and thumb like a ring. I said "I knew Edward was away." She said "How?" I said "I didn't know you would be here." She was wearing an old blue jersey and corduroy jeans. She went to a basin. From the back she was as before. I thought —Perhaps I can make my home in her this winter. Edward might be on the same plane as Elizabeth and Adam. When she had washed she came over to me. Her head was a dark explosion. Her body was in different layers, like demonstrations of history. I put my hand round her. I thought—She is as full as the stomach of a child. She said "Oh how I hate you!" I said

"I hate you too." She moved away. I thought—I will stay still and she will come back on the curve of the universe. And in the spring there would come round again the golden heads of all my children. I sat by the fire. I held my hands out. Between us was a cauldron. She said "What have you been doing?" I said "Working." She said "What at?" I said "Writing." She looked at me with her black gold eyes. These were of the earth, arbitrary: also violent, controlled. She stood by her sculpture. She said "You do like it?" I said "Yes." I wanted to say—It's like God's balls. I said "Come here." I thought—She is like myself: she does not quite believe this. She walked round the room. I thought—Perhaps the old man just got bored and wanted someone to torment him all winter: so he could laugh, being tickled, and keep warm. I said "Come on!" She said "What's the point?" She came and sat on my knee. I thought—They will be getting close to Africa. I put my arm round her. I thought—Natalie, Natalia, nates, my nativity. I looked at the ceiling. It was blank, as if there had been a pattern of a figure there. I thought—I am a man being conscious of being conscious of himself; from where the amoeba split, to where his descendants land in Africa. Natalia leaned down at me. I lifted my head. Clouds broke; gave resurrection. I thought—I have been breathed into; my mouth on hers; have saved; I am destroyed. Natalia was sun and earth; I was gravity. I thought—Not loved nor loving; this is what love is. Where I held her there were small flames like ice. I said "You're cold." She said "Yes." I said "I'll carry you." I thought—We tried this once before; did not quite manage it. I put both arms underneath her: set my two feet on the ground. I heaved. We were standing in the middle of the room like a granary. She had one arm round my neck; another searched for a handhold. I thought—This time we will stay. She said "I thought you hated me." I said "Yes." I remembered—We should be a dancer or Indian goddess; should have more legs and arms.

Thus I could both love and hold her. I said "You're a demon, a demiurge, an agent of creation." She put her other arm round my neck. She said "And what are you?" I thought—In fact, I am better as two persons: then one can stand in eternal chastity while the other moves with her across the room towards the bed. She was smiling. I had forgotten how her teeth came out like stars. I remembered—Or sometimes a skeleton. She too should have other pairs of legs and arms; to give birth and mould me, also to run away. She said "Why are you smiling?" I said "Why are you?" I thought—All these things are growing; have grown, will grow: the sun between the legs appearing and disappearing. I said "Because perhaps now between us we have enough legs and arms—" I could say—two natures, three persons—I put my head back and laughed; I thought—Ah, my loved ones, you will be landing soon in Africa! I said "—to comprehend you."

Nicholas Mosley was born in 1923, the son of Sir Oswald Mosley, the notorious leader of the British fascist party in the 1930s and the subject of his son's acclaimed biography *Rules of the Game/Beyond the Pale* (Dalkey Archive, 1991). He is the author of a dozen novels, including the Whitbread Award-winning *Hopeful Monsters* (Dalkey, 1990; Vintage, 1991), and a half-dozen works of nonfiction. Two of his novels have been made into films: *Accident* (using a screenplay by Harold Pinter and directed by Joseph Losey) and *Impossible Object*. In 1995 Dalkey published Mosley's autobiography, *Efforts at Truth*. His latest novel, *Children of Darkness and Light,* was published in England in 1996 and will be published in the U.S. by Dalkey in 1997. Mosley has five children and lives with his wife in London.

DALKEY ARCHIVE PAPERBACKS

FICTION: AMERICAN

BARNES, DJUNA. *Ladies Almanack*	9.95
BARNES, DJUNA. *Ryder*	11.95
BARTH, JOHN. *LETTERS*	14.95
BARTH, JOHN. *Sabbatical*	12.95
CHARYN, JEROME. *The Tar Baby*	10.95
COOVER, ROBERT. *A Night at the Movies*	9.95
CRAWFORD, STANLEY. *Some Instructions*	11.95
DAITCH, SUSAN. *Storytown*	12.95
DOWELL, COLEMAN. *Island People*	12.95
DOWELL, COLEMAN. *Too Much Flesh and Jabez*	9.95
DUCORNET, RIKKI. *The Fountains of Neptune*	10.95
DUCORNET, RIKKI. *The Jade Cabinet*	9.95
DUCORNET, RIKKI. *Phosphor in Dreamland*	12.95
DUCORNET, RIKKI. *The Stain*	11.95
FAIRBANKS, LAUREN. *Sister Carrie*	10.95
GASS, WILLIAM H. *Willie Masters' Lonesome Wife*	9.95
GORDON, KAREN ELIZABETH. *The Red Shoes*	12.95
KURYLUK, EWA. *Century 21*	12.95
MARKSON, DAVID. *Springer's Progress*	9.95
MARKSON, DAVID. *Wittgenstein's Mistress*	11.95
MASO, CAROLE. *AVA*	12.95
MCELROY, JOSEPH. *Women and Men*	15.95
MERRILL, JAMES. *The (Diblos) Notebook*	9.95
NOLLEDO, WILFRIDO D. *But for the Lovers*	12.95
SEESE, JUNE AKERS. *Is This What Other Women Feel Too?*	9.95
SEESE, JUNE AKERS. *What Waiting Really Means*	7.95
SORRENTINO, GILBERT. *Aberration of Starlight*	9.95
SORRENTINO, GILBERT. *Imaginative Qualities of Actual Things*	11.95
SORRENTINO, GILBERT. *Mulligan Stew*	13.95
SORRENTINO, GILBERT. *Splendide-Hôtel*	5.95
SORRENTINO, GILBERT. *Steelwork*	9.95
SORRENTINO, GILBERT. *Under the Shadow*	9.95
STEIN, GERTRUDE. *The Making of Americans*	16.95
STEIN, GERTRUDE. *A Novel of Thank You*	9.95

DALKEY ARCHIVE PAPERBACKS

STEPHENS, MICHAEL. *Season at Coole*   7.95
WOOLF, DOUGLAS. *Wall to Wall*   7.95
YOUNG, MARGUERITE. *Miss MacIntosh, My Darling*   2-vol. set, 30.00
ZUKOFSKY, LOUIS. *Collected Fiction*   9.95

FICTION: BRITISH

BROOKE-ROSE, CHRISTINE. *Amalgamemnon*   9.95
CHARTERIS, HUGO. *The Tide Is Right*   9.95
FIRBANK, RONALD. *Complete Short Stories*   9.95
GALLOWAY, JANICE. *Foreign Parts*   12.95
GALLOWAY, JANICE. *The Trick Is to Keep Breathing*   11.95
MOSLEY, NICHOLAS. *Accident*   9.95
MOSLEY, NICHOLAS. *Impossible Object*   9.95
MOSLEY, NICHOLAS. *Judith*   10.95
MOSLEY, NICHOLAS. *Natalie Natalia*   12.95

FICTION: FRENCH

BUTOR, MICHEL. *Portrait of the Artist as a Young Ape*   10.95
CREVEL, RENÉ. *Putting My Foot in It*   9.95
ERNAUX, ANNIE. *Cleaned Out*   9.95
GRAINVILLE, PATRICK. *The Cave of Heaven*   10.95
NAVARRE, YVES. *Our Share of Time*   9.95
QUENEAU, RAYMOND. *The Last Days*   9.95
QUENEAU, RAYMOND. *Pierrot Mon Ami*   9.95
ROUBAUD, JACQUES. *The Great Fire of London*   12.95
ROUBAUD, JACQUES. *The Plurality of Worlds of Lewis*   9.95
ROUBAUD, JACQUES. *The Princess Hoppy*   9.95
SIMON, CLAUDE. *The Invitation*   9.95

FICTION: GERMAN

SCHMIDT, ARNO. *Nobodaddy's Children*   13.95

FICTION: IRISH

CUSACK, RALPH. *Cadenza*   7.95
MAC LOCHLAINN, ALF. *The Corpus in the Library*   11.95

DALKEY ARCHIVE PAPERBACKS

MacLochlainn, Alf. *Out of Focus*	5.95
O'Brien, Flann. *The Dalkey Archive*	9.95
O'Brien, Flann. *The Hard Life*	9.95
O'Brien, Flann. *The Poor Mouth*	10.95

FICTION: LATIN AMERICAN and SPANISH

Campos, Julieta. *The Fear of Losing Eurydice*	8.95
Lins, Osman. *The Queen of the Prisons of Greece*	12.95
Paso, Fernando del. *Palinuro of Mexico*	14.95
Sarduy, Severo. *Cobra* and *Maitreya*	13.95
Tusquets, Esther. *Stranded*	9.95
Valenzuela, Luisa. *He Who Searches*	8.00

POETRY

Ansen, Alan. *Contact Highs: Selected Poems 1957-1987*	11.95
Burns, Gerald. *Shorter Poems*	9.95
Fairbanks, Lauren. *Muzzle Thyself*	9.95
Giscombe, C. S. *Here*	9.95
Markson, David. *Collected Poems*	9.95
Theroux, Alexander. *The Lollipop Trollops*	10.95

NONFICTION

Ford, Ford Madox. *The March of Literature*	16.95
Green, Geoffrey, et al. *The Vineland Papers*	14.95
Mathews, Harry. *20 Lines a Day*	8.95
Roudiez, Leon S. *French Fiction Revisited*	14.95
Shklovsky, Viktor. *Theory of Prose*	14.95
West, Paul. *Words for a Deaf Daughter* and *Gala*	12.95
Young, Marguerite. *Angel in the Forest*	13.95